Seeking Space and Time

Praise for Amy's Award-Winning Chincoteague Books
"A beautiful account of the love and healing support of community!"
Island of Miracles, Chandi Owen, Author

"I can already see the Hallmark Channel movie!"
Island of Miracles, Anne, Goodreads

"[Amy] draws you in to the lives of her characters…she paints the picture so eloquently it's almost like you are there.
Island of Promise, Cindy, Amazon

"I love Amy Schisler's books. I cried tears of both sadness and joy while reading this. I read this book in a day!"
Island of Promise, Mitzi Mead, Goodreads

"The romance was pure, refreshing, and beautiful, completely believable and just the right level of sweet. At the same time it was heady and exhilarating–in short: it felt like falling in love–and I was delighted by it."
Seeking Tranquility, Jessica Castillo, Catholic 365

"Five stars -- I was truly blown away by this story and loved every second of it!."
Seeking Tranquility, Cassie, Goodreads

"Part love story, part mystery, *Seeking Sugar and Spice* is mixed with plenty of ingredients for a sweet and spicy summer read.."
Seeking Sugar and Spice, Mary, Amazon

Praise for Award-Winning, *Whispering Vines*
"The heartbreaking, endearing, charming, and romantic scenes will surely inveigle you to keep reading."
Serious Reading Book Review

"Schisler's writing is a verbal masterpiece of art."
Alexa Jacobs, Author & President of Maryland Romance Writers

Also Available by Amy Schisler
Novels
A Place to Call Home
Picture Me
Whispering Vines and The Good Wine
Summer's Squall
The Devil's Fortune

Chincoteague Island Trilogy
Island of Miracles
Island of Promise
Island of Hope

Chincoteague Sunsets Trilogy
Seeking Tranquility
Seeking Sugar and Spice
Seeking Space and Time

Buffalo River Series
Desert Fire, Mountain Rain
Under the Summer Moon
Sapphires in Snow

Children's Books
Crabbing With Granddad
The Greatest Gift

Spiritual Books and Bible Studies
Stations of the Cross Meditations for Moms (with Anne Kennedy, Susan Anthony, Chandi Owen, and Wendy Clark)
A Devotional Alphabet
Meet the Saints from A-Z, A Children's Introduction to the Saints
Clothed With Strength and Dignity: Women of the Bible

Seeking Space and Time

By Amy Schisler

ISBN-13: 979-8-9900644-1-6

Published by:
Chesapeake Sunrise Publishing
Amy Schisler
Bozman, MD
2024

Dedication

To all readers, everyone, especially those who have been
supporting me and buying my books. I write to entertain.
I write to tell stories. I write to bring the people and
places in my imagination to life. I write to release tears in
myself and others, and I write to surprise us all. Thank
you for allowing me to do so.

"No tears in the writer, no tears in the reader. No surprise
in the writer, no surprise in the reader."
--Robert Frost

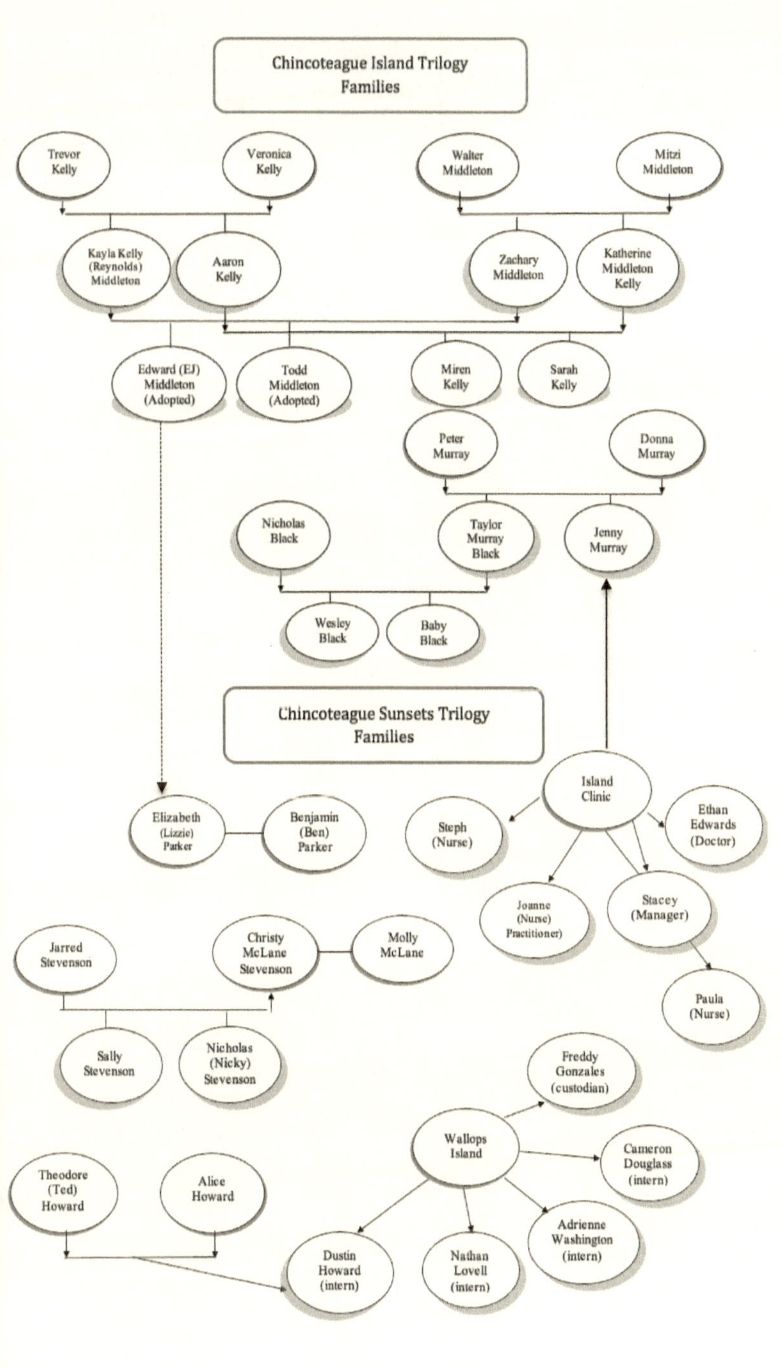

Chincoteague Island Trilogy Families
Trevor Kelly
Veronica Kelly
Walter Middleton
Mitzi Middleton
Kayla Kelly (Reynolds) Middleton
Aaron Kelly
Zachary Middleton
Katherine Middleton Kelly
Edward (EJ) Middleton (Adopted)
Todd Middleton (Adopted)
Miren Kelly
Sarah Kelly
Peter Murray
Donna Murray
Nicholas Black
Taylor Murray Black
Jenny Murray
Wesley Black
Baby Black
Chincoteague Sunsets Trilogy Families
Island Clinic
Ethan Edwards (Doctor)
Elizabeth (Lizzie) Parker
Benjamin (Ben) Parker
Steph (Nurse)
Joanne (Nurse) (Practitioner)
Stacey (Manager)
Jarred Stevenson
Christy McLane Stevenson
Molly McLane
Paula (Nurse)
Sally Stevenson
Nicholas (Nicky) Stevenson
Freddy Gonzales (custodian)
Wallops Island
Cameron Douglass (intern)
Theodore (Ted) Howard
Alice Howard
Adrienne Washington (intern)
Dustin Howard (intern)
Nathan Lovell (intern)

School Notes - Harvard University Announces Top Prospective Graduates, Local Student Makes List

Cambridge, Massachusetts: The Office of Academic Affairs of Harvard University has announced the top students projected to graduate this spring. Honorees include Emily Abbot, School of Public Health, Falmouth, Maine; Dustin Howard, School of Arts and Sciences, Sheridan, Illinois; Molly McLane, School of Arts and Sciences, Chincoteague, Virginia; Robert Shepherd, School of Engineering and Applied Sciences, Atlanta, Georgia; and Alexandra Wilson, Harvard Business School, Philadelphia, Pennsylvania. Rankings will be announced prior to Commencement.

The Chincoteague Herald, May 1

Chapter One

Opportunities, blossoming with promises of wealth and notoriety, dangled before Molly in this season of growth and change, yet she remained a tree trapped in winter, stunted in the ability to embrace the possibilities of new life.

"Graduation's just a few days away," Christy told her sister. "And we're all set. Dr. Johnson will drive everyone to the airport, and we depart at eleven-thirty-five. We'll be there in plenty of time to get to the reception. Did you find a dress?"

Molly made a face that her sister quickly picked up on, even on her small screen.

"I saw that." Christy said. "You didn't get a dress, did you? What about for graduation?"

Molly sighed. "I haven't had time. Besides, I'll have my cap and gown on."

"For graduation, not the reception. Do you want me to bring you something?"

Molly pushed back her chair to look down at her ever-changing, just shy of eighteen-years-old body. Christy, even after two babies, was tall and slim with blonde waves and sparkling blue eyes. Molly wasn't short, but she wasn't close to tall. She wasn't overweight, and not being model thin was okay with her, but her body had yet to fully develop, a collection of large and small bumps in all the wrong places. Her brown hair was flat and straight and worn mostly in a braid down her back. Even three years of college hadn't succeeded in making her a normal, style-aware, shopping mall-crazy teen.

"Mol? Earth to Molly."

Molly looked back at her laptop. Christy grinned, and Molly sighed again. She did that a lot when talking to her sister.

"Whatever. If you insist on bringing me clothes, I won't argue with you."

"Great. Hey, Jared just walked in. Say hi."

Molly's brother-in-law smiled as his face filled the screen on her laptop.

"Hey, Molly. How's it going? Still taking the science world by storm?"

"That's you with your award-winning textbooks."

"Nobody pays attention to textbook awards," Jared said, taking the phone from Christy.

"They should," Molly told him, planting her elbows on her desk and resting her chin on her fists. "Everything okay back home?"

"Everything's perfect. Except that you're up there. We're looking forward to you being home for a while, but don't worry. We won't try to talk you out of one of those high-dollar jobs you've been offered just because we miss you."

Molly squirmed, those offers hanging heavily above her, threatening to fall and rot at her feet if she didn't make a decision.

"Yeah, well, if I want any job, I need to pass my last final. I better go." Better to avoid the subject than talk about her looming future.

"Good luck, but you don't need it. You're going to ace the final and wow everyone with your valedictory speech."

"I have to beat out Dustin first. Our GPAs are really close."

"You've got this. Now, go study. I'll tell Christy you said goodbye. Nicky just woke up from his nap, and Sally will be home from school any minute."

"Okay, thanks, Jared. I'll see you on Friday."

"See you then, Molly."

Jared ended the call, and Molly closed the app on her computer. She stared at the folder that was open on her screen revealing all the tempting propositions she'd received—SpaceX, Blue Origin, SRI, NASA, even the US Space Force, among others. How was she going to break the news to everyone that she hadn't accepted any of them and didn't know if she would? The Tree of Knowledge had been gifted to her from birth, and she feared the consequences of tasting its fruit.

***

"To Molly," Dr. Johnson said, holding up a glass of champagne.

Molly smiled and clinked her glass of sparkling cider with everyone else's glasses of sparkling wine. She didn't care that she was the only person in her graduating class not even close to the legal drinking age. She'd never been one to care about drinking or smoking pot. She understood the effect those things had on the brain, and her brain was what made her who she was, even if she'd been thinking lately that she didn't really know who that was anymore.

"Your speech was beautiful," Diane told Molly.

"Thanks. I wasn't sure anyone would like it. I mean, I was worried, because of my age, nobody would take me seriously."

"Molly," Dr. Johnson admonished. "People have been taking you seriously for a long time. I'll never forget the day Jared dragged me into his office and made me listen to your ideas for the satellite you wanted the interns to build. I wasn't sure even I understood half of what you said, but you knew what you were talking about." He went on to reminisce how, at ten, Molly was far beyond the center's space camp, and Christy and Diane chimed in with their own memories of her as a child prodigy.

"I wish our parents were here," Christy said wistfully. It wasn't often that she referred to their mom and Molly's dad that way—even though Fred had adopted Christy—and the acknowledgment made Molly smile. Fred McLane may not have been Christy's biological father, but he'd loved both his daughter and stepdaughter fiercely.

"Me, too," Molly said, leaning in to give her sister a seated hug.

"So, Molly, have you told Jared and Christy your plans for the summer yet?" Dr. Johnson asked.

"Plans for the summer?" Christy repeated, looking at Molly. "You're coming home for a few weeks before heading to Seattle or Houston or wherever your job takes you, aren't you?"

Molly shot Dr. Johnson a look, but he raised his eyebrows and dipped his chin in a way that told her he already knew she hadn't said anything and needed to come clean. Molly felt temperature in the restaurant rise despite the Boston chill of early May.

"Well, I, um…" She looked at Jared's mentor for help, but he tilted his head to the side and waited for her to continue.

"Salad with ranch dressing," the waiter said, setting a plate in front of Molly and giving her a moment's reprieve.

Once the salads were served and little Nicky happily munched on a sliced cucumber, everyone bowed their heads, and Jared led them in prayer. It was something Molly rarely did anymore. Pray in public, that is. She'd learned to keep her religion to herself and ignore the jabs from her *enlightened* classmates whenever anyone brought up the subject. Praying privately, though, was something she'd been doing an awful lot of lately. At that moment, she was praying they could get through the weekend without any more mention of her summer plans.

***

"Out with it, Squirt," Christy said once the two of them were alone in Molly's dorm room, a luxury the college senior was allowed because of her age. Christy helped Molly finish packing while Nicky slept in Molly's bed and Sally colored at her desk. Jared was giving Simon and Diane a tour of the campus, his Alma Mater, and now Molly's as well.

"Out with what?" Molly paid close attention to the sweater she was folding and refolding.

"What's going on with you and Dr. Johnson? Your summer plans?" Christy said with an edge to her voice.

"Well, you know that he wanted me to intern at Wallops this summer, help him with some research, help Jared with his M29, work on the Antares they're sending up in August, stuff like that."

"And?"

"And I think I'm going to work at the café instead, like I did a few years ago when I helped Holly part-time. Only this time, I'll work full-time for Holly and not work at Wallops."

Christy stood frozen as she looked at her sister. It took several minutes for her to speak.

"Not work at Wallops? Why? You've been working there officially since you were fifteen, and unofficially for longer than that. That college graduate internship is a sought-after prize. Besides, Holly doesn't need more help. She already has Diego, and she's hiring a new pastry chef."

"She still needs more help for the summer, and I like hanging out at the café."

Christy shook her head. "Let me get this straight. You've been offered a $200,000 starting salary by both Jeff Bezos and Elon Musk as well as the biggest internship at Wallops for the next few months, and you're going to spend your time making sandwiches and wiping down tables instead?"

"You know, working at the café was good enough for you when it was the doughnut shop." Molly tossed the sweater into her suitcase and folded her arms, locking eyes with Christy.

"I didn't have a choice. I didn't even have a degree yet, and I had you to take care of. Jared thought you were going to work at Wallops with him. You were going to be his intern. He's got an important probe going to the moon this summer, and he was counting on you. You'd make good money as an intern while you decide where you want to go permanently."

"I'll make good money at the café once the summer gets rolling, and I don't know that I want to do anything permanently. I don't even know what permanently looks like yet!"

"You won't make what you'd be making at Wallops or SpaceX for Heaven's sake. My gosh, Molly. You don't have to take a job and stay there forever, but you need a career. That's why you went to Harvard to begin with. What's going on in that mega brain of yours?"

"This mega brain of mine needs a break. Don't you get that?"

"A break? From what? Reading textbooks and writing papers that you probably composed in your sleep?"

"Yeah, exactly. That's all I do. I read textbooks and write papers and attend lectures on jet propulsion and structural design while solving calculus problems that Eratosthenes and Anaxagoras could never have dreamed of."

"Who?"

"Never mind. The point is, learning and studying and being *that student* is all I've ever done, ever been. I need to do something different, *be* something different, something I've never done before."

"Molly! You're not even eighteen! Do you have any idea how many things you've never done before? You have your whole life for that. But you have to have a job and money and security—"

"I get it!" Molly yelled. "When Mom and Dad died, they left us without any of that. I know. I remember how hard you worked to take care of us, how you had to drop out of school, how we had to sell our house and move to the beach house and work for Diane to make ends meet. I know that. I was there, too."

"Then what is it you don't get about needing to be secure and have money and a stable life?"

Christy huffed while crossing and uncrossing her arms. Sally's eyes were wide as she looked up at them, Nicky stirred, and Molly took a deep breath before speaking.

"I do get it," she said quietly. "I know I need a job and stability and that I have to accept one of these offers. I get it. I just…" She took a deep breath and shook her head. "I just…"

Christy waited, a tight frown on her face and one foot tapping the floor between them.

Molly looked up at her sister and tried to convey her feelings with her eyes. Realizing Christy was the one who didn't get it, Molly inhaled and let out a long, agonizing breath.

"For one summer, I just want to be normal."

It took several seconds for Christy's face to soften and her eyes to go misty. She reached for her little sister and pulled her into a hug. Molly melted in her arms.

"Oh, Mol. You are normal. You're just abnormally smart. There's nothing wrong with that."

Molly felt her own eyes begin to water. She took several calming breaths and pulled back so she could look at Christy.

"For one summer, just for a few short months, I don't want to be smart. I just want to be a teenager and nothing more. Can I have this one summer, please? Then I promise, I'll take one of the jobs I've been offered. I've already talked to HR everywhere. I told them I wouldn't be making a decision until the fall, and you know what? They're actually okay with that. And you know why? Because I'm not normal.

"I'm not just any candidate looking for a job, and they know that. I know that. What I need to know is that I can be a normal person, live a normal life, and not be expected to be the next Katherine Johnson and ensure the safety of rockets and space vehicles with everyone holding their breath while I solve the problems nobody else can. Do you know the kind of pressure that puts on a kid? A kid, Christy. I may be a Harvard grad, but even I know that I'm still a kid, and I want to be a real kid for just one summer of my life before I have to become a real adult with real-world problems at the age of eighteen."

Christy took a long, deep breath, held it, then let it out.

"Jared talks about his childhood sometimes and how he never had any real friends and never did the things other kids did. Some of that was because of Witness Protection, but mostly, it was because he wasn't like other kids. He wonders sometimes how you're able to handle it all. I guess we all just assumed that it came easily for you."

Molly shrugged. "At times, it does. But that doesn't mean I don't know what I've missed out on. I've never even been on a date. Did you know that? No twenty-one year-old wants to take out a fifteen or sixteen-year-old. I got that, and it didn't really bother me. I was there to learn, not to date or party. But still…"

"You'd like to go on a date, attend a party, hang out with kids your own age."

Molly nodded. "I would. I really would."

After one more hug, Christy agreed. "But we might need to talk about the partying and dating and all that before you start going out." She was smiling, but Molly saw the concern in her eyes.

"Don't worry, Sis. I've still got my mega brain to guide me."

***

"It's a pleasure to meet you, Dr. Johnson." Dustin Howard shook hands with the man he was surprised to recognize walking across the campus.

"Likewise, Dustin. I didn't think we'd meet in person for another week." Dr. Johnson gestured to the woman beside him. "This is my wife, Diane. We're getting a tour of the campus."

"Oh," Dustin's heart sunk. "I thought, perhaps, you were here for graduation."

"I am. Dr. Stevenson's sister-in-law graduated. In fact, you must know her. Molly McLane. Jared, this is Dustin Howard, your new intern."

Dustin's heart stopped sinking and began to pound. He had to work at keeping his expression even. He swallowed and breathed deeply through his nose, avoiding the temptation to wipe the sweat from his hand as he extended it.

"It's nice to meet you, Dr. Stevenson. Molly and I, um, we're well acquainted."

Dr. Stevenson frowned as he took a step forward and shook Dustin's hand. "Well acquainted?"

The man didn't look like he spent too many hours lifting weights or punching a leather bag—with his thick glasses and gangly build—but his expression and hard clench of Dustin's hand was enough to make Dustin catch his breath.

"We've been in almost all the same classes since freshman year. She," he stopped and swallowed again. "She beat me out for valedictorian."

"Well," Dr. Johnson said as Dustin continued to eye Dr. Stevenson. "It's too bad, then, that Molly has turned down my offer as an intern. The two of you would've made quite a team."

Dustin blinked as he turned his gaze toward his future supervisor. "Turned down the internship?"

"Yes. I had hoped to have both of you at Wallops this summer, working under Jared. I mean, Dr. Stevenson here, but Molly has made other plans."

Dustin stopped the dismissive sound before it escaped his nostrils. "I see. Well, I hope that doesn't jeopardize my position."

"On the contrary. Dr. Stevenson and I are looking forward to seeing what contributions you can make in our endeavor to study more of the moon."

At that moment, Dr. Johnson's earlier words sunk in. Molly's brother-in-law was also a scientist at Wallops and was going to be his supervisor. Dustin lifted himself a bit taller and looked up at Dr. Stevenson, a tall man with dark curly hair and steely blue eyes behind his glasses, just an inch or so taller than Dustin.

"I need to go find my dad, but it was a pleasure to meet you, Dr. Stevenson and Mrs. Johnson. I look forward to working with you. Dr. Johnson, it was nice to finally meet you off-screen." Dustin shook everyone's hands again and smiled as they all said goodbye, then he turned to go, not letting the scowl take over his features until he was sure it wouldn't be seen.

That child had been a royal pain in his posterior since the day she walked into their first class three years prior. He was overjoyed to hear that she had turned down the internship. He didn't even care about the rumors that she'd been offered some of the most coveted jobs in the universe for his peers. He had those same offers and was pretty sure he knew which one he was going to take. As long as he didn't have to deal with her anymore, life was good.

"Molly turned down the internship?" he heard Dr. Stevenson."

"Simon, you weren't supposed to say anything," Mrs. Johnson admonished her husband, and Dustin's grin widened.

***

Molly frowned as she read the text again. She was sitting at the gate, trying to ignore the anxious expressions and constant whispering between Jared and

Christy. Neither was happy with her decision, but she didn't care. It was her life, and she was getting ready to turn eighteen, so she had the right to make her own decisions. Only now, she was wondering if she'd been wrong about working at the café. She texted back to her best friend, Anya.

What???? Why not???

She watched the dots dance on the screen, her anxiety growing with each passing second.

I'm getting a job here for the summer. Jake doesn't want me to go so far away.

Molly closed her eyes and told herself to stay calm, but before she knew what she was doing, her fingers were feverously tapping the screen, and words were multiplying faster than she could think them through.

Jake isn't worth it. IMO, he's a jerk, and he's just your first love, a high school sweetheart. But we've been BFFs for six years. Let me guess. He says that he'll break up with you or find someone else if you go. Am I right? FWIW, I gave up a good internship to spend my summer hanging out with you at work and on the beach. IDK and IDC what you do. It's your life to screw up.

By the time Molly hit send, tears were sliding down her cheeks, and everyone else was picking up their bags to begin boarding. Molly stood and hoisted her backpack onto her shoulders.

"Hey," Christy said. "You okay?"

Molly nodded. "Just some big changes coming, you know?"

"It's going to be okay, Mol. We'll figure things out together."

Without answering, Molly followed the rest of the group onto the plane. Was she the one screwing up her life? Was she throwing away a good job and good experience just to act like some stupid teenager like Anya? What was so great about being a teen anyway? Or having a boyfriend? Or a first kiss? Once Molly made up her mind about her future job, she would be entering a whole new life, and none of that kid's stuff would matter anyway.

One thing Molly knew for sure. She wasn't going to tell anyone if she had regrets about working at the café. She didn't need to hear any I-told-you-sos. She would make the best of it and use her downtime to make future plans. She didn't need a best friend for that. Anya wouldn't get it anyway. She had the advantage of being normal.

***

"Welcome back!" Diego beamed as he and Molly high-fived each other. "This place is no fun without you." He was pouring oil onto the cooktop behind the counter to prep it for the day.

"Hey, watch yourself," Holly said, playfully punching her young employee in the arm.

"Sorry, Holly. It's not that I don't enjoy working for you. It's just that Molly and I are, you know, close to the same age. That's all."

"Uh-huh. I guess thirty is ancient," Holly said, walking around the counter to give Molly a hug. "For the record, I agree with Diego. I'm so excited you're back for the summer before you head off to galaxies far, far away where no man—or woman—has gone before."

"Um, thanks? Though you're mixing catchphrases. Star Wars and Star Trek are two different franchises."

Diego laughed as Holly sighed. "Glad to see you haven't changed, Molly."

Molly wasn't sure that was a good thing, but whatever. She was happy to be back working with Diego and Holly. Though she only worked part-time the previous summer, she and Diego worked well together, and Holly was always easy going, which made work fun.

"I heard you're expecting," Molly said to her boss and good friend of her sister. "Congratulations."

"Thanks," Holly said with a wide grin, her hand moving instinctively to her swelling stomach. "It took us forever, and we're so excited, but I'm exhausted all the time. I don't know how Taylor did this with a little one at home."

"Yeah, that's one of the reasons I'm glad to be home for a while. Christy has her hands full."

"Well, if you ever need time off to help, just let me know. I can't imagine having two under six and working odd hours as a homecare nurse. Thank Heaven she has Diane and Marge to help out."

"Hey, are you two going to keep gabbing or work?" Diego gestured toward the table where three women, one older and two middle aged, had just taken their seats.

Molly's face lit up. "I'll get their orders," she said, hurrying over to the ladies while tying her apron around her waist.

"Hi, Miss Kayla! Hey, Miss Kate, Mrs. Kelly. How are y'all?"

"Molly! Welcome home," Miss Kayla said, rising to give her a hug. "Congratulations. I heard you took Harvard by storm."

"Thanks. I'm glad to be home."

"Nick says you've had all kinds of exciting offers. He and Taylor brag about you as though you're their own."

Molly grinned. "Yeah, well, Nick's kind of the love of my life, you know."

"You are still talked about by everyone on the island," Miss Kate said. "The way you broke that case years ago when the restaurants were being vandalized. That's the stuff of legend."

Molly knew how much the whole family loved Nick, the best friend of Kayla's husband, Zach, who Molly adored as much as she adored Nick. Nick was the police officer who found Kayla's son, Todd, and rescued him after he'd been kidnapped when he was a little boy.

"What about these big jobs of yours?" Miss Kayla's mother, Ronnie, asked. "Which one are you going to take?"

Molly pressed her lips together. "Honestly, Mrs. Kelly, I don't know. They're all great offers, but I can't decide. For now, I'm working here this summer and hoping to be norm-, to relax on the beach while pondering my future."

"Sounds like a good plan," Mrs. Kelly said. "I hope you have a fabulous summer."

"Thanks. Hey, Miss Kayla, are Todd and EJ home for the summer? What are they up to?"

"You know, I always forget that you had classes with both boys. Todd's home for the summer and heads back to Old Dominion in the fall. He's studying forensics. EJ's home now but not for long," his mother said wistfully. "He ships out in two weeks, so he has to be back on base next week."

"Where is he stationed?"

"Mobile, Alabama, right now, completing his aviation training, then who knows. Once this upcoming mission is over, he'll get his transfer papers, and he could be sent anywhere a pilot is needed."

"I guess that's hard on you."

"Sure, but it's the life he wanted, and I'm happy for him. He followed his uncle and grandfather to the Coast Guard Academy, but he's making his own path as a pilot."

Molly thought about that and was reminded that she had a lot to think about concerning her own future.

"Oh, Molly," Kate Kelly said. "One of the guys at the station has a birthday coming up, and Aaron wants to order coffee and doughnuts for everyone. Can I take care of that for him while I'm here?"

"You sure can, and I'm sure you know that the Coast Guard gets a discount," Molly told her cheerfully.

Miss Kate shook her head. "Aaron doesn't want a discount. He doesn't like to do that to the local businesses."

"Commander Kelly does more for this island than the local businesses could ever repay. Between rescuing boaters, helping during storms, and just being there to assist in any crisis, he and his fellow Coasties deserve more than a discount."

"That's very kind of you and Holly, but please, just charge him whatever you'd charge me. When you get a chance, bring me the order form, and I'll fill it out over breakfast."

"Sure, and thank you. I came to take your orders. What can I get for y'all?"

"You don't need to do that," Mrs. Kelly said. "We can order at the counter like everyone else."

"I know," Molly said. "But I want to do it."

They thanked her and ordered. Then Molly took the ticket to Diego while she made their assortment of coffees.

The rest of the day went pretty much the same as it started. Molly saw lots of people she knew, inquired about others she'd gone to school with before transferring for high school, and heard about the achievements and accomplishments of many of the kids who grew up on the island. It was weird to think that kids she went to school with—like Todd, with whom she was in fifth grade when she first bumped up—were just graduating from high school or only a year into college. Where did she fit in?

***

"Jared, why are you hiding in here?" Simon asked, poking his head into the cluttered storeroom. Shelves lined the walls, overflowing with mechanical parts, wires, rotors, and a vast array of technical gadgets.

"I can't find the parts for the particle detectors."

"For the M29 sat?"

"Yeah," Jared stood and looked at his mentor and longtime friend. He pushed his glasses higher on the bridge of his nose. "I was positive I had them in my office yesterday."

"I doubt anyone would move them."

"That's what I thought, but they're gone. The whole box I put together. I was going to have my intern, Justin, start assembling them."

"It's Dustin," Simon corrected him. "Have you asked him if he saw them?"

Jared shook his head but answered, "Yes, and he didn't know what I was talking about."

"Dr. Johnson," a voice said from the hallway.

"Yes, Ellen?"

"There's a call for you from Houston."

"Go ahead," Jared told him. "I'll keep looking."

Simon walked away, and Jared scratched his head. He knew he had those parts for his satellite. Where could they have gone?

Dr. Ethan Edwards joins the Island Clinic

University of Virginia graduate and former resident of Richmond, Virginia, Ethan Edwards, has joined the Island Clinic as a Pediatric General Practitioner. He recently finished his residency at the Children's Hospital of Richmond. He has two sisters who reside in the Richmond area near his parents, Richard and Judy. His grandmother, Arlene, has been a resident of Chincoteague for almost twenty years, having moved here when her husband, William, joined the Island Dental Group. Dr. Edwards will begin seeing patients immediately.

The Chincoteague Herald, May 5

Chapter Two

"Welcome aboard, Dr. Edwards. I'm Jenny." The embroidery on her lab coat read, *Dr. J. Murray.* He took her hand, which was small but strong, and he wondered how long she had been a doctor. She looked young, and her hands didn't look or feel as though they'd been exposed to constant washing with harsh soaps.

"Are you new, too?" He asked.

Jenny laughed. "That depends upon what you mean by new. I've been here about six months. I graduated a semester early from college by doubling up my classes, and I finished my residency a few months ago. Technically, I'm still new to the clinic, but I grew up on the island and volunteered here when they needed an extra hand. So new is a relative term."

"Nice to meet you, old but new Jenny." He returned her friendly smile. I'm not sure where to begin," he admitted as the familiar scent of antiseptic reached his nose.

"No worries. You're our first official pediatrician, and we're happy to have you here. I've just taken over for Dr. Swann, who was the GP and only doctor on staff, but retirement called." She kept talking as she refilled her travel coffee cup, covered with stickers from campgrounds and vacation spots. "As you know, we're the smallest rural health center on Virginia's Eastern Shore, and we have a growing population on the island. I'm glad the board brought in a second doctor when Lorilee moved, though she was an outstanding PA. Joanne's a fabulous NP, and we're lucky to have her, along with two great part-time nurses, Steph and Paula. There's not an overwhelming demand for more licensed bodies here, but that doesn't mean summer won't be crazy for all of us."

Ethan smiled but wondered, *is she always this talkative?*

"Okay. So, what do I do to get started?" he asked, feeling impatient.

"Stacey's our administrative assistant, receptionist, and jill-of-all-trades. She'll take you to our office and go over the schedule. We're sharing the space. I hope that's okay. I'm not sure how much they told you in your interview, but as you can see, it's pretty tight in here. There's Joanne." She gestured to the woman he saw go into an exam room, "She's our NP, and she'll get you up to speed on the medical stuff. She's been here for a while. And remember this." Jenny paused until he gave her his full attention, forcing himself to stop looking at the outdated equipment and vast wall of cabinets with paper files. "Do whatever she, Paula, and Steph tell you.

In medical school, we're taught that we're in charge, we have all the knowledge, and what we say goes. It didn't take me long to figure out that we doctors take our marching orders from the nurses. If you didn't figure that out as a resident, then it's time for you to get up to speed. We're a small clinic, but we're all the island citizens have. Always listen to the nurse practitioner and nurses, and do what they say. Got it?"

Who is this woman? I graduated from a top school and did my residency at one of the best children's hospitals in the nation. Sure, nurses are valuable, but seriously?

Jenny cleared her throat. "Any questions?" Her narrowed hazel green eyes and watermelon-colored pursed lips made him blush as though she had read his mind.

"No, I'm good. Thanks for the info."

She looked at him for another moment before nodding and calling to Stacey to "take him to our office and show him the ropes."

This was going to be an interesting place to work.

Several hours later, Ethan was exhausted and missing Richmond.

"Not a bad first day," Joanne said. "Things were pretty slow."

"Slow?" Ethan asked, almost choking on the word. "I saw nineteen patients in person, did five tele-med appointments, and barely ate lunch."

"And you have three phone messages from parents you'll need to answer before you leave. Do you need a refresher from Stacey on how to access them?"

Ethan opened his mouth but couldn't find the words. He took a deep breath and tried again.

"Without sounding like a wimp, can I ask how this was a slow day?"

Joanne laughed. "All spring colds, minor accidents, a few well checks, and some camp physicals. Believe me, that's a slow day. Just wait another few weeks for summer to begin. Then you'll see what a busy day is like, especially if we have any emergencies where the Coast Guard has to bring in boating victims, or the lifeguards pull someone from the water, or someone gets too close to a pony. We never know what we'll be facing during the high season."

Ethan's jaw dropped, and Joanne laughed. "Welcome to the world with one pediatrician on staff. Consider yourself lucky. Up until now, we had one PA, one NP, and an RN, no doctors at all. We're moving up in the world."

As he watched Joanne walk away, Ethan had a whole new appreciation for the nurses, as Jenny practically predicted, and he wondered what he'd gotten himself into.

Before she was out of sight, Joanne turned back to him. "By the way, every Tuesday night, there's trivia at Uno Taco, Dos Mojitos. You should come. It's a great way to meet other people on the island. It starts at seven, but we go early for dinner just to get a table. It's always packed. The food is great, so come hungry."

"Trivia night?"

"Yeah, our team is called The I-V Leaguers. Get it? Seriously, you should come."

"Um, maybe. I don't know."

"Be there, or be square, Dr. Edwards."

Ethan shook his head and thought, no way, no how. But as he was walking to his car, after spending thirty minutes trying to talk a mother off the ledge whose child had swallowed a blood tick, he began thinking that a cold beer, a hot taco, and a round of fun might not be so bad.

***

"Seriously?" Molly asked. "Why should I go?" She stood with her arms crossed and scrunched her features together at the suggestion, though EJ couldn't see her on the other end of the phone.

"Because I'm only home for two weeks, and this is what Lizzie and our little brothers want to do, and we want you to join us. Come on. You might actually have fun."

"With a group of people who think they have all the answers but only know what little they glean from watching Jeopardy or doing crossword puzzles?"

EJ's sigh resonated through the phone as distinctively as the squealing wheels of the T Molly could hear from her dorm on exceptionally quiet nights. "Look, Molly, when we were in school, you never let yourself have fun. I imagine boarding school and college were the same. Just for one night, go out with Todd,

Lizzie, Ben, and me, and see what it's like to have a night of fun."

"Did your mother put you up to this? I mean, it's not like we hung out or anything."

"Did you hang out with anyone other than those other science geeks from Wallops? Come on. Give it a try."

He had a point. Lots of them, though she took exception to Chloe and Avi being called geeks. She did say she wanted to be normal for once in her life, and she knew that lots of her classmates had gone to trivia pretty regularly, so it seemed like the cool thing to do.

"Okay, I'll go. But I get final say on the answers." She could practically hear his eyes roll.

"Fine, but we're a team. We discuss the answers. Got it?"

"Yeah, whatever. Thanks." She hung up and looked at herself in the mirror. "What does one wear to trivia night?" she asked herself out loud.

"Trivia night?" Christy poked her head into the room. "Are you actually going out and doing something that regular people do for fun?"

Molly sighed. "I guess so. You didn't tell Miss Kayla to have EJ call me and invite me out, did you?"

"I did not," Christy solemnly answered. "But it's nice that he did. I don't remember you being friends with anyone here when you were in high school."

"That's because I wasn't friends with anyone here in high school. They were all years older and many IQ points under me, and I was away at school most of the time. I have no idea why he even asked. I saw his mom and grandmother yesterday and asked about what he and Todd were up to. I can't help but think one of them had something to do with this."

"Well, whether they did or not, I'm glad you're going. So, what are you going to wear?"

Turning back to her wide-open closet, Molly blew a puff of air. "That might be the hardest question I'll hear all night."

***

"Hey, Molly, I can't believe you're here." A guy from middle school—she thought his name was Rob—sat down beside Molly and smiled at her. She wasn't sure why he was talking to her. They'd never been friends.

"EJ asked me to come, but I haven't seen him or any of his group yet. I figured I'd save the table."

The table had a light wooden top with legs painted a bright blue. All other table legs and the chairs were also brightly painted in pink, yellow, blue, or green. The booths around the perimeter of the room were brilliantly decorated with village scenes reminiscent of small Mexican towns. The smell of fresh tortillas was so strong, Molly could almost taste them. Uno Taco, Dos Mojitos had always been one of her favorite places, and she was happy it hadn't changed.

"So, you're on their team?"

"I guess so. I mean, they asked. Whose team are you on?" She fingered the straw in her iced tea, not confident in her ability to hold an interesting conversation that didn't involve science or space or the latest mystery she was reading. The sounds of clamoring voices, clanging pots, and clattering utensils carried from the nearby kitchen.

"Just a bunch of guys from school. We get together now and then when we're all home and do whatever there is to do. If it's a Tuesday, we're here."

"How often do you get home?"

"Pretty often. I only live an hour away. Sometimes I meet up with them just because I have nothing better to do."

Molly frowned and tried to imagine such a boring existence. A group of guys entered the bar and called to Ron, not Rob, apparently. He waved to them and stood.

"Nice talking to you, Molly. See you around."

Molly said goodbye and smiled. She noticed the way the group kept looking at her, and she felt self-conscious in her V-neck Boston t-shirt and skinny jeans cut at the shins. Maybe this wasn't such a good idea after all.

She went back to watching the door, her fingers still bending her straw back and forth. There were several unfamiliar faces coming and going. A group of Coasties arrived and grabbed a table near the bar. Molly recognized the nurses from the clinic but not the man with them. He was good-looking, really good-looking. But kind of old, too. Old as in older than the guys she went to Harvard with. Maybe her sister's age. When Jenny Murray joined them, Molly smiled and waved at her former babysitter, someone she did consider a friend. Jenny squealed and ran to give Molly a quick hug and chatted for a moment before heading back to her table.

Ron's table continued to fill, and a table was being formed with some of the restaurant owners in town. She waved to Bob and Jane, Jerry, Dawn, and Jake. Molly had gotten to know all of them five years earlier when she'd helped bring down the person sabotaging their restaurants while they competed on a reality show. She watched as Anna, the owner of Uno Taco, Dos Mojitos and another contestant on the show, ran over and hugged them all. Molly smiled.

After a few more minutes passed, and a lot more trivia enthusiasts filled the room, she saw Lizzie and EJ hurry in.

"Sorry we're late," EJ said. "Lizzie got off work late. Mom has a big event tomorrow, so they had a lot to do to get ready. Lizzie, you remember Molly, right?"

"Hi, Molly," Lizzie said with a genuine smile. "It's nice to see you again. Congratulations on all your accomplishments. You look fabulous, by the way. I love your hair that way."

"Thanks, Lizzie." Molly subconsciously ran her hand through her hair, which she had unbraided and left loose. She couldn't compare to Lizzie who had always been one of the prettiest girls she'd ever known with flaxen hair and eyes the color of a robin's egg. "I heard you got your master's. Congratulations to you," Molly offered.

"Thanks. It was kind of necessary for any job prospects, but I'm glad I'm done." She sat next to Molly.

"And what now?"

"I'll apply for positions with some therapeutical practices, but not until we know where EJ will be stationed. I'm working for his mom for the summer and getting my certifications done."

"You mean, you're still dating?" Molly looked between the two in surprise, and Lizzie laughed.

"I know. It's hard to believe, but somehow, we still are."

"How long have you been together?"

"Since we were about twelve, right EJ?"

"Sounds right." He had taken the seat at the head of the table, next to Lizzie.

"Wow. That's crazy," Molly said. "I mean, in a good way," she clarified. She couldn't imagine what that would be like, to be with the same person from the age of twelve for the rest of your life.

Lizzie laughed again. "We get that a lot. But we decided long ago that being young didn't mean being wrong. Whether we were home or miles apart, we could never be away from each in our hearts, and we knew we belonged together."

Molly would've thought Lizzie was just being mushy for her sake, but the genuine love in her eyes, and the loving smile on EJ's face said it all.

Todd and Ben came in and joined them, and Molly had to keep herself from letting her mouth hang open. Ben had grown into quite a good-looking guy with his ocean blue eyes and shoulder-length blonde locks that fell across his face. She could barely utter hello and was happy the DJ was ready to get the game started.

Just then, the door opened again, and her whole world swirled the drain with such strong centripetal motion, she could feel herself whirlpooling into a fathomless abyss.

***

Dustin stopped in his tracks when he saw Molly sitting at the table straight ahead. He blinked more than once and then felt like an idiot. Was he supposed to say hi? They weren't even civil to each other back at school, but they were adults now. At least, he was. He wasn't even sure how old she was. Seventeen? Eighteen? Younger or older? When she first appeared on campus freshman year, she was the talk of the class, but when it became apparent that she wasn't the only child prodigy attending the famed college, the fascination ended. Unfortunately, she and Dustin had nearly every class together, and she bested him in just about every one, always raising her hand and rendering Dustin inadequate.

He felt queasy, and he didn't know if it was due to the strong smell of tacos and tequila or seeing Molly for the first time since graduation. He made a gesture of acknowledgement and followed the rest of the interns to the bar. It appeared there were no tables left, but at least he was old enough to sit there. He couldn't say the same for his esteemed classmate. Former classmate. School was over. And he needed to get over being humiliated by Molly McLane.

However, that was not to be the case that evening.

***

Molly pasted a smile on her face and reminded herself that her specialty was space science; and while she knew a lot about every academic subject, she wasn't as abreast on pop culture as others her age. She needed to be part of the team, not the manager.

"Sure, I'm okay with Lizzie writing the answers. My handwriting isn't that great anyway. I'm not used to writing with pen and paper."

EJ laughed. "Who is? You should see my writing!"

"He's right," Lizzie said. "It's awful."

"He's never allowed to write down the answers," Ben added, those ocean eyes sparkling.

Lizzie wrote something down at the top of the paper. Molly squinted and asked, "You're a Quizzard, Harry? What does that mean?"

"It's our team name," Lizzie said. "Get it? Wizard, quizzard? As in quiz."

"It's not a real word."

"So?" Todd said. "It's a cool word." He narrowed his eyes in suspicion. "You do know who Harry Potter is, right?"

"Of course, I know who Harry Potter is" Molly said indignantly. "And the team name is taken from Hagrid's words to Harry when he presented him with his letter from Hogwarts."

Todd nodded. "Good. Just checking."

Molly rolled her eyes.

At least I read the books. Todd is probably one of those guys who said he read them but only watched the movies.

"Tonight's first category," the DJ said over the music and many voices in the room, "is 80s Television."

Molly's jaw dropped. "What kind of category is that?"

"A very popular one," Lizzie said.

"How are we supposed to know these?" Molly asked, feeling way out of her comfort zone.

"Don't worry. You'll be surprised at how much you know."

Thirty minutes later, Molly felt wholly deficient for the first time in her life. Two categories down—80s Television and Summer Blockbusters—and she had contributed no more than three answers, and she wasn't sure about any of them, though they were all correct.

"The next category is Stuff You Should Know," DJ Charlie said, and Molly wondered if the whole world was made up of knowledge she should know but didn't. Was she too focused on science and not on life? Were there things other people her age knew naturally that she didn't because she had bypassed the age to learn them?

"Question one, how many elements are there on the periodic table?"

All eyes turned toward Molly. "118," she said with confidence. Who wouldn't know that? Maybe this wouldn't be so bad after all.

"Question two, how many bones do sharks have?"

"What?" Ben breathed out loudly, his eyes blinking. "Dude, how would anyone know that?"

"It's a trick question," Molly said, keeping her voice down. "Sharks don't have bones."

"She's right, surfer boy," EJ agreed as Todd nodded. "They have cartilage. The answer is zero."

Molly smiled as she caught the eye of Marian, the longtime school librarian, and Shannon, who recently became the town's new librarian after working for several years toward her degree. Molly waved, and the women waved back. Molly recognized one of their teammates—she thought her name was Tammi—as a friend of Kayla Middleton.

DJ Charlie brought Molly back to focus as he announced, "Question three! What disease stems from the medieval term that means 'bad air'?"

"Malaria," Lizzie and Molly said at the same time as Lizzie furiously wrote down the answer.

"Glad our team has a scientist and the only person in the twenty-first century to still study Latin," Ben said, rolling his eyes at his sister.

"Stultissime," Lizzie said to her brother before sticking out her tongue at him. Molly laughed at the look on his face—eyebrows squeezed together and lips puckered.

"What's that supposed to mean?"

"Too bad you didn't take Latin," Molly said, figuring Lizzie would know better than anyone that her brother was a complete idiot. The two females slapped their hands in a high five.

"Question four, what is the quality of an object that allows it to float on water?"

Molly and EJ both whispered in the huddle, "Buoyancy," and Lizzie wrote the answer with a smile.

"I feel a ten out of ten coming," Lizzie said.

"Don't jinx us," EJ told her.

"Question five, who first came up with the idea of contact lenses?"

"Oh!" Todd exclaimed before leaning into the huddle. "My hero, Leonardo."

"di Caprio?" Ben said, tossing his hair. "I don't think so."

Molly and Lizzie looked at each other and both shouted, "Stultissime!"

Todd rolled his eyes and made a sound of disgust. "da Vinci. Come on. He thought of practically every modern invention hundreds of years before scientists knew how to make them work."

"And he's your hero?" Molly asked in surprise. "I mean he's totally cool. I just didn't think you—"

"I've always been fascinated by him, since I was a kid. Science was my favorite subject, and I thought it was cool that he came up with so many scientific ideas that were way before his time."

Molly was impressed. Todd might be smarter than she thought.

"Question six, what sense is most closely linked to memory?"

Everyone at the table froze.

"Anyone know?" Eddie asked.

"I should know this," Lizzie said. "I really should know this. I took a whole class on repressed memories. Why am I going blank?"

Molly closed her eyes and pictured a page from a book she read recently about the brain. "Smell," she said, her eyes still closed.

"That's it!" Lizzie cried as she wrote down the answer. "Thanks, Molly."

"Question seven, what is the galaxy closest in light-years to the Milky Way Galaxy?"

"Andromeda," Molly said, really feeling as though she was part of the team and enjoying their growing excitement.

"Question eight, the deepest point in all the world's oceans is called what?"

"The Mariana Trench," EJ said quickly. "It's near Guam. Our cutter, the Sequoia, partnered with researchers there to listen to the sounds on the seafloor of the trench. We watched some of the videos in one of my classes at the Academy."

"That's really cool," Molly said. Lizzie looked at her and nodded.

"Question nine, what does CPU stand for?"

"Central Processing Unit," offered Ben. "Finally, a question I didn't have to think about."

"That's because all you think about is computers," Lizzie told her brother as she jotted down the answer. "That and surfing."

"And I'm going to live comfortably off my computer programmer salary for the rest of my life, until I retire young and become a surfing pro, Miss Family Therapist," Ben said with a satisfied grin.

Okay, Ben might not be a total idiot after all. Molly smiled at the thought. *There might be an actual brain under all that hair.*

"And question ten. I'll give it to you if you're within 1,000 miles. What is the distance between the moon and the earth?" DJ Charlie looked around the room. "And some of you probably have an advantage over others with this one."

"238,900 miles," Molly said matter-of-factly.

Lizzie's hand hovered over the paper.

"You know that off the top of your head?" Todd asked.

Molly shrugged. "Um, yeah. It's common knowledge."

Ben shook his head. "Not common to me."

"Can you repeat that?" Lizzie asked.

Molly rattled off the number again. "You guys do know that I majored in astrophysics at Harvard, right? And that my brother-in-law has won awards for his research and writing about the moon?"

As she spoke, Molly happened to look above EJ's bowed head. Her eyes locked with Dustin Howard's. She knew he was working with Jared this summer, and she also knew he was probably the only other person in the room to know that precise answer, except maybe the other interns, of course.

Dustin raised the brown bottle in his hand and tilted it toward her. He smiled, and his eyes sparkled with the knowledge that he was as smart as she was. Well, almost, according to their class ranking. Molly wondered if he would still be smiling at the end of the game.

***

"Seriously? We were beat by a team named, 'You're a Quizzard, Harry?' I mean, what kind of name is that?" Nathan, Dustin's roommate, looked at the group with a scowl on his face.

"They're a bunch of locals," Adrienne said. It was her second year interning at NASA's Wallops Flight Center, just off the island. "They played last summer, too, except for the girl with the brown hair. Molly's her name. She helped out some at Space Camp last summer, but I never really talked to her. She mostly worked with Dr. Johnson, some kind of assistant or something. I think Dr. Stevenson is her brother, so she's basically a nepo baby."

"Brother-in-law," Dustin said. "Dr. Stevenson. She was supposed to be an intern this summer but turned it down."

"Yeah, I heard she decided to work at some restaurant or something instead. Guess she couldn't keep up with the science. I think she's pretty young. Probably decided science wasn't her thing."

Dustin kept his mouth shut. It was one thing to lose to a bunch of locals. It was another to admit that the 'pretty young' 'nepo baby' who couldn't 'keep up with the science' was at least three years younger than he was, finished college in under four years, and vanquished him in his quest for top of the class.

"These questions were bogus anyway," Nathan said. "I mean, who cares about TV shows from the 1980s?"

"Did you ever watch *Quantum Leap*?" Dustin asked before finishing his beer. "It's a pretty good show."

Nathan shrugged. "Never heard of it."

"I'm tired," Adrienne said. "You guys ready to head back?"

She polished off her cosmo, and their fourth teammate, Cameron, threw back his gin and tonic. He slammed his glass on the bar and grinned, pointing at the winning team. He called over to them in a loud voice, "Next time, you bunch of wizard wannabees, you're going down."

"Let's get him out of here," Dustin said to Nathan.

"On it," Nathan said. "Come on, Cam, time to go to bed."

"With you?" Cam laughed. "I'll take the blonde wizard. Hey, cutie. Wanna see my rocket?"

The tall, muscular guy with the buzz cut stood, and the blonde grabbed his arm. "EJ, don't," she said in a loud whisper.

"Hey," DJ Charlie called as the bartender hurried toward the group known as The Mad Scientists. "You want to play next week? Pay your tabs and go home. Now."

The DJ looked from Cam to EJ and back to Cam.

"Come on, Cam. Let's go," Dustin said.

The team was silent as they paid their bar bills and walked out. Dustin felt Molly's eyes on him, and he began to sweat from embarrassment. He left the restaurant grateful that he wouldn't have to see her at work the next morning.

***

Ethan watched the scene with interest. The drunk guy wasn't wrong about the blonde. She was a looker. However, it was the brunette next to her who caught his eye. She looked young, but he wasn't sure she was as young as she looked. There was something about her that made her age indecipherable. He guessed her teammates were in their early to mid-twenties. He had the tall guy pegged for a police officer or military. His girlfriend was refined, a cut above the rest maybe. The two boys with them looked like college students and were definitely their brothers. The resemblance was remarkable in both sets of siblings. But the other girl, she stood out. Why? He wasn't sure.

After the brief non-altercation ended, Ethan told his colleagues goodnight, watched them leave, then took a seat at the bar before ordering another beer. He continued to eye the group across the room as they finished their drinks and carried on their conversations. The brunette talked and smiled but didn't engage as much as the others. She spent a lot of time playing with her straw, answering when spoken to, or offering a thought now and then. She wasn't invested in whatever the others were talking about. As a doctor, he spent a lot of time reading body language, and one thing he knew was that she wasn't entirely comfortable—with them or this place, he wasn't certain.

Despite being unsure about her age, Ethan was intrigued. He tried not to stare but found his gaze wandering toward her more than it should. When the group rose to leave, he motioned to the bartender.

"What can I get you?" the bartender asked.

Ethan nodded toward the door. "That group there. One of them looks familiar to me. Who are they?"

The bartender—Ethan didn't know his name and didn't ask—sized them up before answering.

"Local kids. Good people from good families. The couple, EJ and Lizzie, they've been together since they were little. She just finished school. Master's, I think. Social work or psych, something like that. EJ's a Coastie, graduated from the academy and stationed somewhere…" He scratched his head, and Ethan began to become impatient. "Anyway, he comes from a long line of Coasties here on the island. EJ's brother's in college, so is Lizzie's. Not sure what they're studying, lifelong best friends. Lizzie and her brother—Ben, I think?—are the police chief's kids. EJ and Todd are

Kayla Kelly's, now Middleton's, kids. Their family has been here for years. She's Commander Kelly's twin sister. Their dad's a retired Coastie, Mom's an artist. Kayla and her husband, Zach—he's a former Army sniper—run a catering business." He stopped and straightened up. "Hey, you know that TV show, *Neighbor vs. Neighbor*? The cooking show with all the restaurants from one town?"

Ethan nodded though he was clueless. Medical school didn't allow much time to watch television. The bartender rambled on about the show and Kayla's involvement in it, and Ethan acted interested, asking a few questions for clarification. He'd never keep everything straight anyway. His head was already spinning with all the names and connections. After the bartender filled a few orders and returned to check on him, Ethan again asked about the group that had left.

"I think there was one other person in that group we were talking about. Another female."

"Oh, yeah, Molly McLane. Kind of a local hero. Skipped a bunch of years in school, helped the police solve a string of restaurant vandalisms when she was home from boarding school for the summer, and then went on to Harvard. Just graduated valedictorian. They had a big party for her at the community center. We catered. Not sure what she'll do next. Too smart for her own good sometimes."

Ethan finished his beer and thought about Molly. He didn't ask how old she was—young, apparently, but a college graduate, so not that young. Something about her continued to intrigue him. He'd have to see what else he could find out about her.

***

Dr. Stevenson wouldn't stop looking for that box of M29 parts. There were so many discarded fragments of this and that and odd boxes of metal, he never thought that one would be missed. He was irritated with Dr. Stevenson and with himself.

He'd gone to a darn good school, and he'd done well. He wasn't a legacy student, and he didn't have rich parents, which was why he had to quit. He was deep in debt and wouldn't ever have the money to pay it off if he hadn't secured this job. Not the one at Wallops. The other job. The one that paid nicely for parts and information. He just had to keep his head down and not get caught.

He hoped none of the others figured out what he was doing before his big payday.

Chincoteague Emergency Services Warns of Summer
Dangers

Summer will soon be upon us here on the island, and experts are warning that with the fun and festivities of the season comes increased risk of injury. There will be more cars on our roads very soon, so be alert and aware, not just as a driver but as a pedestrian and biker.

"Look both ways' isn't just a good rule for children," says EMT Tori Spencer. "Even adults have been hit by cars when not paying attention as they're stepping off the sidewalk. And be careful with those grills. Follow all safety guidelines, and never use matches or lighters to ignite your grill when your switch malfunctions."

Other areas of concern, especially on Chincoteague, are swimming and boating. "Never ignore warnings about rip currents, undertows, or impending weather," warns Coast Guard Commander Aaron Kelly. "I've had to rescue many swimmers who got swept out to sea or boats that encountered sudden storms. Always wear proper safety equipment when boating or using personal watercrafts."

"We're prepared," says Chincoteague Clinic Lead Doctor Jenny Murray. "But that doesn't mean we want to see our friends, family, or visitors for more than a routine checkup."

The Chincoteague Herald, May 15

Chapter Three

The moment Molly entered the house after work, the baby's screams alerted her that something was wrong.

"Christy," she called. "Christy!"

When her calls went unanswered, Molly's heart rate increased. She raced up the stairs toward the nursery to find her nephew standing in his crib in the darkened room, his red face soaked with tears.

"It's okay, Nicky, Aunt Molly's here." She gently lifted him from the crib and went in search of her sister, following another series of cries she hadn't realized were separate from Nicky's.

"I don't know," she heard Christy practically shout over Sally's screams. "She's crying, and there's so much blood." She paused before saying, "I don't know why I called you. I panicked." Another pause, and her gaze picked up on Molly standing in the bathroom doorway.

"Okay, I'll call her now. Molly's here. She has Nicky." Molly moved into the small space to get a look at her niece. "Yes, I love you, too," Christy said before disconnecting the call.

"What happened?" Molly asked, watching the blood run down Sally's face.

"She fell and hit her face on her nightstand when she was undressing. I wanted to get her in the tub while Nicky was taking his nap. She was so dirty from playing outside." Christy's words were rushed as she fumbled with her phone.

"Who are you calling?"

"911. Tori should be on call."

"Don't," Molly said, laying her hand gently on her sister's shoulder. "Don't tie up the EMTs. There's an accident on Main Street."

Christy's hand froze as she looked up at her sister helplessly.

"Come on," Molly said, motioning for Christy to stand. She'd never seen her sister at a loss like this. "Let's get her to the clinic. I'll drive, and you can keep an eye on the kids."

Christy nodded and stood shakily, holding the six-year-old tightly. Molly knew right away that Christy was in her own world because Molly didn't even have a driver's license. She also knew how heavy Sally was, but Christy carried her out of the bathroom like she weighed nothing. Sally continued to cry, but she was no longer screaming.

"I was trying to stop the bleeding, but it just keeps coming."

"Christy, you're a nurse. You deal with this type of stuff all the time. It's a face wound. There's going to be a lot of blood."

"I know that!" Christy snapped at her sister then blanched at her own display of hostility. "I'm sorry. It's been a while since I was at the clinic. I don't typically treat facial injuries."

"It's okay. We'll be at the clinic soon. We'll take the back way."

When they reached the bottom of the stairs, Christy reminded Molly to grab the diaper bag from the closet.

"Got it. Is Jared on the way?"

"He's going to meet us there."

Molly strapped Nicky into his seat while Christy managed to get Sally into her booster. The little girl begged her mommy not to put her down, and Molly could see Christy wavering, but she buckled her in anyway.

Taking the back road, Molly got them to the clinic just as the ambulance was delivering the last victim from the accident, and complete chaos had erupted.

***

Ethan's head was spinning. Though the motor vehicle accident had only minor injuries, all required treatment at the clinic. There were no pediatric cases, but he learned quickly that multiple victims necessitated all personnel, no matter their specialty. In one hour, he dealt with more diverse injuries than he had seen since his emergency room rotation in medical school.

"All good?" Jenny asked as he was grabbing a quick cup of coffee.

"All good."

"Great because you have a patient,"

"Someone else from the MVA?"

Jenny shook her head as she downed an entire mug of steaming coffee. "A child. Daughter of one of my sister's best friends. I know you'll take good care of her, but this one's special to me, so I might be poking in to check in on everyone."

"Got it. Thanks for the heads up."

"Dr. Edwards, you have a patient in exam room two," Stacey said as Ethan emerged from the lunchroom.

He thanked her and walked to the door, retrieving the paperwork from the plastic holder on the wall and thinking, again, that they really needed to digitize their records. In med school and in his residency, everything was on an iPad, and he could easily toggle from one patient to the next or link to information online.

He opened the door and walked in while still looking over Paula's handwritten notes. When he looked up, he was surprised to see Molly from trivia holding a baby. She had her dark hair pulled back in a braid and wore no makeup. She had on a uniform with the name of a sandwich shop he'd seen but hadn't been to yet. She looked younger than she had the other night, but he was still intrigued, nonetheless.

"Sally Stevenson?"

"Right here," another voice said, and Ethan turned toward the exam table where the six-year-old looked at him teary-eyed. "I'm Christy, and this is Sally. She cut her face under her eye. Contusion and laceration from falling into her nightstand. Bleeding was profuse, but it has slowed with the steady application of pressure. Sutures are required due to the length of the laceration."

Ethan blinked, then smiled. "Doctor, PA, or nurse?"

Christy looked at him curiously for a moment before letting out a long breath and shaking her head.

"I'm so sorry. I'm a nurse. Molly can tell you I was a total wreck until we got here, and then things just kind of kicked in. I've never freaked out like that before." She looked down at the child in front of her and gave her a weak smile.

"Yours?" Ethan nodded toward Sally with a smile.

"Yeah, but I never thought I'd lose it like that."

"It's understandable. We react differently when we're personally affected." He cleared his throat and pushed visions of Jamie from his mind. "Hi, Sally. I'm Dr. Ethan. Can I look at your eye?"

Sally looked nervously from Ethan to her mother and then slowly nodded at him.

"I'm going to be really gentle," he told her in a low voice. "I need to open your eye a little more and shine a light into it. Okay?"

Sally nodded but huddled closer to Christy.

"It's okay, baby. Let Dr. Ethan take a look."

Just as Ethan was moving toward her to look more closely at her injury, the door burst open. A man stood in the doorway, panting loudly, and wiping the sweat from beneath his glasses.

"Sally, is she okay?" He walked briskly toward the child who held her arms out to him. He leaned down and kissed her on the head before looking at Ethan. "Is she all right?"

"I haven't had a chance to examine her yet," Ethan said kindly, used to parents overreacting when their children were hurt.

"Jared," Christy said firmly. "She's going to be fine. Come over here so Dr. Edwards can examine her."

The small room was getting crowded, but Ethan continued his examination while the family looked on. When he looked up and caught Molly's gaze, he saw amusement in her smirk and twinkling eyes. For a moment, he felt disarmed.

"Well," he said, clearing his throat. "I'd say your assessment is right on, Mrs. Stevenson."

"Please, Christy. She needs stitches?"

"Yes, and a course of antibiotics to prevent infection. This is awfully close to the eye, and she's bound to rub it."

Jared pushed his glasses up on his nose with a finger while asking, "Will it heal properly? Will it scar?"

"It's in a good spot for healing with minimal scarring, but when she comes back in six days to have the sutures removed, we'll determine whether she should see a plastic surgeon. My guess is, she won't need that."

A cry came from the corner along with something that sounded like "Dada." The little boy Molly was holding stretched his arms out to Jared, and Molly handed him over.

Christy sighed. "His only word so far is 'Dada'."

"That will change," Ethan assured her. "Now, let me call Paula in to assist. Um, do you all want to wait in here, or…"

"Come on, Jared," Molly said. "Let's take Nicky to the waiting room. I'd like to hear how work on the M29 is going."

Jared hesitated, but a nod from Christy sent him on his way. Ethan was disappointed Molly was leaving. He watched her walk down the hall, talking to Jared, and wondered what an M29 was.

Thirty minutes later, with a sticker and a date for suture removal, Sally happily went on her way. Before Molly reached the clinic door, Ethan called to her, "Molly," and she turned to look at him, her brow raised.

He felt his cheeks grow warm. "Sorry, I saw you and your friends at trivia the other night and, uh, heard someone say your name. Your team was really good. Congratulations on the win."

Molly grinned. "Thanks. It was fun. I'd give it another try if they let me."

"Let you?"

"Yeah, I mean, I guess they'd let me, but EJ's heading back to base, and I don't know if the others will keep going. I had fun though, which was surprising." A look of contemplation passed over her face before she smiled. "So, maybe I'll see you there."

"Sure. Have a good day."

He had no idea what to think of Molly McLane, but he wanted to explore those thoughts a little more.

***

Molly was wiping down a table at the café when she received a text from Lizzie a few days after they won their second trivia match.

Hi Molly. I know it's short notice, but some of my friends and I are going out tonight, and I thought you might like to go. Don's at eight for shrimp and drinks? It's causal, just a girls' night out. We'll head upstairs to Chattie's bar afterward. There's a band tonight.

"Hmm," Molly murmured.

"What's up kiddo?" Holly asked.

"Lizzie Parker asked me to go out with her and her girlfriends tonight for shrimp and then live music."

"Don's and Chatties? How fun! You should go. They're a great group of girls."

Molly stared at her phone and frowned.

"What's up, Mol?"

"I've never gone out with a group of girls. Like this, to a bar. I mean, I'm not even old enough to drink."

"Molly, do you want to go?"

"I think I do," Molly said, being honest with herself and a little excited about being part of a group.

"Then go, and stop questioning yourself. Have fun, enjoy your youth. Once you start working a real job, your social life takes a serious hit."

"Huh," Molly mused. "I have a social life."

Holly laughed. "And you have a job. Now go wait on that table that just came in, and text Lizzie back on your break."

Molly's mind wandered for the rest of the day. She pictured her former roommate getting ready for a night out. Molly would never feel comfortable wearing the outfits Gabby had worn. So, what should she wear? She only had jeans, t-shirts, and sweats. Did a girls' night out require makeup? Because she didn't have that either. When she had a chance, she texted her former babysitter.

Jenny, what does one wear on a girl's night out?

A few minutes later, her phone buzzed in her pocket.

Where is the alleged girls' night taking place? Will there be men there? Is it casual or nightclub chic?

Molly stared at the screen. Did all of that really matter? What should she say? She watched as three dots appeared.

Sorry, that was overwhelming, wasn't it? Just be yourself. If you want to wear jeans and a top, then wear jeans and a top. If you want to wear a skirt, then wear a skirt. They invited you, not your clothes. How's Sally?

Molly smiled. Jenny knew her well, but Molly still didn't have an answer.

Sally's great. Thanks. She's soaking up the attention.

That's great. Give her a kiss from me. And have fun on your girls' night. Don't sweat about it. Just enjoy.

When Molly got home, she googled *summer outfits for a college girl*. She didn't own a crop top, and maxi dresses made her look like the little teapot—short and stout. She didn't own a romper—too hard to use the bathroom. Sundress? Not really her style. White jeans and a colorful top? She might be able to manage that. With a little help.

She went to Christy's closet and began digging through the ridiculous amount of clothes. Christy's wardrobe sure had expanded since their days of being poor.

"What are you looking for?" Christy asked, coming up behind Molly.

"A colorful top that will look good with white jeans."

"You hate your white jeans. They've been hanging in your closet since I gave them to you for your birthday last year."

"Yeah, well, Pinterest says they're cute with a colorful top."

"Oh, does it now? Well, let's see."

They rummaged through the clothes until Christy pulled out a lavender off-the-shoulder top with a frill across the bust.

"This," she said. "It will go nicely with your eyes, and it's a good cut for most girls."

"I don't know. I've never worn anything like this."

"Did other girls you went to school with wear tops like this?"

Molly frowned. "I went to school in Massachusetts. In winter."

"Okay, but I'm sure they wore cute outfits when they went out."

Molly thought for a moment, picturing her roommate again.

"Yeah, I think so. Can I try it on?"

"Sure. If you like it, it's yours. If Jared gets his way, I'll be wearing maternity clothes forever."

"What? You're not—"

Christy laughed. "I'm kidding, but no, I am not pregnant. Still, I doubt I'll be going out in that again."

Molly took the top into the hall bathroom where they had a full-length mirror.

"Speaking of Jared, he's been kind of preoccupied lately." She faced away from the mirror as she pulled on her jeans and slipped the top over her head.

"Some stuff at work. He'll be fine. Let's see."

Molly closed her eyes as she turned around, took a deep breath, and opened them.

"Wow," was her sister's only comment.

Whoever the girl in the mirror was, Molly had no idea, but she looked good. Really good. Even with hair that was out of shape after being shaken from its braid and no makeup on, she looked better than good. She turned and assessed herself from several angles, and when she caught sight of her reflection, she found herself smiling.

***

Freddy almost dropped his drink when Molly, Lizzie, and the others walked into the restaurant. He knew Molly was only seventeen, but she'd be eighteen later in the summer, and man, she had grown up since they'd worked together at the café back when he was in high school.

He finished his beer and waited for the ladies to be seated before sauntering over to their table.

"Hello, ladies. Lizzie, Carly, Gwen, Molly." He let his eyes linger on Molly for a moment, hoping to convey that she was the reason he was greeting them.

"Hey, Freddy. Where's Maddie?" Lizzie asked.

Freddy shrugged. "We broke up. She met someone at school, got engaged, you know."

"Oh, I'm sorry. I didn't know that. Wow. You guys were together forever."

"Not as long as you and EJ."

"Yeah, well. We dated other people at school, tried to see what else was out there, but we just kept drifting back together."

"That's good. You were always good together."

"Thanks, Freddy. What are you up to these days?"

"Working as a custodian at Wallops and trying to figure out what I want to do with my life, but not having any luck. I heard you finally graduated. Congratulations."

Though he was talking to Lizzie, he let his eyes wander back and forth between her and Molly.

"I thought you wanted to be a chef," Lizzie said, taking a sip of her soda.

"Yeah, well, I dropped out of culinary school. It wasn't as much fun as it was working at the café with Molly. I thought I'd like it, but you know." He shrugged again. "Hey, Molly, Diego says you're back there this summer. No big post-graduation plans?"

"Yeah, but I'm weighing my options."

"I think that's great." He looked at the other girls and back to Molly again. "Well, you ladies have a nice night. There's a band getting ready to start playing upstairs. Are you all staying for dancing?"

"I'm in," Carly said.

"Me, too," Gwen agreed.

"Sure, I'm in if Molly is," Lizzie said, and Freddy thought he saw Molly jump as though she was kicked. "How about you, Molly? Up for some dancing?"

Molly's jaw dropped, and her eyes widened. "Dancing? Um, I'm not sure I know—"

"We're in," Carly confirmed.

"Great. Have fun, and I'll see you later." He said this to Molly who still looked as though she'd seen Chessie, the legendary monster said to live in the Chesapeake Bay.

He walked away smiling, thinking about how Molly had grown, in all the right places.

***

"Oh, my gosh, Molly," Carly leaned in and whispered. "Freddy Gonzales has the hots for you."

"What?" Molly managed to spit out.

"He's totally into you," Gwen said as she nodded. "The best-looking guy who ever graduated from Chincoteague High is into you. Sorry, Lizzie."

Lizzie laughed. "I happen to disagree on that, but it's okay because your statement is half right."

"I don't think so," Molly said, shaking her head. "Freddy and I worked together one summer. Years ago. And he's almost five years older than I am."

"So? You graduated the year after he did, didn't you?" Carly asked.

"Yeah, but I didn't go to school here after sixth grade."

"I know, but still, you just graduated from college, and he's twenty-two, so it's like being the same age, right?"

"Mmm, I'm not sure that logic holds, Carly" Molly said. "Besides, he apparently didn't finish college, so I'm not sure we're on the same path."

"Kind of judgy, don't you think?" Gwen asked.

"Not really," Molly answered. "I'm just not sure what he has in mind for his life, and it sounds like he doesn't either. I want someone more grounded."

"So, what are you going to do, Molly?" Gwen asked. "Date high schoolers or kids just heading to college, or look for older men who are 'grounded'?" She used air quotes, which Molly always found annoying.

Molly was silent for a moment and noticed Lizzie had been silent as well. When she devised her plan to be 'normal,' she hadn't considered the fact that everyone her age was developmentally way behind her.

"You know what? He hasn't even asked me out. If that happens, I can think about whether I'd want to date him. Until then, let's just see what happens. Okay?"

The other girls grinned widely and nodded their heads like a trio of Cheshire cats.

"Good idea, Molly," Lizzie told her with a slight smile. "Let's just see how it all plays out."

Great. Lizzie's friends were just as bad as Anya. All they wanted to do was set her up with a boy. And to make matters worse, Molly apparently needed to learn how to dance in less than one hour.

Then again, wasn't this what she wanted? To be a normal person for a change?

***

The pitfalls of working someplace where almost everyone was single were beginning to become obvious to Ethan. Trivia night was fun, and he appreciated being included, but it seemed that Friday nights were for dancing or karaoke, and he was expected to participate with 'the gang.'

Weren't they tired after a crazy week of seeing patients and patching up the island's entire population? He was exhausted, and he was the doctor on call all weekend.

Still, he was the new guy, and he felt obliged to make them happy. He wasn't going to like it though. Not one bit. He was sure of that.

But that was before he walked in and saw Molly wearing a light purple top that matched the flecks in her eyes—yes, he'd noticed her violet irises—and a pair of tight white jeans. She was smiling and laughing, something he hadn't seen before. Of course, he'd only seen her a few times, twice during the heated competition of trivia, and when she seemed to be the only rational adult in the face of an emergency.

If he wasn't mistaken, the other ladies she was with were teaching her how to dance. Could that be? How had she gotten to adulthood without knowing how to dance? Wasn't dancing around the house with your friends a normal girl thing? He'd seen his sisters do that a thousand times.

"You getting a drink, Ethan?" Paula asked.

"Oh, yeah, sure. A Bud Light, please," he told the bartender.

"What set list are we hoping for tonight, ladies?" Stacey asked.

"Classic Taylor," Paula said, adding with a laugh, "Maybe Ethan will surprise us by getting up to sing." They often played Taylor Swift in the office, low during hours and too loudly after the doors were locked.

"Huh?" he coughed. "I don't think so."

"Come on, you never listened to Taylor back in college?" Jenny asked.

"Maybe once or twice," Ethan admitted. "But I'm not singing in front of anyone."

"Loosen up, doc," Paula laughed. "You're still young, Ethan. Enjoy it while you can."

"You're still out enjoying it," he countered.

"For the second time around," she said. "Believe me, if Bobby and I had sung and danced more and loosened up a bit, maybe things would've turned out differently between us. You've got to enjoy life, my friend." She held up her bottle and waved it at him before downing it.

The band introduced the next song, and a woman with the voice of an angel began singing Heart's *Alone*. Ethan watched as the dancers moved toward the bar, and the couples took to the floor. He took a very long swig of his beer, stood from his seat, and made his move.

"Um, Molly, right?"

Molly turned to look at him, and he saw something in her wide, violet eyes he couldn't quite name, not knowing her at all or understanding her moods. Was she surprised? Confused? Terrified?

"Yes?" she elongated the word into a question. "Dr. Edwards, I presume?"

Was she being coy? Funny? He wasn't sure, but he laughed and said, "Yes, and I feel thankful that I am here to welcome you."

Molly laughed, too, rather loudly, and he liked her hearty tone. "What brings you to the jungle, my good doctor?"

"Well, I'm not sure that Stanley and Livingston ever tried this as a way of getting acquainted, but would you like to dance?"

Molly's smile faltered, and she seemed at a loss for words.

"She'd love to," one of her friends said while pushing Molly in his direction.

Molly looked at the other woman with an open mouth and eyes begging for mercy, but Ethan took the chance and gently cupped her elbow, leading her to the dance floor.

For several moments, they did the usual, awkward swaying back and forth, but their bodies quickly became attuned to the music.

"So, how's your niece? Her cut looked good when the stitches came out. No plastic surgery necessary."

"Thank Heaven for that," Molly said. "Sally's fine. I've never seen Christy like that before, though, not like she was at the clinic. At home, she was completely helpless. It was like she'd never seen blood and certainly hadn't gone to nursing school."

"She's the mom. I've seen some moms go into complete emotional shutdown and not feel anything until the entire ordeal was over, and I've seen some who couldn't state their own name without melting into a pool of tears."

"That was Christy. And Jared." Molly rolled her eyes, and Ethan noticed again how pretty they were, brownish with purple flecks that he could stare into all night. "Well, he's kind of always like that. He gets anxious pretty easily. Except when he's at work. Then he's in total control."

"What's he do?"

"He's a rocket scientist."

"As in, that's his real title?"

Molly smiled. "Yeah. And just as smart as you think he would be."

"I hear you're not too low on the IQ scale yourself." He felt Molly stiffen.

"Well, I guess I can hold my own."

"Did I hear that you just graduated from Harvard? And a year or so early, I believe."

"Maybe. I mean, yeah, I recently graduated from there. And maybe a little more than a year or two early."

"I think that's awesome. What are you? Twenty?"

Molly bit her lip. "Well, my birthday's coming up this summer."

"So, you'll be twenty-one then?"

The music stopped, and everyone in the restaurant gave a rousing round of applause to the lead singer who bowed and blew kisses to the crowd. Ethan and Molly separated and clapped. When the applause died down, Molly smiled and gave him a mock bow.

"And now, Doctor, I must go back and report on my findings. I'm sure you can survive the wilds alone."

With that, she turned and hurried back to her friends, leaving Ethan alone on the dance floor, more intrigued than ever.

"Seriously?" Jenny asked when he rejoined his colleagues with a fresh bottle in hand.

"What?"

"She's a child," Jenny said. "Christy's little sister. I babysat for her."

"She's a college graduate," he countered.

Jenny choked out a laugh. "Yeah, a super-genius prodigy who graduated from Harvard as valedictorian at the age of seventeen."

Beer flew from Ethan's mouth as he coughed and sputtered. "Seventeen?"

Jenny frowned. "Yes, seventeen, and an innocent, inexperienced seventeen. She's been to college, but we've kept in touch, and I guarantee her college experience was a lot different from yours."

"Are you telling me to stay away?"

Jenny's frown softened. "I'm asking you to. Okay? Not as your colleague, but as someone who cares about Molly."

Ethan nodded, but he didn't promise. What did he care what Dr. Jenny Murray thought anyway. They were equals at the clinic, even though she'd been there a few months longer. She wasn't his boss. They both answered to the Board.

He could dance or ask out anyone he wanted, whether she liked it or not.

***

The lights were all off in the white two-story nestled among the trees. He wasn't positive he had the right place, but his intel was rarely incorrect. He checked the address again and was satisfied that he was at the right address, if not the right residence.

He moved like a panther in the night, his eyesight keen as a predator's, and predator he was. Dressed in black, wearing gloves made with material that would leave no fibers behind, he carried no tools but was never without a weapon or two. Tonight, he had three.

Upon inspection of the vehicles—a heavy duty pickup truck and mid-sized SUV—he noted several things. There was a candy wrapper on the back seat next to a child's booster. A hair ribbon—yellow he believed, though it was dark inside the closed car—lay on the floor in a serpentine line. In the back, he could make out a field hockey stick and a small pair of pink roller skates. No signs of boy toys or equipment. That made him all the more certain that this was the right house.

He turned and looked at the building, maybe ten years old, or perhaps much older and remolded. There was a porch that wrapped around the sides of the house with a swing that hung to one side of the front door. A host of Adirondack chairs were scatted along the porch, front and sides. Good quality. Not like those cheap plastic knockoffs.

He'd been told there might be an alarm, but that didn't matter to him. When the time came, he'd be able to get inside undetected. But the time wasn't right. He had more than one house to visit and plenty of time to make his calls. Nobody in the world knew he was there other than the man who paid him, and nobody had any reason to suspect that man still cared about the inhabitants of this house or the others.

Before the end of the summer, three families would pay for the actions of three men, all at different times and under different circumstances. They didn't even know their actions were related. And if he did his job correctly, and he always did, nobody would ever connect the dots.

Wallops Invites Kids to Visit the Moon for a Day

Children, ages nine to twelve, are invited to participate in Moon Day at Wallops this Saturday from nine to four. Participants will learn how NASA engineers are preparing for the next flight to the moon through a series of scientific experiments, hands-on projects, and spacecraft design. The day will conclude with the launch of model rockets built by the students to give them a taste of flying to the moon.

This event is the precursor to the flight facility's popular summer space camp which begins next month.

The Chincoteague Herald, May 20

Chapter Four

Dustin was sifting through the boxes of parts and accompanying instructions to determine if each set was complete when his supervisor walked into the storeroom.

"What are you doing in here?" Dr. Stevenson asked in an angry tone and a scowl on his face.

"Um, I'm just going through the boxes for Saturday. I'm making sure everything is here. I heard that some stuff was missing from the storeroom, and I thought I should check."

Dr. Stevenson's head shot up. "How did you hear that?"

Dustin's heart raced. "From one of the other interns. One of the engineers asked him if he'd seen it, said it was missing."

His supervisor eyed Dustin for several moments, and he felt himself begin to sweat. He resisted wiping his brow.

"Okay, well, you don't have to worry about those. They're good."

Dustin frowned. "No offense, Dr. Stevenson, but if we're going to have all these kids here this weekend, shouldn't we make sure we have complete kits? I've checked with the other interns, and nobody was assigned the job of making sure we have everything."

"It's been done," came the curt reply. "Have you seen the supply of calibration instruments that were delivered yesterday?"

"I believe they're on the table in your office, Sir. Are you sure I shouldn't double check these? I really don't believe anyone has looked at them."

Dr. Stevenson stopped and looked at Dustin as though assessing him. He pushed his glasses up onto the bridge of his nose.

"You can check. They shouldn't have been touched since Molly refilled them last year, but under the circumstances…"

Dustin felt a twist in his gut. "Molly?"

"Yeah, she worked with the space camp kids last summer, and when it was over, she personally made sure all the supplies were ordered and organized for this year because there was some talk about trimming the program's budget. She wanted to use any leftover funds to make sure we'd have everything we'd need for this year."

"I didn't realize Molly was an intern last summer," which was a lie, but he didn't want his boss to think he was asking about her.

"She wasn't. She was a paid employee for the past few years. She revised the space camp program and did a great job of bringing it up to date. Most of the program was still using materials from the last century, which she was determined to change after her first summer here when she was a kid." Dr. Stevenson smiled for the first time since walking in.

"A kid? She knew the program was out of date when she came as a kid? How old was she?"

"Molly was ten when I first met her. Christy had been advised by the school counselor to enroll her in space camp, but it became obvious very quickly that she didn't belong in camp."

"What do you mean?"

Jared chuckled, shaking his head. "When I met Molly, Christy was checking her in for the first day of camp. Molly was reading a book on interplanetary space travel, and Christy was worried that she would be bored at camp. I thought she was over-selling the kid, but I agreed to keep an eye on her for a day or two, and then I heard Molly ask the counselor doing the check-in something like, 'Just curious, but will we dig into the concept of interplanetary travel and patched-conic approximation?' I almost fell over laughing at the look on the counselor's face." Jared laughed as he recalled the scene. "I took Molly straight to Simon, Dr. Johnson, and convinced him to let her shadow me for the summer. She's been coming back to help in some capacity every summer since. Well, except for this summer." Jared's face changed from amusement to introspection, but Dustin wasn't amused or speculative. He was annoyed.

"I guess Molly has quite the reputation around here," he said, hoping as an afterthought that resentment wasn't ringing in his tone. He already knew Molly's reputation. He'd been hearing it for the past three weeks.

Oh, you went to Harvard? Do you know Molly?

Hey, Jared's sister-in-law, Molly, went there. Did you know her?

Dr. Stevenson's wife's sister was valedictorian there. Did you graduate together?

Don't touch that model. It's Molly's.

We always have Reese's Peanut Butter Cups on hand in case Molly drops by.

Dustin was so over hearing about Molly and how great she is. *The next thing you know, they'll be naming a wing after her.*

Jared looked at Dustin for a moment while the silence hung between them and thoughts about Molly's greatness roared through Dustin's head.

"Right," Jared said. "When you're done in here, check to see if Adrienne has made the name tags and if there's anything she needs your help with. I think we're ready for Moon Day."

Moon Day, as Jared called it, as well as the moon camp program were more stunning ideas from the marvelous mind of the remarkable Molly McLane. Dustin was over-the-moon happy that Molly had a new job and a new life and wasn't going to be able to screw up his summer. Otherwise, he'd be tempted to shove her into a spacecraft and send her to the moon herself. It was bad enough that he'd seen her two weeks in a row at trivia, and her team had won both nights. He didn't need the constant reminder that she was smarter than he was.

***

"Have you seen my other tennis shoe?" Molly asked Christy. "I know it was in the coat closet."

"Have not, but maybe if you kept your shoes in your bedroom closet, they wouldn't disappear."

"That doesn't make sense unless you're trying to tell me that this particular closet has a black hole, and since I'm overly familiar with the intricacies of black holes, I doubt that's the case. Furthermore, it makes no sense to keep my shoes in my room since I wear them every day, and you don't like shoes being worn in the house. It's more efficient for them to be kept close to the door."

Molly heard Christy's exasperated sigh.

"Just find it," Christy said. "You and Jared need to get out of here."

Molly yanked the found shoe out from under the couch. "Sally, did you put my shoe under the couch?"

Sally shrugged, her spoonful of cereal halfway to her mouth. "I was playing hide and seek with it."

"Don't say it," Christy warned. "She's six. Logic isn't a thing yet."

"For some of us," Molly said under her breath.

"Speaking of logic," Christy said. "What were you thinking, dancing with a man almost ten years older than you?"

Molly turned to look at her sister. "What?"

"The new doctor. The one who treated Sally. I heard you danced with him the other night. At a bar. You're seventeen, for Heaven's sake."

"First of all, it was at Chatties, inside Don's Restaurant, not technically a bar. Second, he asked me to dance, and Carly said I should. I didn't go willingly. And third, what business is it of yours if I want to dance with somebody? It's not like I went to prom. You said I was too young."

"You were, and you still are. Be real, Molly. What were you thinking?"

"I was thinking that he's nice and that he helped Sally and that it was a public place where other people were, wait for it… dancing!" She flopped into a chair and pulled on her shoes, taking her irritation out on her Nikes that cost more than she wanted to think about but were a Christmas gift from Diane.

Christy again sighed loudly, and Molly realized she had been doing that a lot since Molly had been home from school.

"Look, Molly, you need to be careful. Some older men—"

"For crying out loud, he's not an older man. He's a brand-new doctor, hardly out of school himself. Besides, I just spent the past three years with men who are older than I am, and I was able to handle myself. You weren't there all those years to tell me who to dance with, where to hang out, or what age people I could associate with."

"And from what I understand, you didn't do any of the above."

"You're right," Molly was now shouting. "Because I'm a freak who was treated like a freak and never got asked to go out or hang out anywhere or dance! I didn't do anything but study and read and watch Netflix. And now I have a chance to be normal, to have friends, to go places, and even dance. And if I want to dance with a doctor or a lawyer or a boat captain, it's my decision to do so!"

Jared suddenly appeared between the two sisters. "Let's table this for another day. Molly and I need to get going."

"There's nothing to table," Molly said through gritted teeth. She grabbed her water bottle and stomped toward the door, throwing it open and slamming it shut as she hurled herself onto the front step. She was looking forward to a day at Wallops where she knew she was understood and appreciated.

***

"Hi, Maria. Are you ready to visit the moon for a day?" Molly, who was stooped to the girl's level, looked up and smiled at Maria's brother. "Hey, Freddy."

"Hi, Molly," Freddy looked at Molly like a bear standing over a honeycomb, and she suddenly felt self-conscious in her shorts and NASA t-shirt.

"Are we really going to the moon?" Maria asked.

"Well, we can't actually go to the moon, but you're going to see just what it's like to be on the moon for a whole day. How's that sound?"

"Okay, I guess. I'd rather go to the moon though."

Molly beamed. "I know just what you mean. When I was your age, I couldn't wait to experience galactic travel."

Maria scrunched her nose at Molly. "I don't know what that means. I just want to be as far away as I can get from all my brothers."

Freddy laughed at his sister's words. "Sorry, Molly. She's not the budding scientist you are."

Molly shook her head and grinned. "It's okay. I realized a long time ago that there aren't a lot of kids like I was. Come on, Maria, let's get you to your group."

"Have fun, Maria," Freddy called. "I'll be working today, so I'm here if you need me."

"I won't," was Maria's sharp retort. "And don't try to spy on me or anything."

Molly grinned, suppressing a laugh. She liked Maria. She started to follow the kids inside, anxious to get out of the sun and away from the humidity. She couldn't believe it was only May. What would it feel like in August?

"Hey, Molly," Freddy stopped her with a gentle grasp of her arm. "I was wondering. Would you like to go out sometime. I mean, for dinner or something?"

For once, Molly couldn't speak. Would she like to go out with Freddy? He wasn't the same guy she worked with at the café several years ago, and she wasn't positive he was looking for just a dinner companion. Still, they were friends once, so maybe dinner would be okay. He'd always been nice to her, and he was good looking, even if he didn't have the sense to stay in school. Maybe he'd transferred to somewhere else and was still pursuing a bright future. Maybe she should give him a chance.

"Look, it's okay if you don't want to," he said when she didn't answer.

"No," she said hastily. "I do want to. I mean, I'd like that. When?"

Freddy smiled "How about Monday night? I know the café is closed that day."

Molly thought about all the advice she'd seen on TikTok, and paused. Maybe she'd been too hasty to say yes, too eager. She didn't want him to get the wrong idea, plus all the online advice said to play hard to get, at least at first.

"Monday. Hmm." She tapped her bottom lip with her finger. "I think that will work. Why don't you text me tomorrow so I can confirm?"

Freddy smiled. "Sure. I'll text you."

Molly watched Freddy walk away and suppressed doing a little dance. Even if they were just friends, and even if he was a man now and not the boy she knew, this was what she wanted, right? She had her first date, and it was with one of the best-looking guys on the island.

***

Dustin stood off to the side and watched the exchange between Molly and some guy she seemed to know. For three years, he'd avoided her, never giving a care about she talked to or what she did. He still didn't care. Everything about her annoyed him. He hated that she was part of this event, that it was her idea to have it each year just before summer, that she knew everyone and everything at the facility while he was still feeling his way around. Still, he found that he was inexplicably curious about the exchange.

He waited until later, when the kids were engrossed with building their rockets, to inquire about the conversation.

"So, uh, I saw you talking to Maria's brother this morning. I guess you grew up together."

Molly gave him a sideways glance and shrugged. "Kind of."

"He's not one of your trivia teammates. Different friend group?"

Molly spit out a harsh laugh. "Friend group? Yeah, I guess you could say that."

"Other than trivia, what do you do for fun? You and Maria's brother, I mean. I've seen him around, cleaning and stuff. What's his name?"

Molly squinted at him as if he had a third eye erupting above his nose.

"Freddy. And if you want to know what to do for fun, you can ask him yourself."

With another look akin to a sneer, she walked away and began checking on the progress of one group of kids on the other side of the room.

Until that moment, it had never occurred to Dustin that Molly might dislike him as much as he disliked her. He'd always been popular, even if he was a science nerd. He grew up playing sports and belonging to clubs and doing all the normal things a boy did in the suburbs, and as far as he knew, nobody had ever not liked him.

Despite spending three years doing nothing but giving off negative vibes toward Molly, he now felt out of sorts that she might feel the same way about him.

He frowned as he watched her with the kids. She was so easy going with them, so quick to smile. All the scientists and staff here loved her, even the janitorial staff, apparently. It was like watching a different person than the one he knew. She was not only in her element, she was happy, confident, and looked… He didn't know what the word was. She looked like she belonged here, like she was at home. She looked like he wished he felt, and it made him feel small. It made him feel like she must have felt at Harvard.

He supposed he really didn't know her, and that made him wonder if maybe he'd misjudged her. Or if he'd misjudged himself.

***

Rather than undergo twenty questions and painful scrutiny from her sister, Molly went to Lizzie's to get ready for her date.

"Where are you going?" Lizzie asked as Molly appraised her own appearance in the mirror. "I agreed to drop you off, but you never told me where."

"Lorenzo's. Which is kind of funny since I spend all day working for his wife. Anyway, are you sure I look okay in this?"

Molly turned from side to side, looking in the mirror. She was wearing one of Lizzie's sundresses, which Molly thought would be too small, but didn't look or feel bad at all.

"Better than okay, and it's perfect for a summer evening."

"You know," Molly said. "It's not actually summer yet. The summer solstice isn't until—"

"Molly, it doesn't really matter when the official date is. Summer starts as soon as we all return to the island from school. That's all that counts."

Molly heaved a long exhale. "Old habits die hard."

"I'm surprised your college friends didn't break you of that. Or that you never went on a date. Even if you're shy around guys, one of your girlfriends could've set you up. And look at you. You're beautiful. Why didn't you ever go out with anyone?"

Molly looked down at her freshly painted toes, bright blue against the beige carpet. She didn't look up when she said, "I didn't have any girlfriends in college."

When Molly turned her gaze toward Lizzie, the always-popular girl with a lifelong boyfriend wore an unreadable expression.

"Molly, you had to have friends."

Molly shook her head, avoiding eye contact. "I had lab partners and table mates and roommates, but not anyone I thought of as a friend. Not like Anya and Chloe, but they weren't there, and this summer, they're not here either. I think we've outgrown each other."

"I don't understand," Lizzie said, taking her by the hand and leading her to sit on the edge of the bed. "You're kind, funny, and scary smart. Why didn't you have friends?"

Molly took a long, deep breath and let it out.

"Looking back, I can't blame anyone but myself. Even after years of being the youngest person in school, I felt so out of place there. Not in the classrooms. There, I felt just right, like it was where I belonged. But outside of class? I wasn't just young. I was a minor. I was too young to date, too young to go out, too young to drink, just too young. It wasn't like I was the first person to skip that far ahead and go to college at fourteen, but I was the only person I knew there in that situation. And I didn't know how to fit in with kids who weren't in my place." She began playing with the skirt of the dress, tracing the flowered pattern with her finger. "Sometimes, I'd be invited to join some of the kids to go out or do something, but I never had the confidence to go."

"Molly, I've known you for years. Lack of confidence has never been a problem for you."

"It wasn't that I didn't have confidence in me. I didn't have confidence that they would accept me for who I am. It's one thing to go to school here, where everybody knows each other, and all the adults are friends, and everyone treats each other like family. And boarding school was easy because it was all girls and all smart girls. Up there, it just felt…different."

"Why did you stay? You could've gone anywhere. Even another Ivy League school. Why stay where you weren't happy?"

"I guess I felt like I had to. Christy kept saying how proud my dad would be, me following in his footsteps, and Jared loved it there so much and kept telling me how wonderful it was. And it was. Don't get me wrong. I loved class. I loved the old buildings and the beautiful campus. I even grew to love the weather, though I don't think I'll miss it." Molly smiled. "I'm just happy to be home, to be where I feel comfortable, back with people who always treated me like I'm normal."

"Molly, you are normal. You are the most perfect version of you. Don't try to change that. Freddy didn't ask out the Harvard graduate. He asked out the girl he used to work with at the café. And that doctor the other night didn't know anything about you, but he liked you because you give off this vibe that you're special. Not because you're smart but because of all the things I said before. You're kind, funny, and pretty, too. I'm not just saying that. Everyone has always said so." Lizzie stood.

"Which is why, in that dress, with the confidence you exude, you're going to knock Freddy off his feet." She frowned. "But be careful, Molly. Not everyone who is nice to you will be a true friend. And not every guy you date will end up being nice."

"Thanks, Lizzie," Molly said with a genuine smile, wondering if she might cry and amazed that she never felt such overwhelming emotion before, not even with Anya. "Thank you for tonight, for inviting me to join in with you and your friends, for your advice, and, well, for everything."

"That's what friends are for, Molly."

Lizzie reached over and gave Molly a tight hug before tugging on her braid. "Okay, now for the hair."

They finished getting Molly ready seconds before it was time for Lizzie to drive her to meet Freddy. And for the first time in her life, Molly found herself looking forward to a date as a normal girl her age.

***

Freddy waited anxiously outside the restaurant. The scents of oregano, basil, and cilantro emanated from the building, tempting anyone who was close by. Freddy dug the toe of his shoe into the wooden porch that ran along the front of Speziato, one of the most popular restaurants in town. He hoped it wasn't too much for a first date, but he didn't know what Molly was used to at her fancy college.

When he spotted Lizzie's car pulling into the lot, he straightened and waved. Molly emerged from the front seat of the car, and Freddy's breath was taken away. The pale green sundress flowed out around her legs, and her bare, tanned shoulders glowed in the evening light, which surprised him since she spent so much time working at the café. He rushed to her side and offered his arm when he led her up the steps. Molly gave him a shy smile, and his stomach fluttered as he held the door open for her.

Once they were seated—and the staff all gushed over Molly, congratulating her and welcoming her home—Freddy ordered two iced teas.

"Okay with you? I remember you liked iced tea with extra lemon."

"Perfect. Thanks," Molly said, her cheeks pink, and Freddy wondered if she'd gotten some sun that day, or if she was blushing.

"I guess everyone here is still appreciative of you saving the restaurants a few years ago. They treat you like royalty." He meant it, and without resentment.

"Oh, I'm sure they're like that with everyone," Molly said, making Freddy grin. Her keen intellect didn't typically engender modesty. If anything, she tended to be awkwardly immodest.

"Any idea what you'd like to order? Want to get an appetizer?" Freddy wasn't trying to rush things. He just wanted to get the preliminaries out of the way.

"Calamari?"

"Sounds good. And caprese?"

"Good idea. I bet the tomatoes are just coming in. Produce was always behind in Massachusetts."

"How cold did it get up there?"

Molly answered, and the two continued talking through their appetizers, the main course, and right through dessert, only pausing when Lorenzo, the owner and Holly's other half, stopped by to tell Molly hello. Freddy had forgotten how much fun Molly was to talk to and how interesting she was.

"Is Lizzie picking you up, or can I have the honor of driving you home?" he asked when they were just about finished with the chocolate-hazelnut baci cheesecake, which they split.

"That would be nice. I mean, if you drove me home."

Freddy smiled as his heart flipped in his chest, and he wasn't sure what that meant. He'd gone on more dates than he'd ever be able to count, and he'd had a fair number of serious and not-so-serious relationships, but there was something special about Molly.

As he closed the passenger door and walked around the car, Freddy felt torn. He'd never been attracted to a girl before other than physically, not even his longtime girlfriend, and he wasn't sure about his feelings for Molly. He wanted her, but was that physical or something else? And would liking her ruin his plans to get off this island for good once his big payday arrived?

****

"Molly McLane, you're practically floating on air," Holly said with a large grin. They were ready to open, a little earlier than usual, and Holly was already sitting at a table with her feet up. "What has you so happy this morning?"

"You don't know?" Diego asked.

Molly's smile immediately turned into a warning.

"Molly and Freddy went on a date last night."

Holly's eyes widened. "Really?"

"Yes," Molly said, "but don't you dare read anything into it." She turned and glared at Diego. "It was just a date."

Diego put his hands out in defense. "What? I didn't say anything. I just said you went on a date. You're the one walking around all googly eyed."

The scent of gas from the recently lit stove wafted toward Molly, a fuse ready to ignite.

"I am not," she fired at Diego. "I'm just in a good mood. Saturday's Moon Day went really well, and Christy's planning a birthday party for me later this summer, and yeah, I went on a date and had a good time. So what?"

"Hey, I'm not the one acting all defensive."

"Guys, quit it," Holly said, pulling herself up with some effort. "Diego, maybe we should institute a new rule that we don't talk about each other's personal lives without permission. Okay?"

Diego rolled his eyes and puffed out a breath. "Fine, whatever." He turned his back to them and began prepping the grill for their breakfast orders.

Holly motioned for Molly to follow her into the back where pastry ovens were already hard at work. The aroma of baking dough calmed Molly as she reluctantly trailed Holly to the back office.

"You okay?" Holly asked before Molly could voice the same question of her boss.

"Why wouldn't I be?"

Holly looked at her sympathetically. "I know this is all new to you. When you asked me about working here this summer, I was surprised, but when Christy told me about you wanting to have a normal summer before you settled on a career, it made sense. If you ever want to talk about anything, I'm here. And just because Christy is one of my best friends doesn't mean she has to know what you and I talk about. This place is sacred ground, kind of like Vegas. What we say or do here, stays here. Got it?"

Molly chuckled. "Got it. Thanks, Holly. I've still got a lot to figure out, but working a stress-free job helps."

"Good." Holly started back toward the kitchen but stopped and turned around. "But Molly, about Freddy. You know I like him a lot. He was a great employee, and his family is awesome. He's got a lot going for him."

"I sense a 'but' coming."

Holly took a deep breath and let it out. She looked toward the dining room before speaking in a low voice.

"Freddy has a reputation, you know? I'm not saying it's bad, but he's known for having a lot of girls following him, and for, um, for—"

"Breaking a lot of hearts?" Molly said, not oblivious to the repute of Freddy Gonzales.

Holly nodded. "Yeah, I guess that's what I'm getting at. He does tend to love them and leave them."

"Didn't he date someone from high school for a long time?"

"I think they applied the term 'dating' rather loosely. My sense is that there were a lot of others before, during, and after. I'm not saying Freddy did anything wrong. I think that's what they both wanted, but Molly," she paused and bit her lip before continuing. "Have fun, but be careful."

"Got it. Thanks." Molly hesitated. "Hey, are you okay?"

Holly nodded. "Yeah. My blood pressure's a little higher than the doctor wants it to be, so I have to keep my feet up as much as possible. I may need to hire someone else."

"Oh," Molly said, not sure what else to say.

The bell rang over the door, which Diego must have unlocked. There wouldn't be any more talking for a few hours, but Molly knew she'd be doing a lot of thinking.

***

The café was busier than Dustin had expected it to be. He was still five people behind in line, and the tables were all filled. He watched as Molly and the others rushed back and forth to take care of their customers. After he'd already been there for almost ten minutes,

Molly turned and caught his gaze. Her eyes widened in surprise, but she nodded and gave him a half-smile. Dustin continued jostling along until it was his turn to place an order. The closer he got to the counter, the more the scents of doughnuts, croissants, and cinnamon rolls tempted him.

"I need a dozen doughnuts and six coffees, but they're all made to order. Is that okay?"

"That's what we do," the blonde woman answered with a smile. "What can I make for you?"

Dustin handed her the list and while she read it over, he discreetly watched Molly chat with a family at the far side of the counter. She had a broad grin on her face and talked animatedly, laughing at the responses of her customers. He felt a pang of irritation that she never talked to or laughed with him that way. But of course, he never gave her the chance.

"Okay, give us a few minutes, what's the name for the order?"

Dustin's attention was pulled back to the woman at the register. He noted the name on her shirt—Holly.

"Dustin. It's for Wallops. Dr. Johnson said to put it on their account."

Holly frowned. "I can do that, but I don't know you, so I'm sorry, but I'll have to ask for ID in case there's a problem."

Dustin pulled out his wallet.

"He's legit," Molly said, heading their way behind the counter. "He's Jared's intern, Dustin."

"Still, that's our policy. I don't mind holding accounts for local businesses, but I have to know who's signing the bill."

"I get it," Dustin said as he handed her his license. "Hey, Molly. Um, thanks for all your help on Saturday. The kids had a blast."

"You're welcome," she said slowly, looking at Dustin like he was one of those pod people in that old movie about alien body snatchers.

"Here, Molly. You and Diego get started while I do his paperwork real quick. I'm going to sit in the office to take care of it." She handed Molly the order.

Dustin watched Molly move down to the other end of the counter and continued to watch her while she worked.

"You going to trivia this week?" he asked, moving down to the end of the counter.

Again, Molly looked at him suspiciously.

"Probably. You?"

"Yeah, probably."

He didn't know what else to say, so he just watched her making the coffees until Holly called him back over and had him sign a form verifying his name, driver's license, and that he worked at the flight center.

When his order was complete, it was the guy—Diego, he thought he'd heard—who called his name. Molly was heading back to the floor to wipe down an empty table. Dustin balanced the order as well as he could and headed toward the door.

"I've got it," Molly said. "Let me take something to your car so you don't lose half your order before you get there."

He started to stop her from taking one of the drink holders, but he thought better of it. It had already taken longer than planned to get the order.

"Intern meeting," Dustin said.

"Yeah, I know the drill," Molly answered on their out. "Why didn't Dr. Johnson pick it up? I mean, he lives on the island, and I'm guessing you in the intern dorm."

Dustin shrugged. "He said he had to be in extra early this morning, so I volunteered."

"Oh, yeah. He and Jared had some kind of early meeting about the M29," she said as Dustin opened the car door, instantly greeted by the propulsion of heat that spewed from the car.

"Molly," he found himself saying after they'd put everything safely on the floor behind his seat. "Why are you working here this summer?"

Molly pressed her lips together for a moment before answering. "I like it here. I worked for Holly a few years ago, before I worked at Wallops, and part-time during, and I liked it. She and my sister—"

"No, I mean, why here instead of Wallops? Or any NASA facility, for that matter? Or any space agency? I know you got the same offers I did. Why here?"

"I could ask you the same question." She tilted her head and gazed at him, her expression unreadable, the sunlight bouncing from her purple tinged eyes. How had be never noticed the striking color of her eyes? He shook his head.

"All my offers start at the end of the summer, and I wanted to get some hands-on experience before I accepted anything."

Molly nodded but was silent for several moments before looking him right in the eyes for perhaps the very first time. "I wanted to see what it's like," she said quietly but firmly.

"What *what* is like?" He was perplexed by her answer and her seriousness.

"Being a normal teenager."

Without another word, Molly turned and walked away, leaving Dustin just as confused about her as ever.

Island Preps For What May Be Busiest Summer Ever

Everywhere you go on Chincoteague, there are signs that summer is practically here. Seasonal businesses are opening back up, including the Flying Ponies High Ropes Course, Island Paddle Sports, Grisly Ghost Tours, and of course, the mini golf courses and water parks. There's no shortage of fun on the island for residents and guests. Be sure to sign up at the Assateague Lighthouse for guided walking and biking tours of the trails. Whatever you do this summer, stay safe and always be kind and courteous to those around you.

The Chincoteague Herald, May 25

Chapter Five

"You haven't been out with us for over two weeks. What's up?"

Ethan frowned at Jenny, annoyed that she thought his social life was any of her business. "Is it a requirement that the staff has to spend their workdays and their leisure time together?"

Jenny's mouth dropped open. "Well, no, but I thought you had a good time the couple times you joined us. At least you got to meet some other people on the island." He saw a light go on behind her eyes. "That's it, isn't it? Did I embarrass you the night we went to Chatties? Or overstep? I'm so sorry if I did."

Ethan rolled his eyes. "Your dancing isn't that bad," he told her before turning toward the hall. He was half kidding and half hoping he'd annoyed her as much as she annoyed him.

Jenny grabbed his arm. "Ha ha. I mean about Molly. Hey, I'm really sorry. Maybe the atmosphere made me say some things I shouldn't have at the time. And maybe the cosmos, too," she admitted with a grin. "But seriously, I didn't mean to get into your business."

Okay, maybe she did realize that it was none of her business. And he had to admit that, once he got home and the alcohol buzz wore off, he was second-guessing himself.

"You didn't embarrass me," he said, taking her elbow and leading her into their office out of the hearing of others. He closed the door behind them and stood by what had become his desk, the one closest to the door, though both were in the middle of the room, pushed together to save space. "I guess I embarrassed myself. I really wasn't thinking." He let out a breath and shook his head. "Seventeen, jeez. I had no idea."

"Of course, you didn't. She looks young but not that young, at least with her hair down and makeup on, and she did graduate from college already."

"Yeah, but I knew she went early. I'd heard that from someone at the bar," he told her without admitting that he'd been asking about Molly. "I should've asked you how old she was. It just never occurred to me…" He shook his head.

"I know. Molly's not your average teen. She's miles ahead of everyone intellectually, including me, I'm willing to admit. And I guess because I've known her since she was a kid, I forgot that I still see the little girl in her. I still think of her as the kid I babysat and the reckless thirteen-year-old who nearly got a bunch of us killed, though I'm the one most at blame for that whole thing. I was in college and old enough to know better."

Ethan raised his brow, his curiosity piqued.

"Oh, no, don't even ask. That's a long story for another day. Anyway, I'm sorry I laughed at you that night and gave you a hard time. The truth is, Molly is young, too young for you in years, but maybe not in maturity. I mean, she still has the emotions of a teenager and often says what she thinks without stopping to censor herself, but give her some time. She's not going to be interested in seventeen or eighteen-year-olds who have never experienced the world. She's definitely going to end up with someone 'older and wiser,' as the song says, but I don't think she's going to be ready for that for a while."

"Yeah, no, I mean, she should definitely be a little older before dating someone, er, older."

Jenny laughed. "Yeah, something like that. Anyway, let me know if you want to join us again sometime."

Ethan's annoyance abated, and then something occurred to him. "Hey, Jenny, what about you and me sometime?"

Her head shot up, and she looked startled. "Come again?"

"I mean, maybe we could go out, the two of us, without the group." He put his hands out. "It's just a thought. I mean, two colleagues getting to know each other better."

Jenny looked at him for several moments before answering. "I'll think about it. How's that?"

"Sure, no strings or anything, just casual. And not that kind of casual. Don't hit me for harassment."

"Just two colleagues getting to know each other better," she repeated.

"Just that," he assured her, trying to picture the two of them on a date. No, not a date. Just a night out as friends.

"Let's get through the rest of the month working together and think about it."

He watched her leave and thought it would be nice to get to know Jenny without the rest of the staff around, but thoughts in the back of his mind still lingered on the brown-haired girl with the purple-flecked eyes. What was it about her that he couldn't let go of?

***

Molly was laughing at something Diego said but stopped abruptly when Dustin walked into the café on a bright Saturday morning. As he headed toward the counter, Molly made an excuse to hastily retreat to the kitchen. She hated that she'd let her guard down with him that morning he'd come to get coffee for the intern meeting. He'd never been nice to her in the time they went to school together, so what had compelled her to confide something so personal to him?

She looked for something that needed her attention, but the kitchen was tidy, and no oven timers were ready to go off. Holly and their newly hired pastry chef, Louie, were going over recipes in Holly's office.

"Hey, Molly, can I get some help out here?" Diego called.

Sucking in and releasing a deep breath, Molly closed her eyes and pulled herself together before heading into the dining room.

Dustin was seated at a table with his back to the counter. He ate his breakfast while staring at his laptop. A line was beginning to form, and Molly recognized the beginning of the Memorial Day weekend rush.

She and Diego did their well-choreographed dance behind the counter, and she hurried around the room, delivering orders and cleaning tables. When she finally had a moment to look at the clock, almost two hours had passed, and Dustin was still at the table scrolling on his laptop, the empty plate and cup pushed to the side.

"Would you like me to take these for you?" Molly asked, acting as though he was just another customer.

"Sure, thanks," he said without looking up, a sure sign that things had returned to normal between them. But then, as she turned to throw the trash away, "Hey, Molly."

She inhaled through her nose and turned with a pained grin pasted to her lips. "Yes?"

"I've been thinking about something."

Oh, gosh, here it comes. Will he make fun of me? Ridicule me for what I admitted to him? Say something mean and cutting like he did so many times at school?

"In Dr. Stevenson's book, he talked about the possibility of the presence of lithium on the moon. The NSS believes the moon may have beryllium, zirconium, niobium, tantalum, as well as lithium, and they think we may be able to determine that using a lunar polar orbiter, but Dr. Stevenson, doesn't mention partnering with the NSS in any of his books. When I asked him about it, he kind of brushed it off. Why isn't he in favor of working with them?"

Molly blinked once and attempted to bring his question into focus. "The NSS?"

"Yeah, I mean, I'm trying to do some research on the orbiters while he's at the conference this weekend, and I think it makes a lot of sense, and while he mentions them more than once, he never specifically talks about the NSS."

"I don't think he disagrees with them or has anything against them. He just comes at all this from a different perspective." She pulled out a chair and pointed to the screen. "See, the National Space Society is a non-profit group of scientists, climatologists, normal citizens, and even celebrities."

"Tom Hanks, Hugh Downs, and others."

"Right. So unlike SpaceX, Blue Origin, Honeywell, etcetera, NSS is more of a space advocacy organization. They have great goals and a relevant mission and vision, but they don't really have a horse in the race, so to speak."

"The space race, as it exists today."

"Sure, we can call it that. Anyway, they're all about advocacy for setting up space colonies, and while that's also a huge focus of NASA and the other organizations, it's not the only focus. Jared isn't necessarily against colonizing the moon or working with other agencies or organizations, but he's less focused on colonization and more focused on how to find and use the moon's resources without destroying it like we've done in so many places here on earth. As I said, he's not necessarily against colonization, but he's not really for it either."

Dustin nodded. "I get it. What makes anyone think that moving to another home somewhere else in the galaxy won't take us to exactly where we are now here on Earth? Is that it?"

Molly nodded enthusiastically. "Exactly. And Jared loves the moon, loves studying and learning about it. He wants to learn how to use its resources while, at the same time, protecting it. It's like a child to him."

"Discovering what elements are on the moon is really important to him, isn't it?"

Molly nodded. "Yeah. He thinks there are elements up there that can make a huge difference down here. And if there, why not other places?"

"And then, instead of having to give up life on earth, we can mine what we need from all the other places and hopefully not deplete the resources anywhere."

"Yeah. It's idealistic, but it could work."

"I agree, and he's pretty passionate about it, almost like a little kid himself when he talks about the possibilities."

"Yeah, I always find that really cute." Molly found herself beaming at Dustin, and it felt disarming, like she was letting an alien being see too much of her humanity. "Anyway," she said, getting up and picking up the trash she'd set back down on the table. "I'd better get back to work."

"Sure," Dustin said, looking at her as though he'd never really seen her before. "Hey, I was thinking of trying the ropes course later. Wanna join me?"

"Sorry, I have to work until four, and then I'm meeting my sister and the kids at… Anyway, I can't, but thanks."

"What about tomorrow?"

Molly shrugged. "Work. Sorry." When she saw the look of disappointment on his face, she was surprised. Did he really want to do the course with her, or was this a trick of some kind? She wasn't sure, but he looked sincere. "I really am sorry. We're closed on Mondays, and I'm off on Tuesdays, but you work those days."

Dustin nodded. "What time are you off tomorrow?"

"Four tomorrow, too."

"The course is open until seven, and it takes two hours. How about it?"

Molly rolled her lips, trying to come up with another excuse, but she hadn't done the parts of the course that had been added over the winter, and she'd love to try.

"Um, sure."

"Great. Should I meet you here when you get off?"

Molly nodded. "Yeah, that sounds good."

As if that was all he was waiting for, Dustin closed his laptop and stood.

"Okay. I'll see you tomorrow."

"Sounds good." Molly watched him leave and thought, *Huh, who'd've thought? Dustin might be human after all.* Then she stopped herself. *Which is also how most alien horror movies go. The human-like beings turn out to be aliens in disguise, out for blood.*

***

"You okay?" Christy asked Molly as they walked home from church. The evening was warm, caressed by a salty, ocean breeze. Nicky cooed from his stroller, and Sally skipped ahead, humming to herself.

"Yeah. Why do you ask?" Molly pushed the stroller down the recently paved road, leaving Christy free to run after Sally if she needed to. Traffic in town was just beginning to get busy for the season but their road, just outside of town, was still quiet enough for Sally to walk on her own without holding hands. Molly knew that wouldn't last.

"You're awfully quiet tonight."

"Father Darryl preached about welcoming guests, taking in strangers, and showing them hospitality, like the man did when the Apostles asked about a room for the Passover meal."

Christy frowned and gave Molly a sidelong glance. "Okay, yeah. What about it?"

"What if that stranger was against Jesus? What if he had been one of the people plotting against him, and Jesus was walking right into a trap? What if the man hated Jesus and just wanted to see him fail?"

"Wow. You're introspective this evening. Or cynical. Why are you asking about this?"

Molly heaved a long sigh. "Did you ever know someone or go to school with someone who was mean to you? Like really mean? All the time? And suddenly he was acting like that never happened and wanted you to do something together?"

Christy laughed. "Well, I guess as long as the something doesn't involve going near a cliff, you might be okay."

Molly stopped abruptly, her heart drumming an accelerated beat. Christy stopped and looked back at her, swatting at a mosquito.

"What?" she asked in a bewildered voice.

Molly swallowed. "What if that something involves climbing to great heights and walking across thin boards secured only by a rope and harness?"

Again, Christy laughed. "Molly, what's going on? You love the high ropes park, if that's what you mean. Who asked you to go there? You're talking in circles, and that's not like you. Are you sure you're feeling okay?"

Nicky began fussing, and Molly pushed the stroller ahead, giving him the motion he loved.

"Do you remember Dustin Howard? We went to college together."

"Isn't that the guy who's doing the internship with Jared? Hey, Sally, slow down. Not too far ahead."

"Yeah, that's him."

"What about him? Sally, I said slow down."

Molly watched her niece stop skipping and slow her pace before tossing a quick, backward frown toward Christy.

"He's always been a real jerk to me. We were in almost all the same classes, and we were always competing for the top places, at least he was. I just did my work, but he always acted like we were in some sort of contest against each other, which, honestly, may have pushed me to stay ahead. Anyway, now he's here, and I run into him all the time, and today we had an actual conversation for the very first time. Then he asked me if I wanted to do the ropes course with him after work tomorrow."

"And? What did you say?"

"I said yes, but only because I want to do the new section. But then I regretted it right away. I mean, I want nothing to do with the guy. I always avoided him at school, but today, he actually seemed human. Or semi-human. Maybe alien-in-disguise human. I just don't trust him, and maybe he only asked because he doesn't know anyone else, and in that case, am I a bad person because I don't treat him with hospitality since this is my home, and he's in a strange place?"

"Okay, let me get this straight. You and this guy, Dustin, have had this weird competitive relationship for years, and now that you're thrown together again, so to speak, he's being nice to you, and you don't know if it's for real. Is that about right?"

They turned into their driveway, and Sally bounded up the tall steps leading to the deck on the stilted house overlooking the channel. Christy lifted Nicky from the stroller so Molly could fold and put it away in the cupboard under the outdoor steps.

"Yeah, that sums it up. Do you think I should go? Should I try to be nice to him and see what happens?"

"I think you just answered your own question," Christy said as they headed into the house. "Sally, take your shoes off before you go to your room. Aunt Molly and I are going to get dinner on the table, so don't pull out too many toys, okay?"

"Yes, Mommy," Sally answered as she sat down and tugged off her shoes.

"I should go and be nice?" Molly asked.

"Molly," Christy looked at her sister. "You're almost eighteen. You don't need to be told what to do or how to treat someone. You're old enough and smart enough to figure this out. And you've never questioned your own decisions before. Go with your gut. You always do the right thing."

Molly bit her bottom lip, a habit both sisters had always had.

"I know. It's just that Dustin has always made me question everything about myself. He makes me feel like a kid, like I don't deserve to be where I am. I don't feel like an adult around him, and I don't feel confident around him."

"Hmph," Christy snorted. "Then I'm not sure he's someone you'd want to go out with. Why put yourself through that? Unless you're trying to prove yourself to him, which I don't think you've ever tried to do with anyone. So why him?"

"I don't know," Molly admitted. "Maybe it's more like, I get it to be new around here and not know anyone."

"Well, in that case, Father Darryl's homily might have been just what you needed to hear."

"That's what I was afraid of," Molly said, knowing it didn't take a genius to realize that everyone should be treated with kindness, even if they've never shown that same kindness themselves. Maybe this could be a turning point for them both.

***

"Thanks for coming in on your day off," Jenny said to Ethan. She wiped her brow then took off her lab coat. She was sweating profusely, thanks to the busy day and the Atlantic Coast humidity. "I can't believe we were so busy."

"It's fine. I told Gram I'd be back for dinner, and she was good with that."

"Gram?"

"I never told you my grandmother lives here?"

"Here as in Chincoteague?" Jenny grabbed her purse from the bottom drawer of her desk and turned to look at her colleague.

"No, here as in the clinic. Yes, Chincoteague."

She shook her head. "No, I didn't know that. What's her name?"

She waited in the hall while he shut off the lights and closed the door to the office.

"Arlene Edwards. She lives on Sunrise Drive Circle."

"No way. My best friend from high school lived there. How long has your grandmother been here?"

They stopped to tell the nurses they could leave, and waited, then locked the building on their way out.

"So, how long has your grandmother lived here?" Jenny asked again as they walked to their cars.

Ethan shrugged. "A while. I remember visiting her as a boy, when my grandfather was still alive. I've been here a lot over the years. Gramps was a dentist here on the island."

"Hold on, you grandfather was Dr. Edwards? That's not just some crazy coincidence?"

Ethan laughed. "Nope. That's him."

"He was my dentist growing up. Why didn't we ever meet or see each other? You must've come down often in the summers."

"Along with hundreds, maybe thousands of other beachgoers."

Jenny laughed as they arrived at her car. "True. And I was probably doing something with my friends. We didn't pay too much attention to the tourists." Though they were always on the lookout for good-looking boys. How had they missed Ethan? He was tall with dark hair and a movie star smile, probably thanks to his grandfather.

"To tell you the truth, I was kind of a shy kid." He ducked his head in embarrassment.

"You weren't," Jenny said, genuinely shocked.

"I was," he said with a nod. "I spent most of my days hanging out with Gram and Gramps, so I didn't meet too many other kids when I visited."

"Too bad. We might've been friends." And she certainly would have noticed him.

"We're friends now," he said with a smile.

"We are, and I'm glad you came in today. We needed the extra hands."

"Any time," he said, giving her a wave as he walked on. "Have a great night, and I'll see you tomorrow."

"See you tomorrow." Jenny got in her car, opened the windows, and turned on the AC. While she waited for it to cool down, she couldn't help but wonder what might have happened if they had met years ago.

***

Having lost both her parents at a very young age in a tragic and unexpected event, then discovering after the fact that her sister had been kidnapped by a monster, stabbed in the abdomen, and literally died and came back to life, Molly understood fear and how most people handled it. One either lived in a constant state of waiting for the next catastrophic event to take place, or one rejected the power of fear and lived life for all it's worth. Molly was the second type of person.

Which was why she couldn't understand being paralyzed with fear as she stood on top the highest beam and looked down at the island below. Worse than the fear was having watched Dustin scramble across the beam and repel down without a worry in the world. Molly's fear turned to mortification with the knowledge that he was now seeing her in this vulnerable state.

She closed her eyes and felt her body sway with the brisk breeze that swept off the ocean. Her stomach lurched, and her eyes flew open. Never mind that she was harnessed. Never mind that hundreds of people a day walked across this thin, wooden beam. Molly was frozen in place, her heart racing, and her breathing coming in such increasingly violent waves, she might be the cause of her own demise.

"Molly," a voice called from some distant place. "Molly, you've got this."

She swallowed and tried to nod, forced herself to open her eyes, swallowed again. She stared straight ahead at blue sky filled with a mountain range of puffy white clouds.

"Hey, Molly, remember when Professor Dunn took us to the observatory? He wanted to give us a lecture on the moon in a way that made us feel we could reach up and touch it. But you took over the lecture and ended up teaching all of us more about the moon than Dunn ever could. It was like you'd been there. When I asked you what made you such an authority on the moon, you just looked at me and said, 'Because I've been there a thousand times in my dreams.' We laughed at you."

If this was a pep talk, it was the worst one Molly had ever heard. Figures. He brought her here to demean her. On her island. In front of people who knew her. As if she wasn't already humiliated enough, she felt a tear roll down her face.

"I was such a jerk, Molly, because you were so smart and so brave. Braver than any of the rest of us. You did what none of us could've done. Every single day. You went to class with a bunch of jerks like me who did everything we could to try to make you feel bad about yourself, to make you leave. And you showed us all. Because you don't back down, and you don't give up. Not then, and not now."

Molly didn't know how it happened, didn't even feel her feet slide across the board, didn't register that her heart had slowed, her breathing had softened. Before she knew it, she was rappelling down to the ground, and her heart was trilling like a lark. When her feet hit the sandy ground, it took her a moment to realize that the applause she heard was for her. She felt her face redden, but she wasn't embarrassed, just humbled. And that didn't happen often, but maybe she needed it now and then.

She looked over at Dustin, who wasn't clapping or cheering, but was grinning widely, nodding his head in approval. And suddenly, after all this time, he didn't feel so much like a stranger anymore.

***

Dustin and Molly sat across from each other at a picnic table in the park. American flags were scattered across the park—and across the island—in celebration of the holiday and in anticipation of the memorial service to be held on Monday. Dustin swallowed the last bite of his crabcake sandwich while Molly continued to pick at hers. She'd been quiet since they left the ropes course, and Dustin knew that was not normal.

"I'm sorry," he said quietly.

"For what?" She frowned in confusion. "I said I wanted to go. I've gone lots of times. I can't really explain what happened to me up there. It was like it wasn't really me on top of that thing. I've never felt anything like that. But in any case, it's not your fault."

"No," he said, shaking his head. "I mean, I'm sorry. For everything. For… the way we treated you."

He watched Molly's expression turn from confusion to pain, and he knew he'd caused that pain. He'd seen that look many times, but this was the first time it made him regret his actions or his words.

She put down her sandwich and pursed her lips before shaking her head. "You know, it's not easy. I've lived a lifetime of being different from everyone else. My sister worried about me going to the middle-high school, but those kids were nice to me. They included me on the debate team and MENSA and other things when I was in middle school. I felt like I had friends even though I never did anything with them outside of that environment because I was so young. Boarding school was different. I fit in there because we were all alike, but I was the only one who went to Harvard. Most of my classmates went to Wellesley, Barnard, Smith. You know, women's colleges where they felt comfortable.

"I thought college would give me a new start, a way to meet people who were my peers, intellectually if not biologically. But you all, who were supposed to be smart and mature and enlightened, you were just mean. You made me feel less, less knowledgeable, less capable, less worthy, less of me, the person I am."

Dustin sat quietly, knowing he deserved this.

"I tried so hard that first year to just be normal, but you all acted like I was a leper. All I wanted to do was learn and be among other academics, people who were as curious and passionate about learning as I am."

Dustin swallowed and nodded.

"I don't want you to be sorry, and I don't want your sympathy. I just want to be treated normally."

She took a deep breath and looked down, closing her eyes. Dustin remained silent, the hot sun beating down on his back making him sweat. But was it the sun? He felt the heat of shame coursing through his veins. When Molly looked up, her eyes met his, and he was surprised not to see tears. Instead, he saw determination.

"This summer, this is supposed to be my chance at normal. So, you can put aside whatever feelings of guilt you have and treat me like a peer, or you can leave me alone, like you did most of the past three years whenever I could've used a friend or even nothing more than a study companion. Whatever you decide, that's on you, but I'm going to have a good summer. I'm through with others making me feel inadequate."

Dustin felt a tug at his lips, then he felt a smile, and then he was laughing. He tried holding in his laughter, tried pulling himself together, but he couldn't. He just couldn't. He was so, so…

"Forget it. I knew I shouldn't have come." Molly stood and began shoving her food into its wrappings.

Dustin inhaled and managed to blurt out, "Stop. You don't get it."

"Oh, I'm sure I don't. I don't get why you asked me to come, why you pretended to be nice, why you and all our classmates—"

"Molly, stop. I mean it." He was no longer laughing. He realized he'd reached out and grabbed her without thinking.

Instead of pulling away, Molly looked at his hand on her arm as if it were a snake coiling its way to her throat. He hastily let go.

"I'm not laughing at you. Honestly. It's just that you think we saw you as unintelligent and inadequate. You have no idea how far from the truth that is. At least for me."

Molly looked at him with narrowed eyes. "What does that mean?"

"I knew you were smart. A lot smarter than most of us. And I knew you were more than adequate. It was me. I was the problem."

"You're the Anti-Hero, huh?"

"I have no idea what that means, but sure. I was very much the opposite of anyone's hero. At least where you're concerned. I spent my whole life at the top of the ladder, the top of my game. I wasn't just smart. I was athletic, popular, the All-American guy, maybe even All-American Hero to stick with that image."

Molly slowly sat back down as Dustin spoke, so he did the same.

"When I got accepted into Harvard, I expected life to continue being easy for me. I was going to excel there like I had everywhere else in life. But I wasn't a starter on any of the athletic teams I tried out for. I was a nobody in the halls, and I was no longer the smartest person in class. All that time, I felt like I was in your shadow, in everyone's shadow. I felt like I would never again be the person I was."

It was the first time he'd ever admitted that to anyone, and it was his turn to look away while she pondered his words.

"You made me work harder, you know," she said quietly.

He looked back at her. "I made you work harder?"

She bobbed her head. "It was obvious from the beginning that you had a problem with me, so I was determined to go with it. I wanted to show you I was better, and I goaded you whenever I saw the opportunity. So, maybe I'm the problem, too." She offered a slight smile.

He thought that over for a moment before nodding. If not for Molly always trying to show him up, he might not have been salutatorian. She drove him to work harder, do better. Maybe they weren't so different after all.

"Okay, so how about this," Dustin said. "No more competing, no more trying to see who's smarter. No more of me trying to be the top dog, and no more of you trying to outdo me. How about we just both be normal? We're just two intelligent beings out to have a good, normal summer."

When Molly smiled, another realization hit him. It was the first time he'd ever seen her genuinely smile, a real, honest-to-goodness, send a ripple through his gut kind of smile. And he wondered what he'd deprived himself of for the past three years.

***

Most of the island turned out for the ceremony which took place at noon on Monday. There was a prayer service and flag raising by the Girl Scouts before Jenny's Uncle Trevor spoke on behalf of the many veterans who lived on the island.

"General George S. Patton once said, 'The highest obligation and privilege of citizenship is that of bearing arms for one's country.' I can attest to the truth of this statement. As one who served his country proudly, I stand here today to give praise, honor, and respect to those who paid the ultimate price so that we can live in freedom, celebrating this holiday and every holiday, every day of our lives, as free men and women."

Jenny felt goose flesh tickle her arms as she listened. She looked at her sister, who beamed with pride as she looked on at her uncle-Godfather, as well as her husband

and his two closest friends. Jenny and Taylor grew up listening to the stories their father and uncle told of their days of service, their time at war, and Jenny knew that Taylor had heard tails of glory and of heartbreak from Nick, Zach, and Aaron.

"One of my favorite authors, G. K. Chesterton wrote, 'Courage is almost a contradiction in terms. It means a strong desire to live taking the form of readiness to die.' What more can be said about those we remember today? These brave men and women of all races, all colors, all backgrounds who stood tall in courage while facing their deaths, all so we could eat hot dogs and play in the sand. May we take this day to do more than just celebrate a holiday, another excuse to cook out and be with friends. May we stop and remember those who paved the road of freedom with their bones, watered the seeds of liberty with their blood, enriched the soil of heroism with their ashes, and sighed their last breath upon the winds of independence."

***

It was near dark as he jogged down the sandy strip that ran along the channel at the far end of the island. The houses stood on stilts, away from the danger of flooding. But there were far worse dangers than rising water.

Stopping near the yellow house, he frowned at the big American flag flying proudly by the driveway. After all this guy had been through, he was still proud of that flag, this country? The watcher spat on the ground in disgust. He'd been at the park and had heard the speech about dying for one's country. He was a believer at one time, but no more. One's country had no inclination toward being loyal to its citizens, so why were citizens so unapologetically loyal to their country? He was loyal only to himself.

A woman walked out onto the back deck and hung a pair of jeans over the railing. The watcher pulled his phone from his pocket and looked from the image to the woman, confirming what he already knew. He'd seen her at the park earlier and had easily identified her and her husband. The others had been there, too, listening to the speech with tears in their eyes, unaware that he was watching them, sizing them up, figuring out who was to go first.

The woman glanced toward the channel, and her gaze locked with his. He waved as he turned and continued on his jog. He wasn't worried. She had no idea who he was or that he even existed. In his baseball cap and jogging clothes, he was undistinguishable from anyone else she might see or run into, and this area had more hotels and Airbnb rentals than most of the places he worked. Seeing a stranger jogging on the beach wouldn't cause her to worry. And if it did, it wouldn't matter anyway. They would all be dead before anyone even knew he'd been on the island.

Unprecedented Heatwave Hits Chincoteague

Climate specialists warn that an oppressive heatwave is upon us, and all residents and guests should take precautions. Stay hydrated, remain indoors between noon and 3 P.M., and keep your pets inside. While the ocean seems to promise a respite for beachgoers, the excessive heat can lead to heatstroke, heart problems, lung and kidney issues, and even mental health decline. For all those seeking a vacation on our beautiful island paradise, consider the following options:

Misty of Chincoteague is showing at the island movie theater every day at 1 P.M. Each evening at 7 P.M., a current release is offered.

Visit the Museum of Chincoteague, open every day from 10 A.M.-5 P.M., or take your chance at the Bowling Center, open days and evenings.

The Chincoteague Library offers more than books! Attend story time, check out a DVD, or shop their gift selections.

Don't miss the art galleries along Main Street, and be sure to stop in and say hello to Jane and Jonathan at Sundial Books!

Whatever you do, stay hydrated, and keep your cool!

The Chincoteague Herald, June 1

Chapter Six

Jenny leaned against the door. Her feet hurt. Her back ached. Her head pounded. On top of annual check-ups and standard summer injures, she'd had three cases of heatstroke, and she'd sent a heart attack victim to the hospital. Once the patient was stable enough to make the trip by ambulance, Jenny was ready to collapse.

The door was pushed against her, and she reluctantly moved into the room, her legs unsteady.

"Oh, sorry," Ethan said as he looked inside. "Were you behind the door?" He closed it as he entered the room.

Jenny sighed. "Would it sound terrible if I said I was hoping that my leaning against it would prevent anyone from opening it and finding me?"

"You, too? I thought I was the only one feeling that way. I'm wiped." He went to his chair and collapsed. Sometimes, this tiny room—overtaken by the two desks, several filing cabinets, overflowing bookshelves, and two large windows with heavy curtains—felt claustrophobic. Today, it felt like a safe haven. "I thought Sunday was bad when you needed me to come in. Will it be like this all summer?"

Jenny shrugged. "Your guess is as good as mine. I was only a volunteer here last summer. It was busy, but I don't remember any days like this." She walked around the desks and practically fell into her chair.

"Would you think less of me if I propped my feet on the desk?" she asked.

"Only if they get in the way of mine." He lifted his own legs and dropped them onto his desk. Jenny followed suit.

Neither spoke, and Jenny thought the silence to be more than welcome, comfortable even.

A soft knock sounded on the door before it was opened, and Stacey poked her head inside the room.

"Either of you want to do sutures? I've got Miren Kelly in exam room 2. She stepped on a piece of glass."

Jenny looked warily at Ethan. "I'll take it. Kate and Aaron are like family, and I'd feel bad saying no."

"Are you sure?" he asked without making any sign of moving. "I'm the pediatrician in the building."

"I'm good, but the next one is yours."

"If you say so, but from what I've seen, everyone on this island is like family to you."

Jenny smiled. "Fair enough, but I'm willing to share."

As she walked down the hall, Jenny thought about Ethan's suggestion a week prior that they go out to dinner. Maybe that wasn't such a bad idea after all.

She opened the door and said hello to Kate and Miren with the fleeting thought that her broad smile wasn't just for their benefit.

***

Molly stared at the text as though it was a greeting from an alien planet. She pocketed her phone and finished wiping down the tables before heading to the back of the café. Diego had turned off the ovens and cooktops, and the new guy, Louie, had finished prepping for the next day. They were both working hard to clean up, trying to get out as soon as possible while also attempting to keep Holly off her feet. Their boss was in the office finalizing an order and looked up when Molly entered.

"What's up?" Holly asked, sitting back in her chair.

"We're about done out front." Molly told her, hesitating in the doorway for an extra moment.

"Okay. And?"

"And?"

Holly smiled. "Molly, I've known you since you were eleven. I know that look. What's up?"

Molly closed the door and glanced at the extra chair Holly kept in the room for interviews, talks with employees, and more often, as a placeholder for things that needed to be put away when things got quiet. At the present time, the chair was empty, so Molly took a seat.

"Freddy asked me out. Again."

"Okay," Holly said, stretching out the word. "And do you want to go out with him again?"

Molly shook her head. "Not really. I've given it a lot of thought, and it was nice. He was nice, and I had a good time. He didn't make any moves that made me uncomfortable. I just don't think of Freddy that way, and I don't think I ever will."

"Wow," Holly said with a grin. "You always were different from the other girls."

Molly smiled. "I know. And I get that he's super cute and popular. It's just that, we had a really nice time the other night, but I've known him forever, and I've never, ever thought of him like that. I thought maybe I could like him, but I've been thinking about it all week, and it's just not happening."

Holly tilted her head. "Let me ask you a question, and don't get offended. You haven't exactly had a normal teenage existence, so I'm wondering, have you ever thought of anyone like that? I mean, you went to middle school when boys were a non-entity, then you went to boarding school before you even hit puberty, and college, well, that wasn't normal for you either."

"No, but that doesn't mean I didn't notice cute guys or wonder what it would be like to date. And we had 'mixers', at PEG," she said, using the air quotes she typically detested. She didn't explain the anagram. Holly knew that PEG stood for the Program for Exceptional

Girls at Mary Baldwin. "Mixers is such a stupid, old-fashioned word. Anyway, we had them, but I was so young."

"And nobody special was ever in the picture, I take it."

Molly shook her head. "No, which is why I wanted to have this summer to go on dates, go to parties with friends, and do the stuff I never did."

"So, why not say yes to Freddy? For the experience if nothing else. Well, dating experience, I mean."

"I know what you mean. But every other girl on the island wants to be with Freddy. It just doesn't seem fair. For them or for him."

Holly folded her hands together on her desk and leaned forward. "Let me tell you something, Mol. Freddy isn't going to end up with one of the girls on the island. Whether he dates you or anyone else. Right now, he's the island's answer to Anthony Ramos, and he knows it. He's the town playboy, even if he always was a good, mama's boy, but like I told you last week, I'm not sure he still is. I think he has more experience than most of his friends. I think his goal is to get off the island, and I'm pretty sure he won't be taking anyone from here with him when he goes. He always had his sights set on the bigger, broader world, and he's nowhere near ready to settle down. So, date him if you want. You don't have to have any expectations. If all you want is a summer of fun, then it's not a problem, but be careful. He may be looking for something you're not ready to give. On the other hand, if you want to spend your summer with someone who wants to have a real dating relationship, then you're right to move on."

"I saw him, you know. When I was at school, I went on a bus trip to New York and saw him in Hamilton."

"I assume we're talking about Anthony Ramos and not Freddy."

Molly laughed. "Yeah, sorry. I get what you're saying. I don't want to get serious with anyone, but I don't want to be someone's hookup either."

"And you shouldn't be. You have a lot going for you, more than most girls your age. Whether it's this summer or next year, or whenever you're ready, you're going to have a lot of guys asking you out. You're beautiful, intelligent, confident, and miles ahead of girls your age just heading off to school looking for parties and hookups and experimenting with all the things they're going to regret later in life. You have a lot to offer, and you shouldn't date someone just because he's cute and popular, but you know that. So, what's the real reason you're in here?"

Molly sighed. "I gave Anya a really hard time for having a boyfriend. I haven't returned her texts or answered her calls since I got home. Now that I've gone on a date and am going out with friends, I kind of get it. I mean, I'm still kind of ticked that she chose him over me, but I'm beginning to understand why. I think I'm ready to look for that, not something serious, but ready to test the waters."

"Then you should. It doesn't have to be with Freddy. And you can stay in the shallow waters until you're ready for more. Believe me, I made plenty of mistakes in my past, and I feel so lucky to have what Lorenzo and I have now. Don't rush it. Let things happen, and don't lose your connection to your faith. I did that, and my life fell apart. Stay grounded in what's important, and you won't go wrong."

Molly let all that settle in her mind for a moment. She did want to test the waters without going too deep. She wanted to date and kiss a boy and have friends without losing herself. She liked the person she was, the person she had become, was still becoming, and she wanted to be with someone who liked that person, too. It seemed she was learning a lot about herself this summer, and the season had barely begun.

After they said goodbye, Molly walked to the front of the café and pulled out her phone. She answered two texts, one to Freddy, telling him thanks, but no thanks, and one to Anya, apologizing and asking when they could catch up. She felt better than she had in days.

***

Freddy tossed his phone onto the seat of his car and cursed. Who did she think she was? She probably thought she was better than him, better than everyone on the island.

He could count on less than one hand the number of girls who had turned him down for a second date. No, he could count on one finger, and that's because Erin Roberts found out her father was being transferred to

Texas and didn't see the point in getting involved with Freddy or anyone else.

Disgusted, and maybe a little disappointed, if he'd let himself admit it, Freddy put the car in gear and headed to work. He hated his job, hated this island, hated his life. He wanted out, and he knew just how he was going to make that happen. He just needed a little more time, and he would have the money to leave and never look back.

***

"What's up?" Jared asked, shuffling papers on his desk and nearly knocking over his open water bottle in the process. Dustin's quick reflexes stopped the bottle from toppling over.

"Thanks," Jared said, pushing his glasses up on his nose. Dustin had noticed that Jared did this a lot, whether he needed to or not.

"I was wondering. I mean, I feel like I should ask." He shook his head. "No, this just feels weird. But you're my boss, and—"

"Dustin, take a deep breath. What's your question?"

"Like I said, you're my boss, so this feels awkward, but that's why I'm asking. I don't want there to be any awkwardness on either side. On any side."

"Well, it seems awkward now because I have no idea what you're talking about," Jared said with annoyance.

Dustin inhaled slowly and let out a long breath. "I've been thinking about this for a few days now, and I'd like your permission… Wait. Is that the right word? Your approval? No. Your… Oh, heck. I want to ask Molly out on a date. Will that make things weird between us? You and me, I mean."

Jared laughed, but then his expression turned serious. "Only if you break her heart or hurt her somehow."

Dustin felt his stomach roll. How much did Jared know about his and Molly's past?

"Okay," he managed after swallowing. "Thank you." Dustin stood to leave, but Jared stopped him.

"Dustin, I mean it. You're both adults, er, almost adults. I can't stop you from dating Molly or anyone else, but she's not yet eighteen, as you're well aware. And she's special. If you know that, if you can truly see that, then go ahead and ask her out. But if you have any intention of repeating the past, then you can forget this conversation ever took place and look for someone else to fill your time with this summer."

Okay, so he probably did know. Dustin felt his face grow hot with shame.

"Yes, Sir. I understand."

Jared stared at him long enough to make Dustin want to run from the room, but he held his ground. Eventually, Jared nodded. "I believe you. Now, get out of here. You have work to do in the lab. Bring me your results before the end of the day."

"Yes, Sir," Dustin repeated before hurrying from the room. He felt humiliated, like a child caught wetting the bed at a sleepover. He felt embarrassed that his boss knew about behaviors he deeply regretted. He felt anger at himself for being so immature and just downright mean. But most of all, he felt excited to do what he should've done years ago—get to know the real Molly McLane.

***

"Molly?" Ethan spotted Molly across the library and felt drawn to her like a honeybee to a clover. He almost winced at the inappropriate thought.

Molly looked up from the book in her hand and gave him a tentative smile. "Hi, Dr. Edwards."

Ethan shook his head. "Just Ethan. Are you going to trivia this week?" He looked at the book in her hand, *The Space Barons*.

"Um, yeah. I plan on it. You?"

"Sure, why not? Are you into Science Fiction?"

Molly tilted her head and looked at him with a furrowed brow. He gestured to the book.

"Oh, this? No, this definitely is not science fiction. Well, it kind of is, but only in the sense that they haven't yet achieved all they hope to achieve in this lifetime." She held it up so he could see the subtitle—*Elon Musk, Jeff Bezos, and the Quest to Colonize the Cosmos*.

"Oh, just some light reading, I see," he said with a joking smile.

"Actually, I'm doing research."

"On space colonization?" He was more than intrigued.

"Not exactly. On Musk and Bezos. Trying to weigh my options."

He went from merely intrigued to quite confused. "Are you thinking of packing up and moving to the moon?"

Molly laughed. "Packing up and moving? Yes. The moon? No. But where? California, Washington, Texas, Florida?" She shrugged. "I can't decide."

The confusion expanded with every word. "And this is going to help, how?"

"Maybe it won't help at all. I'm trying to decide which company I want to work for."

Something he'd heard dawned on him, and he felt stupid for being so slow to get it. "You've gotten job offers from space agencies. Is that right?"

She groaned. "Yeah, along with NASA, where my heart is, so I feel stuck. I know I should take one of the big dollar offers, but I can't decide if I want to. It's like being torn between joining the Air Force and serving my country, but having very little to show for it, or becoming an aerospace technician for a major defense supplier and having all I ever dreamed of."

"Hmm, I'm not sure that's fair to those who choose military life. How does it relate to you?"

"How about being a doctor at a small-town clinic that could really use your expertise versus being one of many outstanding cardiothoracic surgeons at Johns Hopkins?"

Ethan laughed. "Now that, I understand."

"Do you have a few minutes?" She motioned toward a nearby table.

"Sure. I ran in on my lunch break to grab something new to read, but I've got a little time to spare." They sat across from each other, and he noticed once again how striking her eyes were.

"How did you decide to come here? Why not some renowned hospital or practice where you could make big bucks and live a lavish lifestyle?"

"Honestly?" he asked, and she nodded.

"Other than living close to my grandmother, I really don't know. I trained in one of the best children's hospitals in the country, under some of the most brilliant doctors, but I didn't really like what I saw. Yes, they had huge houses and fancy cars and lavish lifestyles, but they had so little connection with the patients. Most of the doctors I knew or worked with had little time to get to know the kids and their families. They diagnosed, treated, and moved on. Sure, some patients remained under their care for years and became well-known to the doctors and staff, but most were just short-term cases, and the doctors knew it. I felt like they were missing something, like they were seen as some kind of gods and miracle workers, but they weren't real people. And many of them liked it that way, kind of like they were superheroes, but their superpowers just took them from saving the world one giant event at a time without ever really seeing the people they saved from the bad guys." He shook his head. "Does any of that make sense?"

Molly smiled. "You know? It does. That's why I'm looking at this book, and others like it. I want to know that whomever I work for not only has the same goals as me, but the same moral compass. And I need to determine whether the money is worth choosing one of these guys," she motioned to the book cover, "over the agency I've known my whole life."

Ethan was even more impressed. "You know what, Molly? I think you're going to make the right choice, whatever it is, and that you're going to change the world by doing it."

"I'm not really interested in changing the world, but I want to make a difference. I look at my brother-in-law, an adjunct professor, NASA researcher, and textbook writer. He's not doing anything big or fancy, but he loves what he does, and he's making a difference in his world if not in the world at large. The same went for my dad."

Ethan smiled as he glanced at his watch, disappointed that he needed to get going.

"When do you have to make a decision?" he asked as he stood.

"Before the end of August. It's still weeks away, but it feels like tomorrow."

"You'll figure it out. You're on the right track. I wish you luck in deciding."

"Thanks, Ethan. I appreciate it."

"You're welcome, Molly. I'll see you around."

"Tuesday night, right?"

He smiled. "Tuesday night. I'll be on the team that comes in second to yours."

She looked down at the book in her hand. "Sometimes, coming in second is the better place to be."

"You know, I think you're right, Molly. Sometimes, it is."

He grabbed a new book off the fiction shelf as he went by, an author he read and enjoyed, as well as one he thought Gram would like. He checked them out and hurried back, thorough the light summer rain, to the clinic where he spent the rest of the afternoon thinking, not about Molly, but about his own life decisions. What *had* brought him to this clinic on this little island? Watching his co-workers interact with the islanders and visitors was beginning to make him think that he had taken Frost's road less traveled and ended up someplace where he really could make a difference.

***

"Summertime trivia?" Molly asked. "What the heck? That could be anything."

Lizzie groaned. "Anything and everything."

"Maybe it won't be that hard," Todd said.

"Mind if I join you?" said a voice from behind them.

"EJ!" Lizzie squealed and jumped up, throwing herself into his arms. "What are you doing here? You weren't supposed to arrive until tomorrow."

"I couldn't wait. The second my first month of pilot training ended, I made my way to you." He wrapped his arms around her and kissed her in a way that sent the entire bar into whistles and applause.

Before EJ even pulled out a chair for himself, their waitress, Rachel, was placing a cold beer in front of him. "On the house," she said. "Welcome home, Coastie."

"Okay, everyone," DJ Charlie said into the mic. "No more delays, question one."

"What's the category?" EJ asked.

Molly answered while the rest of the table shushed.

"When you're standing on the beach looking at the horizon, approximately how far can you see?"

"Three miles," EJ quickly whispered. "See? Glad I came home early?" He grinned at Lizzie.

"You bet I am," she replied before giving him another kiss and then jotting down the answer.

They chatted a few minutes before quieting down for the next question.

"Question two, what is the highest-grossing summer blockbuster of all time?"

Molly didn't hesitate. "Star Wars."

Todd shook his head. "Jaws. No doubt."

"Star Wars," Molly doubled down.

Lizzie and EJ looked back and forth between the two. "Which one?" Lizzie asked, her pen hovering over the answer sheet.

"Pick one," EJ said.

"The first night we played, the category was Summer Blockbusters. One of the questions asked how much Star Wars made as the highest grossing summer release of all time. Remember?"

Todd's jaw dropped. "You remember that? How do you do that?" He shook his head but relented. "Okay. Go with it."

"Question number three. In which month are you most likely to see the Perseid meteor shower?"

Everyone turned to look at Molly.

"Seriously? You all grew up here, minutes from Wallops, and you never went out to see the Perseids?"

"Sure," Lizzie said. "But it's Chincoteague. The summer is one long, continuous day broken up by the pony swim. I can't tell one day from the next." She shrugged.

Molly rolled her eyes. "August."

Lizzie quickly wrote it down.

"Hey, Molly, who's that guy who keeps looking over at you?" Ben asked, tossing his blonde mane.

"What guy?" Lizzie asked, immediately turning in the direction to which her brother pointed.

"Someone I went to school with," Molly said, feeling the flush rise to her face when she spotted Dustin across the room.

"He's cute," Lizzie said. "In a nerdy, scientist kind of way." She grinned at Molly.

"Question Four, between May and September, how many hot dogs do Americans consume?"

Molly sat back in her seat and shook her head. "Don't look at me."

"No clue," said EJ.

"A billion," said Ben.

Lizzie shrugged. "As good a guess as any," she said, writing it down.

"He's looking at you again," Todd said. "Maybe he's trying to read your lips."

"From the back of my head?"

"He sure isn't trying to read yours," EJ said to his brother, who reached over and hit him on the side of the head.

"What's the deal?" Lizzie leaned over and whispered.

Molly lifted one shoulder in response. "I'll tell you later." Though she refused to turn around, she felt the heat of his stare for the rest of the game. For almost ninety minutes, she fought the urge to glance over her shoulder, but she kept her gaze on her teammates and their answer sheet.

When the game was over, and scores were being tallied by DJ Charlie, Molly stood to use the bathroom.

"I've got a feeling our streak has ended," she heard Lizzie say, thumbing through Google in the hopes that the sites were all mistaken. "I can't believe we bet everything on the final question, and it's wrong."

"Hey," Ben said. "Maybe we got it right. You can't believe everything you see on the internet."

"Unless it's on every site, you dork. We definitely got it wrong."

Molly smiled as she made her way across the room. This was what she wanted. A summer full of fun and friends and the chance to exchange whispers about a guy who apparently couldn't take his eyes off her.

"How'd you do on that last question?" Dustin asked, coming up beside her as she waited in line.

"Don't ask. How are we supposed to know who the 'girl in the polka dot dress' witnessed being assassinated?"

"I know, right? We put JFK."

"You were closer than we were," she told him. "At least you had the right family."

"Yeah. We never even thought about his brother. Who did you say?"

"Lincoln. We figured, he was at a play. There was probably a girl in a polka dot dress."

Dustin shrugged. "Makes sense to me."

They heard DJ Charlie announce the winner and watched as a group of middle-aged vacationers whooped and cheered.

"You can't win them all," Molly said when the bathroom door opened. She started to move, but Dustin said her name.

"Molly? Do you have plans on Saturday night?"

She hesitated, but when she looked back, she saw Lizzie standing behind Dustin. She was smiling broadly and giving Molly *the look*. The one that said, 'go for it, or I'll never give it a rest.'

"I'm sorry. Saturdays are…not the best nights." She saw Lizzie frown. "But I can go out Friday."

Dustin's face lit up. "Great. What time?"

Molly smiled at Dustin. "I get off at four. Text me." She went into the bathroom, closed the door, and beamed at her reflection in the mirror. There was only one problem. Sooner or later, Dustin was going to figure out where she and her family went every Saturday night, and then the ridicule would start up again.

She looked up at the ceiling and whispered, "And then what do I do? I grew up not believing in you, but Jared changed my mind, only the rest of this world always seems to be looking for ways to prove you don't exist. What's going to happen when I start working with a bunch of scientists who don't see you like Jared does?"

Molly shook her head and got on with her business. This thing between her and Dustin, if it was a thing, was only for the summer, so why worry about it now? If he didn't want to date her because she went to church and believed in God, all she was losing was a summer fling. She'd rather lose that than her faith.

***

"Wanna dance?" Ethan asked Jenny when the cheering ended, and the music started.

Jenny felt the eyes of their co-workers on them and felt self-conscious.

"Go ahead, you two," Paula said. "I'm done for the night. I've got kids at home to yell at."

"Yeah, it's been a long day for me," Stacey said. "And it's going to be another scorcher tomorrow, so be ready."

Their teammates signaled for their checks as Jenny looked up at Ethan. Was it her imagination, or had he gotten taller in the last month? And better looking?

"Sure, one dance."

She let him lead her to the dance floor where she bumped into EJ and Lizzie kissing like there was no tomorrow.

"Uncle Trevor is going to hear about this," Jenny said to EJ with a broad grin on her face.

"Granddad better not hear it from you. And who cares. The wedding is three months away. I'm allowed to kiss my future wife."

"And what about Aunt Ronnie?" Jenny raised her brow.

"Um, she's right, EJ. Maybe we'd better go home. I'm sure your mama has already heard that you're on the island, and your grandmother would not be happy with us making out in public."

"Then let's go make out in private," EJ said with a wicked grin as he took her hand and led her off the dance floor. "See you, Jenny."

Ethan laughed and Jenny let him take her into his arms as she shook her head.

"Young love. Your cousin, I take it?"

"Not quite. EJ's grandfather and my father were lifelong best friends. His grandfather, Uncle Trevor, is Taylor's Godfather. He's always been like a second father to us, especially since Dad died."

"I'm sorry," Ethan said, faltering a step. "I didn't know. Was it recent?"

Jenny shook her head. "It's been almost ten years. I was in high school. He and my sister worked together, and he just collapsed one day. The ambulance got there right away, but it was too late. Heart attack." She smiled. "This rookie cop, first day on the job, was sent to see if the EMTs needed any kind of backup. He had no idea what to do, but I guess he did something right. He and Taylor have been married for seven years. Going on two kids and three dogs and living their best lives."

"What does your sister do?" Ethan asked as they swayed to the music. Jenny self-confessed how easy he was to talk to, to be with, and she found herself relaxing in his arms.

"Like our dad, she's an award-winning landscape artist. Not just muscle, but real brains and talent. And that's not even her claim to fame."

"Oh, really?" he asked, his eyebrows shooting up over his light brown eyes.

"Yeah. She's the island's first Saltwater Cowgirl."

"You mean, the ones who bring over the ponies?"

"I believe the phrase you meant to say is round up, the ones who round up and pen the ponies."

"I stand corrected. My apologies to the cowboys, and cowgirl."

"Cowgirls. There are several now. I'm not sure how many, to be honest. But it was a long time coming. Taylor is seen as a hero to many and a meddler to some."

"I can see that. Change doesn't come easily in a small town."

"No, it doesn't, but it was time."

"What about the rest of your family? Any other siblings?"

Jenny shook her head and noticed the song had changed without her even knowing it. They were off beat and out of step. "Want to sit for a bit?"

"Sure." Ethan followed her back to the table, and they ordered two more beers. "So, siblings?"

"Just Taylor. She and Nick built a house on the ranch. Mama still lives in our childhood home. I've got a cottage closer to town. What about you?"

"Two sisters, both older, married, and having one kid after another. They're back in Richmond near my parents."

"Do you miss them? Your family? Even though your grandmother is here, it's not the same."

"Growing up, I never thought I'd be saying it, but I do. Even when I was in college and then a busy intern, I went home as much as I could. We're all pretty close."

"That's nice. Us, too. I still go home for dinner as often as possible. I know Taylor's right there, but I still worry about Mom being alone."

"I'm sure. My mom is never alone. She works at one of the local hospitals and still manages to volunteer for several charities. She only works part time. We're lucky in that my dad made good money as a surgeon, so she doesn't have to work if she doesn't want to, but she loves being a nurse."

"So, you come from a medical family."

Ethan nodded. "Yeah. Gramp was a dentist, as you know, and my sisters both married doctors, too. One of my sisters is a teacher, and the other is a stay-at-home mom. She calls herself a Household Manager." He laughed. "Which she takes very seriously."

Jenny laughed, too. "I'm the only medical person in my family, but I love it."

"And you're good at it." He smiled, and Jenny felt a tug in her gut.

"So, is your dad one of the doctors who makes big money and gets treated like a god?" She blushed. "Sorry, that was probably rude."

Ethan shook his head. "Nah, it's okay. And no, Dad definitely does not have a god complex. He closed his practice a few years ago and now does a lot of charity cases at a local clinic, not unlike ours, but catering specifically to the underserved. He was a little disappointed when I came here instead of helping him, but he gets it. He respects what I do and why I wanted to come here. Besides, he knows you have to work hard and make something of yourself before you can devote all your time to making the world a better place."

"I think you do make the world a better place," Jenny said, then instantly felt the heat rise to her cheeks. "Okay, well," she said, finishing her beer. "I'd better get home. Sounds like we'll have another busy day tomorrow."

"Need a ride?"

"No, it's a short walk. I never drive when I go out at night."

"It's getting dark out there."

Jenny smiled and waved for their checks. "I'm a big girl, Dr. Edwards. I can handle myself."

"I'm sure you can, Dr. Murray. I'm sure you can."

When they parted ways at the door to the restaurant, Jenny smiled and waved. She wasn't sure about Dr. Edwards when he first showed up at the clinic. She didn't think he'd be able to handle everything he'd have thrown at him. To be honest, some days, she thought the verdict was still out. But Ethan was another story. Once the lab coat came off and the button-down shirt and khakis were changed to a t-shirt and jeans, the hotshot doctor became a real human being, one she wanted to know better.

***

The door opened, and a figure slowly made his way inside. Only a tiny ray of light from a penlight moved in the darkness. A hand hovered over the laptop for a few seconds before typing in the password. Jared was careless about logging in when others were around. He should have a newer computer, one of those with the fingerprint scanner, but that was laughable. This belonged to the U.S. Government, after all. He'd heard that technology was typically ten years behind where it should be in any government office. He smiled as he worked some magic to get into the NASA mainframe. He found the right folder and slipped the thumb drive into its slot.

After a few minutes, he retracted the drive and logged off. He pocketed the drive and all its valuable contents. This should bring a good price from the mysterious man he met just after he accepted the job here.

His days following orders and being a nobody were almost over. Soon, he'd be sitting pretty with no more money problems and nobody telling him what to do with his life.

Carnival Grounds Being Prepped

The Chincoteague Volunteer Fire Company and other local volunteers have been hard at work preparing the carnival grounds for the summer-long festivities. After a rough season of hard rain and strong winds, many of the booths are in need of repair. The pony pen fencing is being replaced as part of a long-term improvement plan. The carnival begins on June 24 and will run every weekend until the pony penning, after which it will run all week until its closure on July 29.

To volunteer to help prepare the grounds, or to volunteer at the carnival, contact the fire company or any of the local organizations listed on the fire company website.

The Chincoteague Herald, June 8

Chapter Seven

Déjà vu wasn't the right word for what Molly was feeling. What are the odds that both of her dates would take her to the same restaurant and order the same meal? Was this a bad sign? There were lots of great restaurants on the island and too many outstanding entrees on the menu for both men to gravitate toward without this being some kind of strange prank.

"You okay, Molly?" Dustin asked, a fork full of linguine inching toward his mouth.

"Yeah, just thinking about the last time I was here."

"I've never been, but Dr. Stevenson said it would be a good choice."

"Dr. Stevenson?" Molly asked, feeling her jaw drop. "You asked Jared where you should take me on a date?"

Dustin shrugged. "Sure. He lives here, knows everyone. I mean, none of the other interns are local. Heck, we don't even live on the island."

That was true, but still. "Does Jared know who you were bringing here?"

At that, Dustin's cheeks began to color. "Well, I did ask him, I mean mention to him, that I thought I might ask you out."

She picked up the napkin from her lap, wiped her mouth, and laid the napkin on the table. Her heart began to pick up its pace. "Whose idea was this? His or yours?"

"What? The restaurant? He suggested it, but I made the final decision."

Molly shook her head. "The date. Whose idea was it that you should ask me out?" She felt herself clench her jaw and took a slow, calming breath through her nose.

"Mine. Why would Jared suggest I take you out? I mean, that's way beyond his job as my boss, and probably a nightmare for HR." He looked at her with narrowed eyes. "What's going on, Molly?"

She surveyed him for a moment before asking, "Why did you ask me out?"

He opened his mouth, then closed it before blinking once and shaking his head. "Why did I ask you out?"

"Yes, Dustin. Why? For years, you were mean to me. You and your friends treated me like dirt, made fun of me, excluded me—"

He held up his hands. "Whoa. I thought we were past this."

"Past this? You think I can just get *past this*? Do you have any idea how hard it was for a fifteen-year-old to navigate all that? Because it didn't get any easier when I turned sixteen or seventeen or when I proved I was smart enough to be there or when—"

"Molly." Again, he interrupted. "Stop. I told you I was sorry. I admitted I was a jerk. What the heck? I thought we were starting over. I want to get to know you, the real you. I wanted to take you out and have a good time." He huffed and looked away, and Molly felt all the air leave her like a balloon a week after a party.

"Dustin, I'm sorry. I thought…"

"Why?" He asked, his eyes conveying the hurt he felt. "Why ask me this? Go off on me like that? I'm trying to do exactly what you said you wanted. I'm trying to treat you normally, help you have a good summer. No, I take that back. I'm not trying to do anything. I like spending time with you. When you aren't acting crazy."

Molly bit her lips so tightly, it hurt. She took a deep breath and closed her eyes, hoping she could stop the tears she felt forming. Why was she so emotional this summer? What the heck was wrong with her? She was stressed and unsure about how she felt about anyone and anything. Why was adulting so hard? She shook the thoughts away.

"I'm sorry. I just, I thought. I'm really sorry. Can we start over, or at least back up to before I made an idiot of myself?"

Dustin looked at her for several moments before shaking his head. "You've got to start believing in yourself, Molly, in recognizing your own self-worth."

"What's that supposed to mean? I know who I am and what I'm worth. I just graduated valedictorian from Harvard, a fact you know very well."

She saw his jaw tense and a flash of anger in his eyes. "Shoot. I'm sorry, again. I didn't mean it like that."

"Look, you know you're smart and capable. That's obvious. What you don't seem to know is that you're likable, too, and that people who don't like you are the ones with the problem. I can say that from a place of experience. Stop worrying about what people think or if they like you or why they want to be with you. Stop questioning everyone's motives. Be proud of who you are and what you've accomplished. People will naturally gravitate toward you because they like you. You're an adult now, out of school, and getting ready to enter the real world. Act like it."

He said the words without criticism, without judgement, and without cruelty. He spoke softly and kindly even if his words were harsh, and Molly knew instinctively that he was right. What he said wasn't too different from what Lizzie had told her. Molly was used to not being accepted, not fitting in, always being the odd one in the room, but the past few weeks, that hadn't been the case at all. EJ and Lizzie liked her. Jenny no longer treated her like a little kid. She had real friends and was on her second date. Why was she acting like she was five? Maybe if she wasn't always looking for people to judge her, she could've had more than one or two friends ages ago.

"You're right," she finally told him. "You're one hundred percent right. I've been a total idiot. I really would like to go back and try this again. If you're willing."

It felt like forever before Dustin's mouth twisted into a smile. "We make an odd pair, Molly, you know that? Despite everything, I think we can have a great summer together. Are you willing?" He threw her words back at her, and she returned his smile.

"Willing and ready. What's next on our summer agenda?"

"Finish eating, and I'll show you."

Molly's heart skipped a beat as she put the napkin back in her lap and picked up her fork. She was going to start looking at the world differently, beginning with herself.

****

The thought crossed Dustin's mind to take her hand as he and Molly walked down Main Street, trying to avoid the many passersby sharing the sidewalk. He was surprised to experience an unexpected feeling of loss every time they had to separate to allow a large group to go by.

They tried on hats in Blue Crab Treasures, marveled at the kites in the Kite Koop, and laughed at the shirts in the T-Shirt Factory. Dustin had never seen Molly smile so much, and it was doing something to him that was completely unexpected, and he wasn't sure how it happened. He liked Molly McLane, seriously liked her.

"What about this one?" Molly held up a shirt with a saying that made Dustin guffaw, a term he only associated with cartoon characters, but there it was. He guffawed. And the shirt wasn't even that funny.

"Ready for dessert?" he asked when they left the store.

"I'm always ready for dessert," Molly told him. "Where to?"

"I'm surprised you're asking. This is Chincoteague, after all."

Molly's smile turned into a broad grin. "You're learning, out-of-towner. Lead the way."

He didn't lead the way. They walked side by side to the Creamery, the most well-known eatery on the island. When they reached the tail end of the line of families, groups of teens, and couples of all ages, a signboard a few feet ahead read, "You're forty-five minutes from the best ice cream you will ever devour."

"Wow," Dustin said. "I'd heard the line could take a while, but really?"

"Have something better to do?" Molly asked with that killer grin, her purple eyes twinkling. He wasn't sure he'd noticed their color before that day he stopped her and made her sit with him in the café. Since then, he couldn't forget them.

"I've never had anything better to do than this," he answered, and he knew his grin was just as wide as hers.

It felt strange, to look at her this way, to feel what he was feeling. And all the while, he couldn't help but wonder what college would've been like if he'd only been nice to her.

"You weren't alone, you know," he suddenly said, and Molly looked at him with a furrowed brow. "At Harvard, I mean. I read somewhere that it has one of the highest rates of mental health issues with a large number of students feeling isolated, afraid to talk to anyone about their worries or problems—to either faculty or fellow students—and lack of social acceptance and connection. It described the school as having a 'toxic campus'."

Molly didn't say anything, and he worried that their relationship had just taken a giant step backwards. Again. He'd always had a problem with speaking before thinking, and he wished he could take it back.

Finally, she said, "I wonder if that was before or after the pandemic. I bet it got worse."

Dustin nodded, relieved. "It seems like that was the case everywhere. Some of this was before, but they've had plenty of time to fix things, and the article went on to say that nothing much had been done to make things better even after 2020."

"When teens and young adults everywhere really began struggling," Molly said.

They took a few steps forward.

"Tell me more about your dad." Molly looked at him, wondering if they looked alike.

Dustin made a noise of amusement and smiled.

"My dad is the greatest. He's supportive, kind, funny, loving, exactly what you'd want in a dad." He looked back at Molly and remembered. "What about yours?" he asked tentatively. "Was he a good dad?"

Molly nodded. "As good as yours. He used to bring these giant books home from work and read them to me. He never asked if I understood them. He just read and answered any questions I had. I always asked for more. I just wanted to soak up everything he knew, everything anyone knew, about space. My mom used to laugh at us. Christy thought we were weird, but I loved learning from my dad."

"He didn't do that with your sister?"

Molly tilted her head. "Christy's dad died when she was a baby. Cancer. She was twelve when my dad met our mom."

"Was there ever, like, any weirdness between you two? You know, because she didn't have your mom all to herself anymore?"

Molly vehemently shook her head as they progressed in line. "Never. She says she loved my dad from the start because he never made her feel like he was taking her mom away from her. They were a unit from day one."

Dustin thought about that. His father had never dated, and he wondered how he would've reacted if his father brought home a woman, wanted to marry again. Dustin wanted his dad to be happy, but did that mean he would've been open to having a mom, or a stepmom?

"What about you?" She broke into his thoughts. "Any brothers or sisters?"

"Not that I know of. I mean, I haven't seen or heard from my mom since, well, ever. I suppose there could be siblings out there somewhere."

"Have you ever thought about doing a DNA test to find out?"

Dustin shook his head. "Not really. Dad and I have always been happy. He's a great dad and a good person. We had money—my grandfather was wealthy by inheritance and by hard work—so we had it pretty good. Dad worked but always had time for me. I have no regrets about my childhood. My grandmother was there, and my dad was pretty good at being both a dad and a mom. Still is." He shrugged. "I was lucky, I guess."

They talked more about their parents, their lives growing up, and their school experiences before college. The time passed unbelievably fast, and before he knew it, they were walking outside with one Mud Marsh and one Wallops Rocket Fuel. Dustin's eyes watered with the infusion of chili pepper and cinnamon mixed with his chocolate ice cream.

They continued walking toward the park, eating their ice cream, and talking between bites. Dustin tried to think of something else to do, somewhere else to go, after they finished their cones. He wasn't ready for the night to end.

***

"Hey, Mol!" Jenny waved at Molly and the boy she recognized from trivia. She thought he was one of the Wallops kids.

"Jenny!" Molly squealed, just like she had when she was ten and Christy dropped her off for Jenny to babysit.

The two hugged, and Molly said hello to Ethan before raising a brow in question and smirking at Jenny.

"Hi Molly. Nice to see you again."

"Ethan and I just saw the new Austin Butler movie. It was good. I'm Jenny," she said to Molly's companion.

"This is Dustin. We went to school together," Molly jumped in before Dustin had a chance to introduce himself.

"As in Harvard?" Jenny asked.

"Yep. We, uh, didn't really know each other there."

"And she wouldn't have liked me much," Dustin added. "Like most college guys, I was a knucklehead."

Jenny noticed the look that passed between them and wondered what the deal was. Something was being left unsaid.

"Looks like you made it through the line." Jenny gestured toward their quickly dwindling ice cream cones.

"Forty-five-minute wait when we got in line. I think it's shorter now."

"Good. You know I never pass up a chance to have homemade ice cream. It was nice meeting you," she said to Dustin, making a mental note to call Molly over the weekend and get all the deets. She watched Ethan as his eyes followed Molly and Dustin. "You're not still thinking of dating her, are you?"

Ethan looked at Jenny and smiled. "To be honest, I was thinking that she's pretty darn impressive. I ran into her the other day at the library, and we had a long talk. She's every bit as smart as people say she is, and more mature than her age, obviously, but there was something else. She's…"

His features turned pensive, and Jenny found herself torn between amusement and maybe a bit of jealousy.

"Intriguing?" Jenny supplied. "I get it. She's not your average almost eighteen-year-old."

"She's not, and intriguing is a good word for her." He turned his gaze on Jenny. "No, I'm not still interested in dating her, but she's definitely somebody I'd like to count as a friend. I get the feeling she's someone you'd want in your corner."

Jenny turned back toward the direction in which Molly and Dustin were headed and nodded. "You've got that right. More than one person on this island count themselves extremely lucky to have Molly as a friend and someone who looks out for them. Admittedly, I'm one of them."

"I can see that."

Ethan held out his arm, and Jenny took it, sliding her arm around his. She felt a tremble in her mid-section that she liked quite a lot.

"So, show me this ice cream place," Ethan said, and Jenny led the way, not unlocking her arm from his until they reached the inside of the shop thirty minutes later.

During the time they waited in line, they talked about their families, their education, and even the cliché, 'where do you see yourself in five years.' Jenny was surprised by his answer but realized she shouldn't have been. Ethan wanted to be married, have at least one child by then, and feel like he was making a difference in the world. He admitted that it was a new realization for him, but one that had always been in the back of his mind. He told Jenny that he'd gone to medical school to help people, graduated with a desire to make big money, and gradually found himself thinking less about the money and more about the helping.

After taking several licks of her Iced Nirvana—she craved coffee and espresso any way she could get it—Jenny pointed to a nearby bench under a streetlight and took a seat. Once Ethan was settled beside her, she returned to their conversation.

"So, why Chincoteague? I know you wanted to do something different from your father and the other doctors, but why here? You could've worked at a hospital or a clinic or other healthcare center where you would have patients without all the glory. "

Ethan took a bite—he was an ice cream biter and not a licker, which Jenny found funny—of his salted caramel pretzel and nodded. "I hated the rat race at the big hospital. It had me questioning what I was doing this for. I mean, I was helping people and making good money, and it was nonstop excitement, but something was missing there."

"Connections." Jenny said, remembering their previous conversation. She knew she would feel the same way after growing up in such a close-knit community.

"Yeah, exactly. I wanted to know the people I was treating, what happened to them when they left my care, and if what I did for them really mattered. When I talked to my dad about the way I was feeling—after he got over my decision not to work in his clinic—he suggested I look for a place that was the total opposite of Richmond." He shrugged. "So, here I am."

"Yet the pace is pretty hype some days," Jenny said with a laugh.

"Yeah, but in a good way. I mean, I'm exhausted at the end of one of those days, but I'm also kind of excited. I know what to expect the next day, and I start looking forward to it. Even with the curveballs we get thrown."

"Those are what keep it exciting."

"You've got that right. It's like a Ferris wheel that keeps going round and round, but we can stop and get off, and the view constantly changes, like looking down at the ground and realizing there's grass on one side, a parking lot on another, and a beach and seashore on another."

Jenny tilted her head and watched a seagull swoop down to rescue a lost piece of soft pretzel as she thought about his analogy. He wasn't wrong.

"So, do you think you'll stick around after the summer? Things get pretty slow here when the season dies down."

"I think that's the time I'll enjoy the most. I'm looking forward to being part of the community, meeting my neighbors, doing some volunteering, putting down roots, all that stuff."

Jenny looked at Ethan and felt a broad grin tugging at her lips. "You know what, Dr. Edwards? I think you're going to fit in just fine 'round these parts."

Ethan grinned back at her in a way that made her heart miss a beat.

"You know what, Dr. Murray? I think you're right."

***

"Hi, Molly."

Molly looked through the display case and smiled at the best-looking man—not boy—on the island. He was well over six feet tall with close-cut, dark hair and piercing dark eyes that almost made Molly feel like he could see right through to her soul. Maybe he could. His reputation as a former Army sniper—information she found online and knew in-person—profiled a man with the speed of a cheetah, the eyes of a hawk, and the mind of a wolf. Molly knew there were people in this world whose blood turned cold at the mere mention of his name, but not Molly, not anyone on the island.

"Zach!" She ran around the counter and threw her arms around him, and Zach Middleton enfolded her against him like a giant teddy bear.

"I haven't seen you since your graduation party. How's your summer going, kiddo?"

"It's going."

"Any decisions yet?"

Molly twisted her mouth and shook her head. "Still researching and weighing my options."

"Any praying? There's no better way to find the right answer."

Molly bit her lips together. "Um, not really. I guess I hadn't even thought about that."

Zach narrowed his eyes at her. "That big fancy school with all those scientific minds didn't steer you away from the truth, did it?"

"Absolutely not," she said, though her gut twisted a bit. She hadn't turned away from the Church. She just tried to hide it from everyone she knew. "I just, well, there wasn't a lot of praying going on up there, you know?"

"I do know. You ever hear the saying, 'There are no atheists in foxholes'"?

Molly nodded then frowned. "What does that have to do with me and school?"

"When I was at the academy, I ran into plenty of people who had no need for God or religion. That changed for a lot of them when we arrived in the desert. Sometimes, we don't think we need God because things are good. We might not even believe in him because who needs to believe when everything seems to be going right? But as soon as you're surrounded by mortar shells and bullets and people dying all around you, you start looking for some meaning, some stability, something to hold onto when there doesn't seem to be anything else there."

Molly slowly nodded, unsure of where this was going.

"You've got your whole life ahead of you and probably offers of the kind of money and perks that could change your life forever in ways you can't even imagine yet."

She inhaled through her nose, held it, and slowly released the breath. He was right.

"Those are some big things, life-changing things. Don't take them lightly. You need to keep yourself grounded, and the only real way to do that is to keep yourself close to God. You're going to be faced with big questions, big decisions, and big changes, and there will be times you don't know what the answers or paths are." He pointed upward. "But he does. Ask him. Listen for him. He'll tell you where to go and what to do."

"But what if he doesn't? What if he wants me to make my own decisions, using my own free will?"

"He always wants that, but he gave you free will not to do what you want but what is right. And you can't do that unless you stay close to him."

The bell over the door rang, and Molly looked past Zach, her eyes widening.

"Um, yeah. I hear you, Zach. I'm glad you stopped by. I need to get back to work though."

Zach turned to look behind him. He let his gaze settle back on Molly as though he knew exactly what she was thinking. It unnerved her in a way that it never had before.

"Just remember what I said, Molly."

"You bet, Zach. Thank you." She meant it and hoped her eyes conveyed that. "Oh, did you want to order something?"

Zach looked up at the menu and ordered a breakfast sandwich and black coffee to go. Molly rang him up, and he moved aside, picking up the local paper that was on the counter for customers to read.

"Hi, Dustin. What can I get for you?" She tried to act casual, but she couldn't control the smile that spread across her face.

"Hey, Molly." He smiled broadly, gazing at her for a moment before looking up at the menu. He gave her an order and paid but didn't move on. "Um, I know you said Saturdays are complicated for you. I'm not sure what that means, but tonight is going to be the best night all summer to see the Summer Triangle and I thought, maybe, we could look for it together."

"Well, I guess that would be after dark." *That would work.*

"That's when you tend to see the stars, as far as I know." He was smiling, but he kept blinking, and his voice wasn't as steady as usual, a layer of nervousness peeking out under that bright smile.

"Do you think we'll be able to see all three constellations?"

He nodded. "I think so. And Hercules, too."

She sensed Zach's interest in their conversation even though he appeared to be engrossed in the newspaper.

"I'd like that. I just can't do anything before seven. I have something I do with my family on Saturday evenings. Something important to me," she added for Zach's benefit.

"Sure, no problem. Can I pick you up? Will you have eaten?"

"You can pick me up, and yes, I'll grab something to eat."

"Great. I'll be at your house at seven. We can watch from the beach. Does that work?"

"Not for seeing the stars. The beach closes at ten, but I know a place we can go for that."

"Awesome."

"Molly, you've got an order ready," Diego called.

She retrieved the order and called Zach's name. When she handed it to him, he gave her a long, hard look.

"See you later, Molly," he said. "Think about what I said."

Molly swallowed. "I will, Zach. Thanks."

"And Molly." He glanced toward Dustin, who was scrolling through his phone, and spoke in a low voice. "If you need to hide who you are and what's 'important' to you, think about whether that's worth it in the long run. If it's important to you, those who care about you will understand and will find it to be important to them, too. If not…" He stood and gave her a knowing look before turning away.

"Order, Molly."

Molly grabbed Dustin's order and called to him.

"Who was that guy?" Dustin asked. "Kind of scary looking."

Molly smiled as she reached for a lid for his coffee. "Nothing scary about Zach. He's a good guy. Former military who consults with the local police sometimes. He helped me with that restaurant stuff you've probably heard about."

Dustin raised a brow.

"Another time," Molly told him. "Here's your coffee. Careful, it's hot. See you at seven?"

"Yeah," Dustin said slowly, eyeing her warily. "See you then."

Molly watched him leave and thought about what Zach said. Deep down, she knew he was right. About everything. She wasn't so sure that Dustin would feel the same, but what did it matter? They were just having fun, right?

Internal Memo

Do not remove items from the storeroom or warehouse that you did not purchase or were not ordered for your project. Be sure to fill out the proper paperwork before taking anything from storage or claiming any packages.

Thank you.

Dr. Simon Johnson, Director
Wallops Island Flight Facility

Chapter Eight

Ethan didn't quite know how it had happened, but he wasn't complaining as he and Jenny spent another evening together. It was her weekend off, but she'd shown up at the clinic around lunchtime and asked him if he and his grandmother would like to join her and her mother for dinner that evening.

"Nothing special," she said. "It turns out that my mom and your grandmother have known each other for years. They're in the garden club together. At their meeting the other night, your grandmother mentioned that you were the new doctor at the clinic, and my mother gave me the third degree for not inviting you for dinner."

Ethan laughed. "I guess you offended her sense of island hospitality."

"That, and…" She paused and looked around before leaning closer and whispering, "I think they may be scheming to fix us up. You know, two doctors, shared interests, island roots." She shrugged.

Ethan was amused by this but found that he wasn't entirely opposed to letting the women pursue their scheme. He accepted the invitation and now found himself sitting across from Jenny and Donna Murray in an elegant dining room on a ranch on the far side of the island.

"So, how do you like it here so far?" Donna asked.

"I like it a lot," Ethan said, smiling at Jenny.

He had a hard time suppressing a laugh at her coloring cheeks and the looks being passed between the older women.

"Things are going well? At the clinic I mean?" Donna asked.

"Yeah, well, he's learning the ropes," Jenny said. "The verdict is still out on whether he'll be able to cut it here." She gave him a wicked grin, and he feigned feeling insulted by making a noise in his throat and clutching his chest.

"I think I'm holding my own," he shot back, realizing there were sparks flying between them, and they weren't going unnoticed.

"You've got some areas where you still need to prove yourself," Jenny said, grinning with twinkling eyes. "But you're getting there."

"I think it's time for dessert," Jenny's mother said. "Jenny, help, please?"

Ethan watched them leave, unable to take his eyes off his colleague.

"Well," his grandmother said when they were alone. "Jenny hasn't changed. She always did keep everyone on their toes."

He turned and looked at Gram. "You've known Jenny for a while?"

"Yes and no. I've seen her around the island and at the clinic. I've known her mother for several years, though, and I've heard her talk about her girls. They're both go-getters who let nothing stand in their way, but Taylor was always focused on the future, on being a Saltwater Cowgirl, taking over the family business, getting married, while Jenny…" She cocked her head to the side and stared at the family portrait that hung over the massive marble fireplace in the next room. In it, Jenny and Taylor were teenagers, and their parents beamed with pride at the camera. Ethan realized it must have been taken shortly before Jenny's father's death.

"Jenny is also focused on her future," Gram continued, "but she's more independent."

"What's wrong with that?" Ethan asked, not sure what she was trying to say.

"She had a boyfriend for a long time, a local boy, but I've always had the feeling that she's one of those modern women who doesn't want to settle down. Her mother is determined to prove otherwise."

Ethan looked toward the kitchen and wondered if Gram was right. Was that why Jenny didn't want to go out with him right away? Or why she was friendly but didn't put out any vibes that she wanted more? Was she uninterested, or was she waiting for him to take the first step?

"Well, I guess that's Jenny's business," he said, as he thought about his grandmother's assessment. Maybe Gram was worried she'd break his heart, and he needed to put her at ease. "She and I are just friends and colleagues, so whether she settles down isn't really my concern."

Gram turned to him and gazed thoughtfully at him for several moments. "Are you sure about that? You've been talking about her a lot lately, and here we are, having dinner in her mother's home."

"Which the two of you organized. Jenny and I had nothing to do with this."

"Donna wanted to see how you two acted together, and I wanted to see if Jenny had wised up."

"And you don't think she has." He sat back and clicked his tongue. "Though I doubt she'd appreciate you comparing her lack of desire to settle down as being unwise. Perhaps she just wants to establish her career first."

"Perhaps. I suppose time will tell."

Ethan smiled and picked up his glass of wine, tilting it toward her in a mock toast. "Then I guess we'll just have to wait and see, won't we?"

"Wait and see about what?" Jenny asked as she placed in front of him a slice of blueberry pie topped with vanilla ice cream and garnished with a piece of fresh mint.

"How the summer unfolds," Ethan said with a smile.

Gram's brow arched, and he wondered if she truly had something against Jenny or just wanted to give him a challenge.

Jenny looked inquisitively between Ethan and his grandmother. "Did I miss something?"

"No, not at all, dear," Gram said, patting Jenny's hand. "In fact, I think this summer is going to be very interesting."

"I'll drink to that," Ethan said, taking a long sip of his wine as he held Jenny's perplexed gaze.

***

"Okay, this question doesn't count. Do you want a soda?" Dustin pulled a Miller from the cooler that sat in the sand next to the blanket.

"No, thanks. Not a soda drinker. I stick to water and tea. I hate all the added sugar." She held up her water bottle then put it back on the blanket. She had finished her sandwich and was lying on her stomach, her elbows propped up so she could look at him. Dustin sat in front of her, his back to the water.

Dustin popped the top and took a sip. "Next question. Have you ever had a drink?"

Molly frowned. "Why?"

Dustin shrugged and took another sip. "Just curious. I know you weren't part of the party scene at school."

"I'm not really the party type, but yes, I've had wine. Kind of. I've tasted it."

"And what? You don't like it?"

"It's okay. It's just not something I've ever cared about."

Dustin nodded. "Ever smoked pot?"

Molly's eyes went as wide as a pair of Frisbees, and Dustin laughed.

"Sorry. Didn't mean to put you on the spot."

"No, and again, not really any desire." Her Frisbee-like eyes narrowed like lab tweezers. "Why? Have you? It's my turn, by the way."

"True." He thought about how to answer for a moment. "Once. Hated it. Hated the thought of not being in control of my senses."

"Yet you drank heavily, from what I heard."

He shrugged. "You got me there, but that was different."

"Different, how?"

"I don't know. Just different. I knew it was something I was doing as part of the crowd, and then wasn't likely to keep it up after graduation, not more than one or two at a time anyway. Drugs, though, that's another thing entirely. Addiction always scared me. Still does. If I thought I was heading that way with alcohol, I would've stopped drinking. I used to talk to my dad about it, and he always told me to be careful and not let it control me."

"How would you have known if it was controlling you, if you were heading down the wrong path?"

Dustin had wondered that, too, more than once. "I guess just the fact that I could say no if I wanted to. And

I never, like, craved it. I just enjoyed it when I was hanging out with friends."

"Okay. I asked a bunch of things in a row. Your turn."

He thought it over. What did he want to know? His curiosity about her present life was stronger than about her past. "What's the deal with Saturday nights? What do you do with your family?"

She visibly stiffened and looked down at the blanket. "Nothing really. Just family stuff. My turn."

"I don't think so. That's not an answer." Now his curiosity was truly piqued. He put down the can and folded his hands in his lap. "What do you do?"

Molly looked around him, out toward the glowing pink horizon for several minutes. The beach was going to close soon. She rolled her lips together and took a deep breath before pulling herself up to sit up on the blanket.

"What's your take on the big bang theory?"

"Wait. You didn't answer my question."

"I'm getting there."

He wasn't so sure about that, but he gave her the benefit of the doubt. "Well, everything points to a big bang."

"Genius." She rolled her eyes. "And what do you define that as?"

He blinked. "Well, the same thing other scientists define it as. It was a small but dense explosion of a singularity of atoms that continues today, ever-expanding in space and time."

"That's pretty good. It's actually almost exactly the way the original theorist explained it."

"Okay, so what does that have to do with anything?" He picked up his can and took another sip then took the last bite of his sandwich.

"It has to do with everything. It proves that the universe was nothing, a great void of nothingness that spontaneously combusted into this ever-expansion of space and time, as you put it."

"So? What's that have to do with you and your family's secret Saturday night adventures?"

Molly laughed. "I wouldn't call them adventures."

"Then what?" He was trying not to get frustrated by her beating around the bush with scientific riddles.

"Do you know who proposed the theory?"

"The big bang theory? Lemaitre in 1927. We had to know that for a test in astrophysics, remember?"

"I remember. I also remember that we weren't taught anything about Lemaitre himself, about who he was and his background."

Dustin shrugged. "We weren't taught that about most scientists. We were taught what they did, what they discovered. That's what matters."

"So, who they were and where they came from has no bearing on their intelligence or ability to impart scientific knowledge, right?"

He leaned forward with his elbows on his knees, feeling like there was some sort of catch in her question. "No. Yes. I'm not sure. What are you getting at?"

"Lemaitre was a Jesuit."

"Okay, so he was from… Where is that exactly?"

"Not where he was from, what he was. He was a Jesuit priest."

"A priest? Like a religious priest?"

"A Catholic priest."

"Okay. I still don't get it."

"Most of the people at school—students and professors—believe there is this dividing line that separates religious people from scientific people."

"Rational people from irrational people, you mean."

Her jaw twitched, and she frowned.

"Why are religious people irrational?"

"Oh, come on, all that stuff about the world being created in seven days—"

"Six. The seventh was for rest."

He raised a brow, surprised that she had corrected him, and kept going. "Okay, six. And the stories about floods and burning bushes and people coming back from the dead. Irrational stuff."

"So, no such things as miracles?"

"Nah. Everything has an explanation."

"Like the entire universe being created from absolutely nothing and suddenly having intelligence and reason and perfect order and design."

"Which can all be explained by math and science."

"Yet math and science are human creations. The field of mathematics is a mode of measurement realized and put forward by man, not a reality, but a way of measuring and ordering. Science is man's attempt to explain the unexplainable."

What the heck is going on here? Is she trying to throw me off? Trying to make me feel stupid? Is this some game about whose mind is more scientific?

"Molly, what the heck? I asked you about what you do with your family. If you don't want to tell me, then just say so." He threw his arms up in exasperation.

"Catholics believe, on faith, that God created the universe from nothing, going from absolute nonbeing to a vast collection of planets, stars, and creatures of the highest intelligence, save his own."

"And?" He forced himself not to shout. This was going nowhere.

Molly just sat there, calmly looking at him. She blinked once, then said, "I go to church on Saturday nights because I work on Sundays. I'm Catholic. This is what I believe. And I have one of the greatest scientific minds since Lemaitre, since his friend and colleague, Einstein. And he, a Jewish, scientific genius, also believed."

***

They never made it to the star gazing. The evening went downhill from there. Molly saw the change come over Dustin immediately. He completely shut down. He was at a loss for words, which she had never witnessed before. At first, he tried to play it off like she was joking, but she never gave in.

He pressed her to admit that the whole religion thing was far-fetched. She pointed out flaws in his arguments—she'd had a lot of time to read Augustine and Aquinas while he was out partying—and told him stories about miracles, but he was unfazed. The only thing she didn't tell him was her family's own miracle, her sister's vision of Christ just before her heart stopped beating. How Christy reached out for him, reached out her arms in surrender, giving her life for Jared's. How her heart miraculously began beating again, and she survived internal injuries she should not have survived, and went on to have a baby a year later.

She knew that Dustin would blow it off, find some reason for what happened. She'd shared the story once with her roommate in boarding school. The girl had changed rooms soon after, telling her friends that Molly was a weirdo whose family dabbled in the occult. She learned her lesson then.

Molly and Dustin packed their things in silence. On the way to the car, she asked, "Would you mind if I skipped the star gazing? I think I'll walk home. I'm more tired than I thought I'd be, and I have to work tomorrow."

"Um, sure, if you're okay walking."

"I'm good. See you later."

"Yeah. Have a good night."

She stood in the parking lot and watched him drive away. When the car was no longer visible, she pulled her phone from her pocket and called Jared. Between tears, she asked him to pick her up in the Assateague Beach parking lot.

While she waited, she imagined all the ways the conversation could have gone. Dustin was intelligent, he could conduct a respectable debate and articulate a fine point with the best of them. It was almost as though he just gave up, just decided the debate wasn't worth it. That made Molly realize that he didn't think she was worth it, worth exploring something he didn't know or understand--both her faith and her as a person.

Jared was furious that Dustin had left Molly so far from home, that he didn't stop to think about her welfare, and didn't make sure she got home safely. He let her know that he was irritated that Dustin didn't have the courtesy to listen to Molly's beliefs, to try to understand that this was important to her. Most of all, Molly sensed that he was sad that someone so smart could be so stupid.

***

"So, you and that guy from Wallops looked like you were enjoying each other's company the other night." Jenny watched as Molly made her an iced coffee.

"Yeah, we were, but don't read anything into it. He's just a friend." Molly scrunched her cheeks and mouth together. "Maybe. Not sure that's true anymore." Molly's voice dipped low, something Jenny recognized.

"Hey, Mol, you okay?"

Molly nodded, then looked around at the busy café. "Jenny, have you, I mean, are you...? Never mind."

"What? Did something happen? Did he do something to you?"

Molly fervently shook her head. "No. It's just." She let out a long breath. "Nothing. I can't get into it. Not now." She handed Jenny the cup, and Jenny grabbed her hand.

"Hey, we've known each other a long time. I used to braid your hair and make sure you brushed your teeth."

"I always brushed my teeth."

"You know what I mean. What's up?"

"Are you on your way to work?"

Jenny looked at her watch. "Yeah, why?"

Molly turned around. "Diego, can you handle things for a few minutes?"

"I've got you," Holly said, coming out from the kitchen. "But not too long."

"Thanks," Molly said before racing around the counter and dragging Jenny out the side door by the arm.

"I don't have a lot of time, so I'll try to compress."

Jenny listened as Molly gave a quick, breathless rundown of her conversation with Dustin.

"You really like him, don't you?"

Molly jerked back as though Jenny was a snake poised to strike.

"No, I mean, maybe. No." She shook her head. "Yes, I like him, but it's not just him. Will I ever find someone whose intellect matches mine who believes in God? Did you run into that in med school? You're technically a scientist, too."

Jenny's thoughts ran to some discussions with her classmates. "I did, but I went to a Catholic school, so it wasn't as big a deal. As to your other question, Jared believes. He believed even when you and Christy didn't."

"Yeah, but Jared was raised in a home with a mother and a stepfather who are intelligent and knew how to explain things to him in a way that prompted him to explore and find answers. Dustin doesn't want answers. He wants logic."

"I know plenty of men who believe, and they're men of logic."

Molly gave that a thought. "True."

"Dr. Johnson is a scientist. Zach and Aaron are no dummies. They both graduated from military academies."

Molly looked pensive. "It was actually Zach who prompted me to bring it up to Dustin. He said I shouldn't hide my faith, or something to that effect."

"And he's right. If Dustin doesn't appreciate and accept that, then he's not right for you. But someone will be. You've got a long time to find him."

"But how will I find him where I'm heading?"

"You will. I promise. And he doesn't have to be someone you meet at work, another scientist. He could be a doctor or lawyer, maybe someone you meet at church."

Molly nodded. "Okay, you're right. Speaking of which, what about your doctor?"

"What about him? I mean, not that he's *my* doctor, just a colleague and friend."

"Uh-huh. Anyway, what does he believe?"

"Molly, girl, we barely know each other. That's not something I'm worried about at this point." *Or am I?* "Anyway, I've got to get to the clinic. It's just Steph and me today."

She grabbed Molly's hand. "Don't worry about this now, Molly. Enjoy your summer. Figure out what you want to do with your life. The rest will come in time."

They hugged and said goodbye, but Molly's question was a phantom hovering behind Jenny all the way to work. What about Dr. Edwards?

***

"Hey," Nathan said, taking a seat beside Dustin on the sand.

"Hey," Dustin answered back.

"You okay? You got back a lot earlier than I thought you would last night, and today, you seem off."

"I'm fine. Just tired this weekend." He had no intention of telling his roommate what was on his mind. Even though he had very mixed feelings about Molly at the moment, he still felt protective of her.

"You and Molly have a fight?"

Dustin picked up a handful of sand and let the grains slip through his fingers. He watched the sand, an unenclosed hourglass slipping into a mound of grains upon grains without structure or meaning. He wondered about the concept of time, another invention of man to keep track of his days on earth, to give it structure and meaning.

"So, you did have a fight," Nathan said as he shaped granules into a pile, time adding up, never ending yet always signaling the end of something.

Was this the end of something? Or was it the beginning of new thoughts and ideas, runes Dustin didn't know how to decipher?

"I don't know if it was a fight. More like a general philosophical disagreement about life."

"Man, you're too young to be having philosophical discussions about life."

"Oh, yeah? How old do you have to be to start thinking about life, the future, things just beginning, or time slipping away, serious stuff that adults are supposed to care about?"

"Oh, I think about that stuff all the time. Ever since my old man left us, and my mom had to scrape together every dime just to feed my sister and me, I've thought about my future and about everything that is always a moment from slipping away. I just didn't think it would involve trying to figure out how to pay off thousands of dollars in student loans. I've still got a year to go in school, and the bills are already more than I'll ever be able to repay. I'm beginning to think it's not worth it. I'm ready for the future to start now."

Dustin stopped thinking about Molly and looked at his roommate. "Are you thinking of dropping out of school? You only have one year left, and you've got a good chance at the intern scholarship."

"Nah, this is Adrienne's second year here. She's got that in the bag."

"I don't know. Dr. Johnson is always saying what a bright future you have in rocketry. Adrienne's more interested in weather. I think you'll get the scholarship."

"Maybe, but I've got a contingency plan. I'm working on something with a guy I met at school."

"So, you might be the next Watson and Crick or Jobs and Wozinak? What are you working on?"

Nathan shook his head. "Can't tell you. Maybe someday I can let you in on it, but not now."

"Now I'm really intrigued."

"It's nothing." Nathan squashed the mound of sand and stood. "I'm getting fried, and I'm past bored. You ready to head back? Adrienne fell asleep reading, and Cam is wasted, as always. This beach thing is getting lame."

"Sure, we can get them moving and head back." Dustin stood and wiped his sandy hands on his bathing suit, which had dried quickly after his tumbles in the waves. He followed Nathan back up to the umbrella and gently roused Adrienne while Nathan helped Cam find his shoes.

They were an odd bunch, but Dustin liked them. He felt old next to them even though he was only a year ahead of them in school and life. When he'd taken this internship for some hands-on training and time to think about what to do with his life, he hadn't realized he'd be the senior intern. And he certainly never saw himself thinking deep thoughts about what he wanted for his future, about whom he wanted in his future.

He hoped Nathan and his mysterious partner rocked the scientific world with something that would help Nathan find the fame and fortune he sought. He knew Adrienne would go far, and he had a feeling Cam could be the next Thomas Edison if he got a handle on his drinking.

But where did that leave him?

Nathan's potential lucrative partnership had Dustin thinking about more than future endeavors. He found himself contemplating famous pairs in science and tech history. He had never thought of himself as being partner material, but his thoughts wandered to some of the other successful pairs he and his classmates had learned about—Marie and Pierre Curie, Frederic and Irene Joliot-Curie, and Marie-Anne and Antoine Lavoisier. Was Dustin screwing up what could be another famous coupling in the world of science?

He thought there might be someone he could go to for answers. It was risky, but Dustin thought it might be worth it.

***

"Yeah, I'm making my move in the next couple days. Have that wire ready to go as soon as you get my call."

He hung up and smiled. They didn't get any easier than this. Not a soul within miles knew who he was or what he was up to. Nobody would be on alert or suspect something big was getting ready to happen.

He laughed to himself as he strolled down the beach, tossing his long, thick mane like the ponies he passed. He changed his looks every few days, so he was always just another tourist. A wave kissed his bare feet, and he felt the icy water between his toes.

He might be on the job, but there weren't too many places as nice as this to take a long business trip. He might even miss it when he was gone.

Farmers and Artisans Market Has Something for Everyone

Chincoteague's Saturday Morning Farmers and Artisans Market has been a staple of the community for many years. Farmers, artists, and craftsmen come from up and down the peninsula to share their homegrown and homemade products. You can find anything from fresh fruits and vegetables to local honey and jams. Check out the inspirational pieces by artists Ronnie Kelly, Cheryl Taylor, Dora Todd, and Sharon Lupton. Purchase amazing decorative pieces by Ocean Wood Designs or engraved gifts from High Tide Fabrication. Decorate your beach home with goodies from Yellow Rose Sewing and Ocean Soaps. You never know what you'll find at the market!

The Chincoteague Herald, June 15

Chapter Nine

Dustin waited three days before knocking on his boss's door for something other than work. There had been this weird vibe between them, and he wondered what Dr. Stevenson knew. He'd gone back and forth about talking over his thoughts with his boss, and he still didn't know if he was doing the right thing. Was this some sort of breech of work etiquette? Having never had an adult job, Dustin didn't know. Maybe he should've asked his dad instead.

"Come in, Dustin. What's up?" Dr. Stevenson sat back in his chair and pushed his glasses up his nose, giving Dustin no choice but to go in and face his boss. The man's dark, curly hair bounced as he moved, and it reminded Dustin of the dark-haired poodle his late great-grandmother once had. His face was pinched in annoyance, and Dustin wondered again if he was doing the right thing.

"Everything okay?" Dustin asked.

Dr. Stevenson shook his head. "Have you seen my legal pad? The one I make notes on?"

Dustin shook his head in reply. "Not today. You had it yesterday when we were working on the rocket specs."

His boss sighed, and Dustin took a deep breath before plunging ahead.

"Dr. Stevenson, can I ask you a question?"

"Does this have anything to do with me picking up Molly the other night in the beach parking lot?"

Oh, crud. Dustin hadn't expected that. "You picked her up? She said she wanted to walk."

"And you thought that was a good idea? A safe alternative to being driven home and dropped off in her driveway? Do you know how long a walk that would've been? How dangerous?"

"No, no, I didn't," Dustin assured him. "I wasn't thinking. I'm sorry. Molly said some things that I, well, that got to me. That's what I wanted to talk to you about."

Dr. Stevenson's eyebrows raised, and he leaned back toward the desk with a now unreadable expression. "Go ahead," he gestured to the chair opposite the desk, though his voice was cautious.

"I'm curious," Dustin began but stopped. He remained standing, thinking he might need to make a hasty exit. He was having second thoughts. Heck, he was past that. He was having third or fourth thoughts. Was he violating some workplace rule about what should or shouldn't be discussed with one's boss?

"Dustin?" His tone was firm and hinted at impatience, maybe annoyance.

Sighing, Dustin shook his head. "It's a stupid question, and maybe it's nothing. Means nothing. I don't know."

"Dustin, I don't have all day." Dr. Stevenson looked back at the papers on his desk. "Do you need to know something from me or not?"

"It's something I heard, something I can't quite wrap my head around."

"I'm waiting." His tone was just on the edge of anger, and Dustin knew he was pushing him beyond his patience.

"Do you think science and religion can co-exist?"

Dr. Stevenson's brow shot up, and his eyes narrowed. His head gave a small shake.

"I must say, I'm surprised you came to me about this."

"I'm sorry. I know that's bordering on personal beliefs, which should have no place in our world, but I didn't—"

"No place in our world?" He stood and walked to the window, looking out briefly before turning back to Dustin. "Do you know that all scientific theories begin as beliefs? Beliefs about what if, how to, and is there? Nothing we do is based on anything we pull from the air."

Dustin stared at his boss, perplexed beyond understanding.

He continued. "No great scientific mind begins any study without having some kind of belief in mind, some kind of working theory."

"Okay, but that's not the same as personal beliefs about such mythological concepts as the existence of gods in the universe."

"Isn't it?" he asked matter-of-factly.

"Excuse me?"

"Isn't it the same?" He began pacing as he spoke. "Aren't personal beliefs or personal theories what lead to all great discoveries?"

"I'm sorry. I'm not sure we're on the same page."

"Did you know that some believe that the Christian doctrine of creation may have encouraged scientists to seek answers to a universe that is both intelligent and orderly, leading to the discovery of many modern laws of science?"

Dustin merely shook his head, unsure of how to answer.

"Scientist Wentzel van Huyssteen argued that science and religion exist in a 'graceful duet.' Think about that. What a wonderful way to picture the two, not just an open dialogue but a harmonious song or dance between the two."

"But didn't Comte state in the eighteen-hundreds that all societies, in an attempt to explain the world, go through stages of development, beginning with religion but ultimately ending with scientific explanations and empirical observations?"

"Sure, but should that discount religion as invalid? There are a number of modern Christians as well as Islamic scholars who contend that there can be no conflict between God's word and God's work, that religion and science are entirely compatible."

"Scholars, not scientists," Dustin contended.

Dr. Stevenson stopped pacing and shook his head. "Scholar scientists, or scientific scholars." He resumed pacing as though movement helped him think.

Dustin had witnessed this on prior occasions and was always fascinated as he watched the concepts and arguments develop in his boss's brain. He found that this time was no different.

"Many confuse science with scientism. Scientism is what a lot of scientists practice today as religion, but science doesn't always hold all the answers. Even Einstein recognized that as he got older."

"Science as a religion?" Dustin asked.

He stopped and looked at Dustin as if suddenly surprised to find him in the room.

"Scientism is the excessive belief in the power of science. It has become a religion, a way to put all faith and reason in science without ever considering the possibility that there are things which cannot be explained through scientific inquiry."

"Isn't that the way it should be?"

He leaned his head to the side and studied Dustin for a moment. Dustin felt the weight of his stare and shifted uncomfortably from one leg to the other.

"How do you explain miracles?" Dr. Stevenson finally asked.

"Miracles? They're supernatural nonsense."

The scientist made a noncommittal noise before proceeding. "A woman has pancreatic cancer, confirmed by three different doctors. She knows this is a death sentence, so she goes to a cousin who is a religious sister and asks for prayers that she won't suffer too much before dying. The sister lays her hands on the woman and prays over her. The woman goes back to the doctor a few days later to begin treatment. A routine check of her condition reveals no cancer. Another doctor is called in who confirms this. The doctors are stunned as the woman's x-rays and test results are laid out before them. She lives another twenty years and dies of heart failure. As a scientist, what is your theory?"

Dustin realized his mouth was hanging open in shock, but as he regained his senses, his intellect returned him to a state of realism. "The initial diagnosis was incorrect."

"Ah, but there are tests and scans to back it up."

"Then it's a made-up story with nothing to back up the claims. Hearsay, I believe a court would conclude."

"I can assure you it's not made up."

"You mean this is a real person? No way."

Dr. Stevenson nodded. "My aunt, who was sick, and my stepfather's cousin, a nun. We just attended the funeral not long ago. There isn't a person in the family who doesn't know the story. We all witnessed it."

"That can't be. There had to be some mistake."

"The mistake, Dustin, is made when mere mortals become gods. As the great philosopher, mathematician, theorist, and scientist Blaise Pascal once said, it is better to believe in God than not, since the gains in believing far outweigh the risks of being wrong if, in death, we find that God exists." Dr. Stevenson returned to his desk and stood by his chair. "Science doesn't have all the answers, Dustin, and those who claim it does have shut their minds and hearts to any possibility that cannot be proven. There are many things in this universe that must be taken on faith, and the most intelligent beings will admit this. Humans are not omnipotent, and we must accept that there are things we do not know and will never fully understand. To think otherwise is to see ourselves not as human but as divine, and therein lies the problem with scientism."

***

Ethan stood beside Jenny in the doorway and watched as the little boy was hoisted into the airlift. As the chopper took off, Jenny breathed an audible sigh of relief. The metallic stench of blood hung in the air, and Ethan felt his stomach rebel.

As though awaking from a dream, or a nightmare, Ethan became aware of his sweaty palms and shallow breaths. Without a word, he turned and hurried down the hall into the bathroom where he vomited into the toilet. When he was finished, he splashed cold water on his face and took several deep breaths. He looked down and saw the blood that covered his lab coat and felt a fresh wave of nausea.

This wasn't the first time he'd experienced this, but it had been a while, and he'd so hoped he was past it.

"Dr. Edwards, Ethan?" came Jenny's voice from the other side of the door. "Are you all right?"

"Fine," he said quickly, wondering how many people saw his hasty retreat to the bathroom. He tore off his coat and threw it in the trash can.

"Are you sure?"

"Yeah." He waited until enough time passed to ensure her withdrawal before he opened the door and ducked into the office to grab another coat.

The rest of the day proceeded without incident, and he thought they'd all forgotten, but Jenny waited for him outside after everyone else had left.

"What happened earlier?"

"What do you mean?"

She stopped walking and looked at him. He paused at the edge of the parking lot and sighed.

"Do we have to do this here?"

Jenny shook her head. "Anywhere you're comfortable talking. Just name the place."

He thought for a moment and came to the realization that this was inevitable. He owed her an explanation, as her colleague and friend. "Want to take a walk on the beach?"

They drove together in his car, and the silence seemed to speak volumes. She didn't press him, and he gathered his thoughts, aware that she was giving him the space and time to say what he needed to.

They took off their shoes at the edge of the sand and walked for several minutes before Ethan felt the urge to finally unload, to share with Jenny what he'd never shared with anyone except his parents.

"That kid today. I thought we were going to lose him."

"I did, too," Jenny admitted. "It was scary. He needed to be at the hospital. We aren't equipped for that kind of injury. His parents should've called 911 instead of bringing him to us."

"But they did bring him to us, and it was too late not to do something. We had to do everything in our power to keep him alive until he was stable enough to be air-lifted out. Whether we're equipped or not, they were counting on us."

"And we did it. By the skin of our teeth, but still, we kept him alive. What happens next is out of our hands."

"But he was in our hands then. He was depending on us. They all were."

"Ethan, what's going on? What aren't you telling me?"

He stopped and looked out at the endless stretch of ocean extending from the Assateague shore to miles beyond their limited vision. The sun hung low in the pink and blue, cotton candy-streaked sky, and gulls swooped in and out of the waves as a frothy, low tide went in and out.

"You know how many ships there are on this ocean right now?"

Jenny shook her head. "A lot, I guess."

"A lot. Some big, some small, all designed for specific purposes." He took a long breath, let it out, and stood still as the tide washed over his feet. His pants were rolled up, his socks stuffed into the shoes he held in one hand.

"Big hospitals, experienced doctors, they're made to handle what we faced today. Small clinics, remote medical sites, places with doctors and nurses ill-equipped for life-threatening emergencies aren't supposed to deal with that kind of stuff, but sometimes we do. Sometimes, we have no choice."

Jenny didn't comment, and he appreciated her silence, her ability to just listen, to hear him out.

"My best friend died when we were ten. He was hit by a drunk driver on a back road with nobody else around. Lots of internal injuries. We didn't know any better, my other friends and me. We should have, but we didn't. We took him to a local clinic near our suburban neighborhood because it was close. None of us had cell phones. We were at the age when kids were first beginning to get them, but none of us had one yet. We never thought to go to someone and ask them to call 911. We just carried Jamie as fast as we could. The clinic couldn't help him. They called for an ambulance, and they did the best they could, but they weren't fully staffed and didn't have the equipment. I watched through the glass door as Jamie died on the table. I didn't know that, not until my parents told me that he was already dead when the ambulance arrived to transport him to the hospital."

He turned and looked at Jenny. "If they had been better trained, more qualified, had better equipment, Jamie might've lived."

Jenny grasped his arm. "You don't know that."

"Logically, I agree. Emotionally, I wish we'd gotten him to a hospital. No, I wish we'd called 911. Anything other than what we did."

"Ethan, you were a kid."

He nodded. "Yep, and I vowed that day that if I could, I'd make it up to him. I would make sure that nobody under my watch would get less than the best care under the best circumstances I could offer."

"So you decided to work at a small town clinic instead of a big state-of-the-art hospital."

He nodded. "My dad didn't get it at first, but then he realized what I needed to do."

Jenny let go of his arm and laced her shoe-laden hands around his waist, laying her head on his chest.

"You saved that kid's life today. You kept his parents from losing their son, another boy from losing his best friend." She looked up at him. "You didn't need fancy equipment or years of experience. You did it with your own human hands and God-given skills. But you can't save them all."

"I know that. That's what's so hard."

She pressed her cheek back to his chest, and he rested his chin on the top of her head. They stood there for a long time before he gently shook her lose.

"It's getting late. Let's go."

"Thanks for letting me know," Jenny said.

"Thanks for... you know."

He didn't take her hand or put his arm around her, but he felt like they were connected, nonetheless.

"Anytime, Ethan. I'm here for you."

He looked into her eyes and realized she meant it, and he didn't think she was only referring to their work at the clinic.

At that moment, Ethan realized he was falling, and no doctors or fancy medical devices would be able to save his heart if she decided to break it.

***

"Are you ready to talk yet?" Christy walked down the steps of the back deck and sat next to Molly on the beloved backyard swing that had been a wedding present from Jenny's Uncle Trevor.

"About what?" Molly stared intently at her lap as she used her toe to gently push the swing back and forth.

"About what went wrong on your date and why you've been avoiding me ever since."

"Who says anything went wrong?"

"Maybe the aforementioned avoidance."

Molly continued to rock the swing while her sister waited patiently. When it was obvious that Christy wasn't going to leave it alone, Molly sighed.

"The date was fine. Maybe even great. We had a really nice time."

"Okay…" Christy dragged out the word. "Then what's got you so down?"

A voice came from the deck. "God, perhaps?"

Both women looked up to see Jared standing on the deck.

"You're home early," Christy said.

"Something happened at work today, and I thought I should come home and make sure everything is okay. Molly, do you want to talk?"

Christy looked back and forth between the two, then stood and made her way toward the house. "I think I hear Nicky crying. I'd better go check on him." She gave Jared a kiss as she passed by him on her way into the house.

Jared sat next to Molly on the swing. "Are you still upset about what happened with Dustin?"

"No. Yes. Why?" She looked up at him. "Did you say something to him?"

"Other way around. He came to me."

Molly nodded. "I think it's a deal breaker," Molly said. "With him. And with me, I guess. I hid my faith throughout college. Nobody ever asked where I went on Saturday nights while they partied or on Sunday mornings when they slept off the partying. I attended a local Bible study on Monday evenings, but nobody ever noticed I wasn't around. I was pretty invisible outside of class, so it was easy."

"But now that you're ready to start dating, not so much?"

Molly shrugged.

They sat in silence for a while, long enough to hear Nicky crying when he awoke and see Sally's bus pull up in front of the house. Molly's day off was quickly nearing its end, and soon she'd be helping Sally with homework and preparing dinner with Christy.

"There aren't a lot of us out there," Molly said.

"Geniuses?" Jared asked.

Molly laughed. "Scientists who believe in God."

"I bet there are a lot more than you think," Jared said.

"You know, I was like him. Dad was like him."

Jared nodded. "I know. It was the one and only thing I didn't admire about your dad, but I did admire the fact that he was open to any possibility. He never discounted anyone's faith."

"I think that's what made it easy for me to listen when you talked to Christy about your faith. And then, after what happened…"

She didn't elaborate. That day, when they almost lost Christy, was something they never discussed even though it ended well, miraculously well.

"Here's one thing I learned a long time ago, Molly. Don't compromise your morals, your principles, or your beliefs. Those are the things that make you who you are. If someone doesn't appreciate that about you and isn't willing to look at things from your perspective, he or she will never truly value you as a person."

"What if I only meet people like that?"

"You're young, Molly, and you've never really been out in the world. You'll find that person, those people, who love and accept you and even have the same beliefs as you. They're out there. You just have to look for them. And praying for help in that department never hurts."

Molly nodded, remembering Zach's similar advice.

"I'm going to head inside. It's too hot for me out here. And too buggy." He swatted the mosquitoes. They never bothered Molly. "You good?"

"I'm good." She offered him a smile. "Thanks, Jared." She did feel better, and she loved that he came home early just to check on her. "Oh, Jared," she called. "What did you say? To Dustin?"

"I told him to be careful not to make science his religion, and I recommended a couple podcasts to help him see that the two don't have to be at odds."

"Smart. He's into podcasts."

Jared smiled. "I know. Sometimes I do notice things about people, and sometimes, I'm even a little smart."

Molly laughed. "You and me, both."

She watched him go into the house but sat on the swing a little longer. She was only on the island until the end of the summer. She'd focus on having fun with Lizzie—who was turning out to be a real friend—going to trivia—from which Dustin was noticeably absent the previous night—and hanging out with the girls while also narrowing down her career choices. She didn't need to date anyone to be normal or have a good summer. She just had to be herself. She realized that's what she'd been doing wrong for a very long time. She was hiding her true self, hiding her feelings, and hiding from the world. She just needed to let herself enjoy life and be the person she was created to be. The rest would come in time.

***

"What are you doing this weekend?" Ethan asked. The day was winding down, and Jenny looked forward to her time off.

"Tomorrow night, I'm going out with my girlfriends. Saturday, my mom and I are doing the farmer's market, and Sunday, I'm going with Mom, Taylor, and Nick to dinner at Aunt Ronnie and Uncle Trevor's. Aunt Ronnie does a big dinner after church every Sunday, and anyone considered family heads over as soon as Mass ends." She considered this for a moment. "Would you like to go?"

"I'm not sure I feel comfortable going where I'm not invited."

Jenny laughed. "You don't know Aunt Ronnie. There are no invitations. If you're family, thought of as family, or brought by family, you're invited and welcomed."

"Do you all go to church together, too?"

Jenny felt an invisible lasso take hold of her gut and cinch it like one of the ponies at the penning. "Typically. Sometimes one or more of us will go to church Saturday evening for one reason or another."

"Saturday night? That's a Catholic thing, right?"

The lasso tightened.

"It is." She didn't know what more to say.

Ethan shrugged. "I was raised Episcopalian, so I'm kind of familiar with Catholicism. Haven't found an Episcopalian church here on the island."

"No, we have a few churches, but not that." She hesitated. "You're welcome to join my family on Sunday."

Ethan seemed to give it some thought before answering. "Thanks. I'll consider it."

"And dinner? Too much? I mean, it's not like we're dating, but you have met my mother. Your grandmother would be welcome to come, too." She tried to read his expression but couldn't discern his thoughts.

"Maybe. Let me think about it, okay?"

"Sure. No pressure."

"How about doing something on Saturday? Not a date. Just a continuation of friends getting to know each other."

It was her turn to consider. Should she say yes or play it cool? She wasn't good at relationship games, hated them in fact. So much so, that she'd pretty much given up on dating after she and her high school sweetheart broke up halfway through college. She focused on medicine and little else. Even her current social life revolved around the people she worked with and the couple girls she grew up with. Maybe it was time she gave Ethan a chance.

"What did you have in mind?" she asked noncommittally as she straightened her desk.

"I was thinking something casual, maybe on the water. Kayaking? And a picnic dinner?"

"That could be fun," Jenny admitted. "I haven't been kayaking in forever."

"I know there are rental places all over the island. I can check them out."

Jenny shook her head. "No need. Taylor and I have kayaks. I can borrow the trailer and haul them. Where do you want to go?"

"Oh, I, uh, hadn't thought that far ahead. Where should we go?"

"There are a few good spots on Chincoteague to put out the kayaks, and there's Assateague as well. Are you seasoned?"

"You mean, have I kayaked before? Yeah. Lots of times."

"Great. Let me get the boats and figure out where to launch. Just tell me when."

"Well, neither of us is on call this weekend, so how about as soon as you and your mom finish at the market?"

"How about a little later in the day? Maybe kayak out to an inlet, have that picnic dinner, kayak back at sunset? I have some things I want to get done in the afternoon."

"Sounds good. You figure out the logistics, and I'll supply the food."

"Hey, guys," Joanne said, poking her head into the office. "Since I'm on duty all weekend, I'm heading out. You two good?"

"We're good, Joanne." Jenny answered. "Have a nice night. See you in the morning." She turned to Ethan. "I have things I want to discuss with Stacey before we head home, so if I don't see you at closing, I'll see you tomorrow."

They said goodbye, and Jenny headed toward the receptionist's desk. She knew Stacey was an expert kayaker and worked for a local rental place on weekends. Jenny had an idea about where they could launch the boats and thought she'd run it past her, but she would ask discreetly. While it was a small island, nobody at the clinic seemed to know that she and Ethan had gone out to a movie and then went for ice cream together, and Jenny wanted to keep it that way for a little while longer. She would tell Stacey that she was asking for a friend and hope that the cliché excuse didn't give too much away.

Chapter Ten

Friday came and went quickly, and Molly was happy to be off her feet once she and the girls arrived at Uno Taco for karaoke night.

"I'm beat," Lizzie said. "I thought working for EJ's mom all summer while I got my certifications together would be perfect, but she's so busy all the time, I hardly have time to breathe."

"Tell me about it," Molly said. "I haven't worked at the café since I was thirteen, and I'd forgotten how exhausting it is. I imagine catering is just as much work."

"Yeah. Even if we don't have an event, there's planning and marketing, and baking for the farmer's market, which I'm working tomorrow. I had no idea how much work goes into what she and Zach do."

"You call him Zach?"

"That's what he tells me to call him. Don't you call him Zach?"

"Yeah," Molly admitted, "but he's not my fiancé's father."

"He's not EJ's father, either. EJ was twelve when his mom and Zach got married. I still call her Miss Kayla, by the way."

"I forgot Zach isn't EJ's and Todd's dad. They seem like the perfect family."

"It wasn't always like that. I don't remember EJ's dad since they didn't live here when he was alive, but I know it was hard on him and Todd not to have a father when they were little. Well, I guess Todd was still little when Zach and Miss Kayla got married, but EJ had grown up so much by then."

"He'd been through a lot."

"Yeah, and he liked Zach right off the bat, but there was that whole sniper deal. Miss Kayla had a hard time with that considering EJ's dad was killed in a shooting."

"Hey, ladies!" Carly and Gwen took seats at the table. "I'm so happy it's Friday," Gwen said. "I hate my job."

"Get a new one," Carly said. "I've been telling you that for ages."

"Choices are limited here, you know."

"Then leave. You could go anywhere," Molly said.

"I know." Gwen sighed. "I really don't hate my job. I just hate that school runs so late into the summer. The kids are restless, the teachers are burned out, and summer school starts just ten days after school gets out."

"You don't have to teach summer school, you know," Lizzie pointed out. "Isn't one of the advantages of teaching that you have summers off?"

"Yeah, it should be, but we get paid less than plumbers, work harder than doctors, and deal with more messes than attorneys."

"True," Molly agreed. "I've always felt that teachers are the most underpaid professionals in the nation."

"They are," Gwen said. "If I want to earn what I deserve, I have to move to Scandinavia."

"Where there's no such thing as summer," Carly reminded her.

"And I can't move anywhere until I have enough money to move out of my parents' house."

They all laughed knowingly. "Let's buy drinks and toast to that," Lizzie said.

They ordered drinks and snacks and watched DJ Charlie set up for karaoke.

"Hey, Molly, isn't that the guy you went out with?" Carly asked, motioning toward the door.

Molly turned and locked eyes with Dustin. He nodded but didn't smile before taking a seat at the bar. He was with one of the guys from his internship, his roommate, Cameron, she thought.

"Yeah, that's him," Molly acknowledged.

"Didn't go so well?" Gwen asked.

"No, it went well, but I think we're looking for different things in life." *Or look at life differently.*

Lizzie gave her a quizzical look, but Molly ignored it.

They continued to drink, eat, talk about a million things, and take several turns at the mic. Eventually, Molly and Dustin met face to face on the dance floor. Both stopped and stood staring at the other before Dustin motioned for her to follow.

Molly hesitated but ended up following him to a quiet corner in the back of the restaurant.

"Hey," was all he said.

"Hey," she answered, not knowing what else to say.

"I talked to Jared."

"Yeah?" She wouldn't let on that she and Jared had talked about their conversation.

"He gave me some things to think about."

"Okay."

"Look, I don't know what to think about all that stuff, but I know I like spending time with you. I missed you this week. I'd like to hang out again."

Molly started to speak, but the words didn't come. She missed him, too, but she had already decided nothing was going to happen between them.

Dustin looked at her expectantly, and she tried to think about what she should say.

"Look, Dustin. I had fun when we hung out, but I'm not sure—"

"Molly, you wanted to have a normal summer. Let's just do that, okay? Hang out. Do summer things. Enjoy each other's company. That's all. We don't need to get any deeper than that."

She raked her lips in thought before answering, "Okay, sure. We can hang out."

Dustin's smile grew like the Grinch's heart, and Molly felt the tightening in her abdomen she had been noticing lately, a strange but exhilarating feeling that was new to her.

"Great," Dustin said. "Tomorrow evening? After you go to church, I mean. The interns are all getting together on the beach for dinner, some friendly beach volleyball, maybe take in the sunset before the beach closes. It's the last week of school, and camp starts the following Monday, so we're having a beach party before we're too tired to do anything but sleep on the weekends."

"I won't be able to get there until seven. Jared can probably drop me off. You'll have to let me know where."

"No problem. I'll text you. I would offer to pick you up, but I don't know who's driving."

"It's fine. I'll work it out. Plus, once you have a parking spot, you don't want to give it up."

"True. See you then, Molly."

She watched him head back to his seat at the bar. This could work out, she thought. They could be friends, and she could have her normal summer. Yeah, this could work.

If only she could stop that tingling in her stomach every time she thought about him.

***

"Is that a dolphin?" Ethan called from his kayak.

Jenny stopped paddling and turned to look. She shrugged and called back. "Maybe. I didn't get a good look at it. Could be a sandbar shark."

"Did you say shark?" That wasn't something Ethan had bargained for, especially in a kayak.

Jenny paddled over to him and smiled. "Sandbar shark. Nothing to worry about. A big game fish around here, but not harmful."

"So, I'm not going to be somebody's dinner?"

"I can't promise that. If you wander off into the ocean, a great white might decide you look tasty."

Ethan felt his stomach drop. "Seriously?"

Jenny laughed. "Seriously, but don't worry. We're not going out there. The currents can be pretty strong, and I'm not kidding about the great whites, but they're as uninterested in seeing you as you are in seeing them."

"Good to know."

They paddled beside each other for several lengths, pointing out seabirds and waterfowl.

"This is a good place to stop for a while," Jenny said, pointing to a small cove. "It's private, but I know the owners, and I checked with them about us using the beach for a picnic."

She led the way, and Ethan followed her. He liked how confident she was, at work and at play. She was serious but not stern, and she was cautious without being scared. He let her beach her boat first, then followed her lead. They pulled Jenny's waterproof backpack from her kayak and removed their PFDs.

"I'm so happy to be out of that thing," Jenny said, tossing hers onto the beach. "I get so hot and sweaty."

Her tanned skin glistened, and Ethan thought it looked sexy, but he pushed the thought away. Friends. They were just friends. He still didn't know if she was willing to entertain anything more than that, and he wasn't going to initiate it, though it killed him to spend so much time with her and not be able to touch her.

She went to a spot a little ways upland and dropped the backpack in the sand.

"What did you bring for us?" She unzipped the pack and pulled out a towel, gently laying it in the sand, before taking a seat.

Ethan dug into the pack and produced several brown bags and plastic containers.

"Classic picnic fare," he said, opening a bag of fried chicken. "I can't guarantee it's still hot."

"Picnic chicken doesn't have to be hot."

He opened a container of coleslaw and another of potato salad. A third container provided pickles, and the second bag held chips and pretzels.

"One more," he said, reaching into the bottom of the pack and pulling out another container. He opened it to reveal fresh, dark pink slices of watermelon.

"My favorite!" Jenny exclaimed. "How did you know?"

Ethan felt his heart swell, and he beamed. "I didn't. It's my favorite, too."

They ate and chatted while they watched the gentle waves lapping the shore. The time went by as quickly as the tide rushed out to sea, and Ethan was disappointed when Jenny pointed out that it was time to head back.

They loaded their gear, put their PFDs back on, and tugged the kayaks back into the water.

"The tides may have shifted while we were on the beach, so be careful. Let me know if you have any trouble," Jenny said, and Ethan appreciated her advice. He was smart enough not to pretend he knew everything about kayaking. Mansplaining aside, he didn't know the waters, and he'd kayaked enough to know he should listen to the wisdom of a local.

As soon as they were several yards from the beach, Ethan could feel the difference. He paddled hard, but he didn't seem to be getting anywhere. Jenny was half his weight and three-quarters his height, yet she seemed to be paddling and moving with ease. Just when he thought she'd unknowingly leave him behind, she turned around to check on him.

"You doing okay?" she called.

"Truthfully? Not really. I'm not used to the strong current."

Jenny turned and headed toward him. The tide hurried her along, and she carefully maneuvered her kayak alongside his.

"I'm going to turn around and come up beside you and hand you the tow rope. Do you know what to do with it?"

"Um, tie it on the boat somewhere?"

Jenny shook her head. "Tie it around your waist. I'll lead, but you need to help. Paddle with me, as hard as you can. Don't let the kayak broach, or we'll both be in the water."

"Broach?"

"Go sideways. One good wave, and you could capsize."

"This isn't how I pictured this evening going. I'm not impressing you with my skill and strength." He managed a feeble smile.

"You're impressing me by not arguing or telling me you can handle it."

"I never said I was stupid."

Jenny smiled. "I'm turning around now. I'll be right back. Keep paddling. We're getting caught in the tide."

He paddled as hard as he could, watching from the corner of his eye for her to come back, somewhat afraid she'd be swept out to sea trying to rescue him. After what seemed like forever, she was back, tossing him the rope, and yelling instructions.

"Put the paddles in the boat, and quickly tie the rope around you. Make sure it's tight. Good. Grab the paddles and start working."

He did as he was told and felt the paddling get easier as she pulled him along. Where did she get the strength to paddle against the tide while dragging him and his boat behind her? Talk about impressive.

They were halfway back when he heard a motor and felt the current shift. He looked back and saw a Coast Guard boat slowly approaching. Jenny looked at the boat and stopped. Ethan thought he saw relief cross her features.

"You guys okay? Oh, Jenny! I didn't realize that was you. Are you good?"

"Just okay," she admitted, her voice straining as she puffed out the words. "The outgoing tide's stronger than I thought, and we were struggling."

"You want a lift?" the officer asked.

"Is it too much trouble?"

The man laughed. "It's what I do, remember?"

Jenny looked back at Ethan. "My arms are about to give out. How do you feel about a wet exit?"

"A what?"

"Do you know how to roll your kayak and exit?"

"I'm not sure. You mean, like, flip it?"

"Don't worry, Jenny," the officer said. "You get out, and we'll fish out your friend."

Jenny nodded before she expertly rolled her kayak into a capsize. He held his breath until she sliced up through the water. She held onto the fin of the kayak, kicking her legs, and breathing hard.

"I don't know if I can do that," Ethan admitted.

"Do you know how to exit onto a dock?" the man asked.

"Yeah, I can do that."

"Okay, here's how this is going to work." The man explained to Ethan how he could maneuver to the Coast Guard boat and use the low gunwale like a waterside dock. Ethan could see how that would work and managed to get up into the boat without any problems.

"What about Jenny and her kayaks?"

"No worries," the man said. "Jenny, you good to swim, or do you need help?"

"I'm good."

Ethan watched in amazement as she righted her kayak, held onto the lip that ran around the seat area, and pulled it toward the boat. She helped the second crewman lift the kayaks on board, then climbed up onto the boat.

"Thanks, Aaron. I really appreciate it."

"No problem, Jenny. Brock, can you grab some blankets?"

Once Jenny and Ethan were settled inside the cabin, wrapped in warm blankets, the Coast Guard men went to the front of the boat—Ethan knew there was a word for it but couldn't think of it.

"If I hadn't been here," he said to Jenny, "you wouldn't have needed help, would you?"

Jenny gave a little shrug. "Well, my arms were tired from paddling."

"You mean tired from pulling me and the kayak."

"You don't weigh that much," she said, playfully punching his arm.

"I mean it. You could've fought that tide and been just fine."

"Yeah, but I grew up on these waters. You did fine. Don't beat yourself up over this. These guys live for this kind of thing."

As if summoned by her words, Aaron appeared in the doorway. "You good?"

"We're fine, Aaron. Thanks. This is Ethan, my colleague."

Ethan felt a bit wounded by her introduction. Not even a friend? Just a colleague? He pushed away the thought and reached out to shake Aaron's hand.

"Thanks for the help, Sir. I was struggling out there."

"It happens all the time," Aaron said. He looked at Jenny. "Mom says your family is all coming for dinner tomorrow. Dad's barbecuing ribs, and Mom's doing all the fixings. Will we see you there?"

"I'm in for sure." She looked at Ethan. "I invited Ethan. I hope that's okay."

"You know it is," Aaron said with a grin. The other officer called, and Aaron looked up and nodded. "We're at the station. I'll give you guys a ride back to your vehicle, but you're going to have to come back here for your kayaks."

"That's fine. Thanks again," Jenny said.

She stood, and Ethan followed her off the boat. It seemed he was going to the family dinner whether Jenny was into him or not.

***

Molly felt awkward as she walked toward the beach. It was still sunlight, but she could already see fires along the sand. She was pretty sure one of the girls she'd seen on Moon Day and at trivia was a second-year intern, but Molly didn't really know her. After spending the entire Mass praying that these interns would be as nice to her as Jared's first set of interns had been all those years ago when she first met Anya and Chloe, Molly felt slightly more at ease and ready to meet them.

She wasn't sure which group was theirs, but she straightened up and walked with confidence down the beach, checking out each set of faces she approached.

"Molly, over here!"

She turned to see Dustin and the others further down the beach, closer to the marsh grasses than the water, which was smart. The tide was going out now, but high tide would begin to rush in before sunset.

Molly made her way toward the group and smiled broadly at them. "Hi, everyone."

"Hey, guys, this is my former classmate and friend, Molly."

"Hey, I know you. Aren't you the girl from trivia, the one who used to work at Wallops?"

Molly nodded, her grin still plastered on her face. "Yeah, I remember you from last summer."

"I'm Adrienne. You're working in town this year, right?"

"Yeah, I wanted to do something different this year. I've been spending my summers at the center since I was ten."

"Ten? You were a camper before you started helping Dr. Johnson?"

Molly looked at Dustin, unsure how to answer. What had he told them?

"Molly was never actually a camper. She started working at camp when she was ten and helped Dr.

Stevenson with his first cube sat. After that, she did research for Dr. Johnson. She's taking a break from science this summer before she starts her career in the fall."

"Career?" Adrienne asked. "For some reason, I thought you were a lot younger than me, but I guess you did say 'classmate,' didn't you?" She looked at Dustin. "As in, Harvard?"

"Molly was valedictorian," he said proudly, as though it was his honor as well as hers.

Molly blushed. She hadn't expected Dustin to be so forward about how they knew each other.

"Wow," the blonde boy said. He reached to shake her hand. "I'm Cameron."

"I'm Dustin's roommate, Nathan," said the boy Dustin had been with at the bar, reaching for her hand. She thought he was Cameron, so she'd have to work not to mix them up. "Dustin talks about you a lot. Too bad you didn't cross paths at school. He said you would've been fun to hang out with."

Molly gave Dustin a look, and she saw that he was blushing. *Embarrassment over the white lie, or something else?*

"Have you eaten, Molly? We have some hot dogs left," Adrienne offered. "The rest of us are ready for s'mores."

The smell of charred marshmallows tickled Molly's nose. "I grabbed something on the way, but a s'more sounds great."

"We can eat all night," Dustin said. "How about a dip in the water before the sun goes down?"

"It's still pretty cold out there this time of year," Molly said. "I don't typically go in until after the Fourth."

"Oh, come on. It's not that bad," Dustin encouraged, pulling off his shirt. "Do you have a bathing suit on?"

"I do." Molly hesitated. She'd put one on at Christy's urging, though she hadn't really planned to strip down to it.

"Come on. Just a quick dip," Dustin said.

Molly sighed. "Fine. Just a quick one."

She tossed her bag into the sand and pulled off the sundress she'd worn to church. She felt Dustin's eyes on her as she dropped the dress beside her bag and took off her flip flops, and she became self-conscious. She looked up and saw the admiration in his eyes, maybe something else, too, and it made her stomach twirl. She wasn't used to people looking at her that way.

She knew that her body had begun to transform a lot in the past several weeks. Each time she looked in the mirror, she saw that her teenaged body was finally filling out in places she never thought it would. She equally wanted to hide it and show it off, and the conflicting emotions toyed with her self-esteem.

Dustin grabbed her hand and dragged her down the beach. She felt light in the sand, like she was flying with the gulls. When her feet hit the water, she shrieked, but Dustin didn't let go. He pulled her farther into the crashing waves, and the biting cold took her breath away. Or was it the look in his eyes when he turned back toward her?

"You're in now. Better get used to it," he said, a wicked smile on his lips.

"You knew it would be freezing," she said, longing to pull her hand away to wrap her arms around herself, while simultaneously, not wanting to let go.

He was wading now, kicking his legs under him, and she realized she was, too. She let him pull her closer, and he put his arms around her.

"I've got you," he whispered. "Don't even try to head back in."

Molly just nodded, unable to speak. Her heart was thrumming to a frantic beat, and she felt almost dizzy. Her stomach was going crazy, as though it was turning itself inside and out. She swallowed as she stared into his green eyes.

"I like this a lot better than high ropes climbing," Dustin said, his voice close to a whisper. "How about you?"

"I, uh, yeah. Me, too." She felt her breath coming in little waves as the bigger waves pounding against them began to feel less cold. She licked her lips and tasted the salty ocean.

"Molly, I..." Dustin began, stopped, and took a deep breath before continuing. "I know I've been a jerk for most of the time I've known you. You have no idea how sorry I am about that. I don't know how to make it up to you, but I want you to know that I..." His words broke off, and he looked out to the horizon for several moments before turning back to her. "I know we said we'd just be friends and hang out this summer for fun, but I like you, Molly. I really like you. I don't want to be a jerk anymore. I don't want to hurt you, and I don't want you to think I look down on you. On the contrary, I look up to you. I admire you, and I know I can learn a lot from you, and not just about space stuff." He smiled, and she literally felt the contractions of her heart. "I don't know where you're heading in the fall. Heck, I don't know where I'm heading in the fall, but for the summer, anyway, I want to be more than friends. I'd like to explore this. See where it goes. Are you good with that?"

Was she? She'd already made up her mind that they would just be friends, nothing more. Did she want to date someone for just the summer? Did she want to date anyone at all right now when she was so uncertain about her future? Sometimes she did, and other times, she wasn't sure.

Dustin frowned. "I don't want to rush you or scare you off. We can take it slow." He started to release her, but Molly's body protested.

Before she knew it, she was doing something she never thought she would do as she leaned toward him, her eyes closing. Molly McLane was kissing a boy under the summer twilight sky beside a beach of young people roasting s'mores, singing songs, and living normal lives.

***

He stood outside the last house he needed to scope out. Like the others, it was secluded, on a road outside of town, away from the tourists and crowded streets and busy traffic. This would be an easy job. The easiest in fact. It wasn't far outside of town, within walking distance of the main street and shops. It would be easy to slip in and out, no vehicle necessary.

He watched from the trees as a young couple walked onto the back deck and then descended into the yard. The man sat on a loveseat-style swing, and the woman eased onto his lap. They talked, laughed, and then began to kiss. He found himself smiling at them, urging them to enjoy each other. He hoped they'd go inside and continue their interlude. After all, time was running out for them both.

Carnival Opens This Weekend

The Chincoteague Volunteer Firemen's Carnival opens this weekend. Dating back to 1924, the annual Firemen's Carnival was first held when the volunteer fire company was created and needed to raise money for equipment. The event has been going strong ever since.

The carnival offers something for kids of all ages from rides and games to local foods and live entertainment. Come enjoy pizza, oyster and clam fritters, funnel cakes, ice cream, pony fries, and baked goods from our very own Sand and Sugar Café and Second Helpings Catering. Try your luck at bingo or one of the many raffles.

The fun never ends at the Chincoteague Volunteer Firemen's Carnival!

The Chincoteague Herald, June 22

Chapter Eleven

"This is always the best way to start the week," Jenny's mother, Donna, said as she placed her tray of fresh fruit on the long picnic table.

Ethan watched Donna and the woman he presumed to be Jenny's Aunt Ronnie do double air kisses, and he smiled.

"We're so happy you came," Aunt Ronnie said before turning to Jenny. "You, too. Come give me a hug."

Jenny hugged her 'aunt' and then gestured to Ethan. "Aunt Ronnie, this is my friend and colleague Ethan."

"Oh! Arlene's grandson. I've known you since you were a boy, but I don't expect you to remember me. Welcome. It's so nice to have you. I'm sorry Arlene couldn't make it."

Ethan reached for her hand, but Aunt Ronnie pulled him into a hug. "We hug around here," she said before releasing him. "Come meet my husband and my boys."

"He's so cute," he heard Jenny's mother whisper as they moved toward the men surrounding the grill.

"And my colleague," Jenny said.

"Nothing wrong with that. At least you'll always have something in common."

"Mother," Jenny warned.

"Fine. I'll behave."

"Fat chance," Jenny said.

Ethan tried not to laugh, but he couldn't suppress his grin.

"And these are the boys," Aunt Ronnie told him. "My husband, Trevor. Our son, Aaron."

Aaron gave Ethan a wave. "We've met. Good to see you again."

"Thanks," Ethan said, grateful Aaron didn't launch into the story about their rescue.

"And Zach, our daughter Kayla's husband." Zach shook Ethan's hand.

She gestured to the volleyball game on the other side of the yard. "The dark-haired boy on the other side of the net is their son, Todd. The other boy is his best friend, Ben. The young blonde woman is Ben's sister, Lizzie."

Ethan recognized all of them from trivia.

"Lizzie's engaged to Kayla and Zach's oldest, EJ, who's in the Coast Guard. Playing on her team are Kayla and my granddaughter, Miren." She paused and looked around. "Somewhere around here is Aaron's wife, Kate, and their youngest, Sarah."

Ethan was already lost. He'd never keep them all straight.

"Sarah was hungry," Aaron offered. "Kate's making her a snack."

"Sarah is always hungry," Jenny's Uncle Trevor said. "Why don't you two grab a drink and jump in on the game. Kayla looks about worn out."

"Come on," Jenny said, pulling Ethan away before he had a chance to argue. When they were out of earshot, she whispered. "Kayla had cancer several years ago. She's fine, but her parents still treat her like she's fragile. Believe me, she never was."

"There are so many of them. I'll never remember who everyone is."

"You will," Jenny told him. "We're doctors. We're good at that."

"Aunt Jenny!"

Jenny smiled as she was pummeled by a little boy who threw himself into her arms. "Hey, kiddo."

"Who's this?" Ethan asked, stooping down to the boy's level.

"Who are you?" the boy asked, his nose scrunched.

"I'm Ethan. I'm a friend of your Aunt Jenny."

"I'm Wesley." He looked at his aunt. "Are there cookies?"

"Are we at Aunt Ronnie's house?" she answered with a grin, and he took off toward the kitchen.

"Wesley, no snacks before dinner," Taylor called, slowly coming around the side of the house. Ethan recognized her from their family portrait.

"Oh. My. Gosh. You're huge." Jenny said before clamping her mouth shut and covering it with her hand.

"Thanks, Sis. Love you, too."

A loud laugh followed Taylor into the yard. "Don't mind her. She's hangry."

"Taylor, Nick, this is Ethan. He's the new doctor at the clinic."

Nick's gaze bored into Ethan, maknig it obvious that he was sizing Ethan up. When they shook hands, Nick's grip was more than firm. "Ethan. Welcome."

"Knock it off, Nick," Jenny said, pushing him away. "Ethan's a good guy."

"He better be," Nick said.

"How far along are you?" Ethan asked Taylor.

"Just about seven months," she said. "And I could eat a horse right about now."

Nick placed his hand protectively on Taylor's back. "Let's get you some food, babe. You and I will talk later," he said pointedly to Ethan.

"Don't mind him," Jenny said. "He thinks he needs to protect everyone on the island."

"Is he Coast Guard, too?"

"First of all," she said, handing him a beer. "They're called Coasties. Second, he's a former Marine and island police officer. He has quite the reputation. If not for him and Zach, many people here tonight, and elsewhere, wouldn't be alive. Honest truth."

"I thought this was a quiet little island." He took a sip of the beer.

"You'd be surprised," Jenny said with an air of mystery.

Despite the overwhelming amount of people and the intimidating looks he intercepted from Nick and Zach, Ethan enjoyed the afternoon immensely. When things quieted down, he found himself sitting next to Jenny in a backyard swing overlooking one of the island's many canals.

"Not too bad, was it?" she asked.

"Other than feeling like I was being surveilled throughout the meal? No, not bad."

Jenny laughed. "Don't worry. Their barks are worse than their bites." She stopped and bit her lip. "Well, not quite, but as long as you don't kidnap anyone, hold anyone hostage, try to run someone off the road, operate an illegal drug ring, or do anything else along those lines, you'll be okay."

"I think I can manage avoiding those things," he said, casting a backward look toward the house. "Did they really—"

"Yep, and more. I'll tell you about it all sometime."

A gentle breeze broke through the humidity of the late afternoon, and Ethan was pleasantly surprised when Jenny settled a little closer to him on the swing. His arm automatically went around her shoulders, and they sat in silence gazing out at the canal. Ethan had never felt so content.

***

"Sorry, gotta go!" Molly yelled as she ran out of the house, the swinging door banging behind her. She opened the car door and slid inside.

"High school?" Dustin asked.

"High school," Molly confirmed.

"You sure we won't get into trouble?"

"Positive. Everybody goes there. You'll see." She turned her gaze on him. "Are you sure about this? We don't have to do it."

"Positive," he echoed her previous answer. "Are you?"

"Yep," she said while exhaling.

Molly was a jumble of nerves and excitement. She never had an interest in doing this before, but this summer, everything was changing so fast. In just two months, she'd be leaving the island, probably for good, and there were things she needed to know and do before she left. She would be an official adult in a little over a month, and it was time to start acting like one.

Dustin pulled to a stop in the high school parking lot and cut the engine. There wasn't another soul in sight, and Molly hoped it stayed that way.

"Ready?"

"Yep."

"Nervous?"

"Yep."

They both laughed, and Dustin took her hand in his. "You're going to be fine. It's a piece of cake. I'll ease you into it. I've got lots of experience, and you're not my first. We'll be safe, I promise. Don't worry."

Molly took a deep breath. "Okay. Let's do this."

He leaned over and gave her a long kiss, and the butterflies in her stomach began to settle their frantically flapping wings into a steady, peaceful rhythm.

They both got out of the car and switched sides. They buckled in, and Molly placed her hands on the wheel.

"Um, Molly, you have to start the car first."

A nervous giggle rose up from her chest, and Molly nodded, reaching for the push-start on the dashboard. Nothing happened.

"Put your foot on the brake, and hold it down."

"Oh, okay. Sorry. I knew that." She pressed down on the brake and started the car.

"It's okay. Don't be nervous. You said you've driven before. You know what to do."

She took a deep breath, held her foot on the brake, and shifted the car into drive.

"Good, now just make your way to the course. You know how the car works. Just follow the lines."

Molly did what she was told and eased the car toward the driver's ed course that was painted on the lot. She thought back to the few times she'd moved Jared's car for Christy so she could get out on time when she worked nights. The day of Sally's accident, Molly had driven to the clinic without either sister thinking anything of it. Dustin was right. She knew how to do this.

After completing the course a few times, Dustin suggested they go out on the road.

"What if I get pulled over?"

"Don't do anything to make that happen," Dustin told her.

She blew out a long breath. "Okay. Here goes."

They stuck to the backroads, and Molly gave Dustin a tour of the island, pointing out the Murray family ranch and landscaping business, the beachfront home where her friends, Zach and Kayla, lived, and the Kelly family home. It looked like they were hosting one of their Sunday family dinners.

Giving a tour and telling Dustin about everyone on the island put her at ease, and the driving came naturally. Now and then, Dustin gave her pointers, but for the most part, Molly didn't need his help. When it began to grow dark, they switched sides, and Dustin drove them to JR's for dinner. As was the case whenever she entered one of the island's restaurants, Molly was greeted by the staff like she owned the place. Over dinner, she reluctantly told Dustin about the summer she helped Zach and Nick catch the local restaurant owner who was trying to sabotage his competition.

"You're pretty amazing, you know that?"

Molly felt her cheeks grow warm. "Not really. I was a stupid kid who almost got herself killed."

"No, really. I wish I'd known you, you know, before. We all judged who we thought you were instead of getting to know you as a person. We were the stupid ones."

"Dustin, do you think we could forget about all that? Not keep looking back on that time?"

Dustin's eyes fell to his lap. "I'm sorry. I don't mean to make you uncomfortable by bringing it up." He looked into her eyes. "The truth is, I don't want to forget it. I want to remind myself every day that I will never, ever be that person again. I hope that I've grown up enough just in the past several weeks to be a better person than that. I'm ashamed of the person I was, and I'm even more ashamed to think about what my father would think of the way I behaved and the way I treated you."

"I'd like to meet your dad someday," Molly said, not intentionally changing the subject, but being honest.

"I'd like him to meet you. Actually, he's going to come out next week for the rocket launch and stay through the Fourth. Maybe we could all do something together."

"I'd like that."

"Good. So would I."

"Hello, Molly. Care to introduce me to this young man?"

Molly looked up to see her former babysitter, Marge. Though Jenny always watched Molly in the evenings, when Christy was out with Jared or with friends, it was Marge who drove Molly to space camp every morning and looked after her all the times Christy was working. Molly and Christy would've been lost that first summer if not for Marge and Diane.

"Hi Marge," Molly said with a wide smile. She stood and hugged the older woman. "This is Dustin," she said, sitting back down at the table.

"Ah, so this is Dustin," Marge said knowingly. "Simon has good things to say about you."

Dustin looked at Molly with a confused frown.

"Marge and Dr. Johnson's wife are best friends," Molly supplied.

"Nice to meet you," Dustin said, standing to offer his hand.

"Sit, sit. Enjoy your dinner. I just wanted to come over and say hello."

"Who are you here with?" Molly asked, looking around.

Marge gave her a shy smile. "Tom Donovan. Remember him?"

"Didn't he and his wife teach at the high school?" Molly asked.

"Yes, but he lost her a few years ago, God rest her soul. She was such a lovely woman. He's been so lonely without her."

Molly grinned. "Well, I hope he finds happiness," Molly told her, and Marge grinned back at her.

"So do I," she said before wishing them a nice evening and hurrying back to her table.

Dustin laughed. "You're never too old to find happiness."

"I'll drink to that," Molly said, lifting her iced tea in a toast.

After dinner, Dustin drove Molly home. He put the car in park and reached for her hand.

"That was fun."

"It was. Thank you. I wish I could get my permit right away, but if I wait a few more weeks, I won't have to take the class. This is one of those times I'm grateful we moved to Virginia. Christy told me the Maryland permit rules are much stricter."

"What do you want to do for your birthday?"

Molly shrugged. "The same thing as always, I guess. Christy's throwing me a party."

"Yeah, but you're not a kid anymore. In fact, you'll be a real, legal adult. What do you want to do to celebrate adulthood?"

Molly hadn't really thought about it. She'd lived an older person's existence for more than half her life. She'd never stopped to consider that she was going to be an actual adult in a few weeks.

"Wow. I never thought about that. I have no idea what to do to mark the occasion."

"Think about it," Dustin said. "We can do whatever you want."

"Mmm… I know what I want to do right now." She gave Dustin a mischievous grin, and he unbuckled their seat belts without breaking eye contact. He pulled her closer, and their lips came together.

After several moments, Molly stopped and gasped for breath. She held her lower lip between her teeth as she gazed into Dustin's eyes.

"Goodnight, Dustin. Thanks again."

"Goodnight, Molly. I'll text you later."

"Okay. Goodnight." She forced herself from the car and made her way to the front door.

Dustin waited until she opened the door and waved to him, and she stood watching as he drove away.

"There was a lot of steam rising off that car," Christy said from the living room.

Molly's smile fell. She closed the door and turned around. "Hey," she said.

Christy's stern look morphed into a broad smile. "So, the summer of being normal seems to be going well."

Molly heaved a long sigh and plopped down on the couch next to her sister. "I'm in serious like," she said.

"As it should be at your age. All that stuff from last week under the bridge?"

Molly shrugged. "I don't know, but I figure, it's one summer, my summer. I'm not going to let heavy stuff weigh me down."

"You just remember that as the summer goes on and your 'serious like' develops. No heavy stuff."

"Don't worry. I know. I could live forever on kisses alone."

Christy laughed. "I hope it stays that way for a while, Squirt. A very long while."

They said goodnight and headed upstairs. Molly never touched a single step the whole way.

***

The parking lot was lit up like the Fourth of July. But the flashing red and blue lights bouncing off the building were an unwanted fireworks display, a week too early.

"I don't understand," Dr. Johnson was saying to a man in a black suit. "This makes no sense."

"Dr. Johnson, you need to stand down. This is an official government matter."

"I am official government. I run this place. Tell me what's going on."

Dustin watched, helpless, as Jared was pushed into the car, his hands cuffed behind his back.

"This is a mistake. Tell me what he's supposedly done, and we can get to the bottom of this."

"Dr. Johnson," the man snapped, out of patience. "If you don't stand back, you will join Dr. Stevenson on his ride to D.C."

"He's done nothing wrong."

"And he will have his chance to defend himself." The man closed the door and walked around the car, entering on the passenger side. An equally imposing man started the car and drove away.

Two more men emerged from the building carrying Jared's government computer, his personal laptop, and several boxes of papers, notebooks, and who knew what else.

"You can't take those!" Dr. Johnson yelled. "They have classified information on them."

The men ignored him, put everything in the second car, and drove away.

The facility had been evacuated, and everyone stood outside gaping at each other, nobody knowing what to do. Dustin took out his phone and sent a text. He needed to get out of there, needed to get to Chincoteague, needed to make sure Molly was okay.

"Dr. Johnson, what do we do now? Are we allowed back inside? Do we go back to work?"

Dr. Johnson's phone began to buzz, and he answered it without acknowledging Dustin.

"Sam. What the hell is going on?" He walked away, leaving Dustin and the others at a loss.

Adrienne walked over to Dustin, and he imagined his face held all the same emotions hers did—disbelief, alarm, worry, and anger, all rolled into one expression.

"What do we do now?" she asked.

"I don't know what we're supposed to do, but I know what I have to do."

"You're going to see Molly?" Nathan asked, joining them, looking every bit as upset as they did.

"Yeah. I need to make sure she's okay."

Nathan nodded. "Let us know what you find out, okay? I mean, if she's okay and what's going to happen to Dr. Stevenson."

"Do you want me to go with you? She's going to need all the support she can get. The whole family will," Adrienne said.

Dustin shook his head. "No, but thanks. If I need you guys, I'll call."

"Let us know if you find out anything about Dr. Stevenson," Nathan said again, looking as worried as Dustin.

Dustin nodded and hurried to his car, squealing tires as he left the lot. His text had gone unanswered, and he didn't know if that was good or bad.

***

The kitchen was filled with people. Surrounding the table were Lizzie's father, who was the chief of police, Dr. Johnson, Zach, Aaron, and Nick. All were at a loss. Dustin and Molly sat on the couch holding hands, neither saying anything to the other.

Molly saw Christy reach for her phone. "Hi Dr. Patterson. Sorry, Sam. Yes, we're all here. I'm going to put you on speaker. What have you found out?" She laid the phone on the table.

"Christy, it's bad. Really bad. There was a security breach. Someone used Jared's computer to download massive amounts of information from the NASA server. This happened a couple weeks ago, and the FBI and NASA have been investigating it twenty-four-seven. This morning, they were able to trace it back to Jared."

"I don't understand. Jared would never do that."

"I know, but with his past—"

"His past? He has no past. He was a ghost until six years ago."

"Yes, but his family has big ties, a bigger reach than anyone ever suspected. Drug lords, Russian crime bosses, even ISIS. That makes Jared look like a prime suspect."

"But he has nothing to do with his family. He was in witness protection from the time he was five years old. He didn't even know his real name until the Feds took the whole family down when they tried to kill me to get to him."

Christy never talked about that day, about what she went through. Just like then, this wasn't about her feelings. It was about Jared. About saving Jared. Like it had been for her that night.

"I understand that, Christy, but these ties are strong. These families have ways of—"

"Stop! Just stop. There is no way they got Jared to give them classified information, to work with them in any way. He did not do this." She placed emphasis on every word in her last sentence.

"Christy, give me some time to find a way to help him, okay? Just hang tight."

"Sam, Sam!"

Silence filled the air. Christy flopped back into her chair and looked around the room. "Now what?"

"I wish there was a way we could help you," Lizzie's dad said. "I just don't know how. We have zero jurisdiction in this."

"It didn't even happen on the island," Nick said. "So, we had no warning, no time to give you or Jared a head's up."

"Chief Parker," Christy said with pain in her voice, "Jared would never go to work for his family, or do anything for them. And I thought their whole operation was shut down when the Feds arrested his uncle after Jared's cover was blown."

"Those families are hard to keep down," Aaron said. "I dismantled a lot of Mexican crime families involved in the drug trade during my time in the Gulf."

"And dealing with those kinds of families were my specialty in Afghanistan," Zach said. "You take down one, and three more rush in to take his place."

Dustin leaned over and whispered, "What are they talking about?"

Molly pointed to Aaron. "Part of drug cartel intervention in the Gulf of Mexico years ago." Then she pointed to Zach. "Army sniper in the Second Gulf War, one of the best in the world."

"That explains a lot," Dustin said, in awe of the men in the next room.

"I have some connections in D.C.," Zach said. "Higher than your friend, Sam, does at NASA. Let me see what I can find out."

"Thanks, Zach. I appreciate that."

"I just don't understand how this happened," Dr. Johnson said. "How did somebody get into Jared's computer, and how did they know what to find and where?"

"Somebody way above your pay grade told them how," Nick said. "And I'm willing to bet whoever did it, works inside your facility."

"I can't believe that. We vet everyone thoroughly before they can enter the private areas of the building."

"Well, somebody got to Jared's computer," Aaron said. "And I think Nick's right. Paul? Anyone you can spare from the department to go over their employment records, see if anything stands out?"

Paul shook his head. "About as many as you have to spare going into July."

"And that's all private information," Dr. Johnson said. "I can't let anyone outside the facility do that."

"What about me?" Dustin spoke up.

"Dustin," Dr. Johnson said. "I'm sorry, son, but you'd have no idea what to look for. I wouldn't even know what to look for."

"Any kind of discrepancy," Molly said. "Any red flags, suspicious family history, drug use, money problems, that kind of stuff."

"Molly," Zach warned. "Not again."

"But we could do it," she insisted. "You'd have two of the best brains NASA ever employed looking into it. We can find the leak. I know we can."

"Heaven, help me," Dr Johnson said, eyes raised to the ceiling. "I'm actually considering this."

***

"You're letting them do this?" Diane asked Simon after he arrived home and told her all that transpired that day.

"What choice do I have? We must figure out who did this so Jared is exonerated."

"I would think Jared would be able to do that himself without two kids having to get themselves involved in something that could go wrong for all of you."

"Darling, I know this looks bad, but you know Molly. She's no ordinary kid."

"And how well do you know Dustin? Wasn't he Jared's intern? Didn't he have access to Jared's office?"

Simon nodded. "I've considered that."

"And?"

Simon placed his elbows on the table and cradled his head. "I just don't know what else to do."

***

"Are you kidding me?" Kayla looked at Zach like he was an alien from Mars. "Molly? Hasn't that girl gotten into enough trouble trying to play detective?"

"It's not about that," Zach said. "She can think things through like nobody else can. Her mind works differently. She sees things others miss."

"She's a child, not even eighteen. I don't even think she drives a car. Would you let EJ do something like this? Possibly put himself in harm's way?"

"EJ is an officer in the United States Coast Guard, Kayla. Why not ask your brother about putting himself in harm's way."

"That's not the same. She's digging into things she shouldn't be, putting herself in danger without proper training, putting her family in danger." Tears began to run down her face. "She could get herself killed!"

Zach wrapped his arms around his wife. "She's not Eddie," he said quietly. "We're not going to let that happen to her."

Kayla let herself cry against Zach's chest and prayed that he was right. She knew all too well what happened when ordinary citizens tried to do the Fed's job.

***

"What? Is he crazy?" Kate asked, doubting she'd heard Aaron correctly. "He's really going to let two kids investigate a federal crime? Can he even do that?"

"Legally? Probably not, but the Feds don't seem to be trying to help Jared. They're convinced that he's joined his family's business and is selling secrets to the Russians."

"What can we do?"

"We're less worried about the Feds and more worried about whoever stole the info to begin with."

"You mean, they might still be around."

Aaron shrugged. "We don't know. We don't know anything. Why they took it, for whom, how they got into Jared's office, what they're doing with the info, if it was an inside job—"

"Meaning someone who works there, someone who might be part of the community, even our community."

"It's possible," he admitted.

"So, what are you going to do? I know the men in my life well enough to know that you're not going to stand by and let two kids do all the work, or put themselves in danger."

"We're going to keep an eye on them."

"Who's we?"

"Me, Zach, Nick, whoever we can trust."

Kate dragged her hands down her face and let out a long breath. "Don't get yourself killed, Aaron Kelly, do you hear me? Don't let anyone get killed."

***

"Holly, this is Gwen. She's a teacher, and school just let out, so she's looking for something to do this summer to make some money."

Holly smiled at Gwen. "Sorry I can't shake your hand." She gestured to the pastries she was icing. "Molly can take you in the back and get your paperwork filled out, but I'd like a minute with Molly if you don't mind."

"Sure, I'll wander around the front and begin familiarizing myself with everything."

"See? She's great already. I knew this would work."

"Molly, are you sure about this? I mean, I know you like Dustin, and I remember what first love feels like, but you really shouldn't throw away your summer plans for a guy."

"I told you, I'm not doing that. Dr. Johnson really needs my help at the center now that Jared's not there."

Molly looked away, her face red with the knowledge that the entire island knew about Jared's arrest.

"I still can't believe what happened. I mean, I know the details are sketchy, but I can't imagine Jared breaking any kind of laws."

"I know," Molly said. "It's hard to believe, but the evidence is pretty clear." She said a silent prayer asking for absolution. They'd all agreed to go along publicly with what was being said. They didn't want the real perpetrator to know they were digging into things, and they certainly didn't want the Feds to know either. Plus, it was the only way the 'men' would allow Molly and Dustin to help. They thought it would keep them safe. Molly knew there was still danger involved, but they needed to clear Jared and get him back home. Somehow, any fear she should've felt dissolved into pure excitement about investigating another crime on the island.

"And Christy believes it, too?"

"Of course not, but what can she do? She got Jared an attorney, and she's hoping she can get him off, but I don't know how they can fight Uncle Sam."

Holly shook her head. "What a mess. And you're sure you aren't going to work at Wallops just to be close to Dustin?"

"Holly, you know I'm smarter than that. I doubt we'll even cross paths that much. He may not even have a job anymore with Jared gone."

"Oh, I hadn't thought about that. Wow. This sure has a ripple effect, doesn't it?"

"You have no idea," Molly muttered. "Let me get Gwen started on the paperwork. I'll let her shadow me for today, but I've got to be at Wallops tomorrow."

"Okay, but I really hope you're not making a mistake."

So do I. More than you could ever know. Jared's entire future depends upon us playing everything just right.

***

I'm good on my end. I can start tomorrow. How are things on your end?

Not great. I'm already overwhelmed. There are a lot more people working here than I ever imagined. And we need to look into all the ones who come and go from NASA, and then there are the marine biologists and meteorologists who use the center for their research purposes. Not to mention all the Scout groups, school kids, campers, volunteers, you name it. This place gets a lot of traffic.

We only need to worry about the people who had access to Jared's office, not visitors. Just gather what you can. We'll look at everything and develop a systematic approach. We've got this.

Dustin wasn't so sure about that. He meant it when he said he was overwhelmed. This wasn't like cramming for an exam or writing a research paper. Someone's life depended upon what they found, or didn't find. And that person's life was connected to so many others. They had to find something, but he didn't know how. This was worse than trying to find a needle in a haystack. It was like trying to locate the smallest star in the universe.

When his phone rang, Dustin assumed it was Molly, but his father's image came up on the screen instead. Shoot! He was due to arrive later this week.

"Hey, Dad. What's up?"

"Just checking in. I didn't hear from you over the weekend."

"I'm sorry. I was busy."

"Hanging out with the girl from school?"

"Yeah," Dustin admitted, a smile forming on his lips.

"Not getting too serious, right? I mean, you just graduated. You haven't even decided on a job after your internship is finished."

"Yeah, I know, and Molly's in the same boat. We've had most of the same offers, so we're weighing our options."

There was a beat of silence before his father said, "Not weighing them together, right? She wants to go somewhere, so you pick the same place so you can be together? Don't go down that road, Dustin."

The weight on Dustin's heart mirrored the heaviness in his father's voice.

"I know, Dad. I won't let that happen. We need to choose what's best for each of us."

"Neither of you will be happy if one of you makes sacrifices for the other that are too big to live with."

Dustin knew the speech, understood the warning. When two people had so much promise and such big dreams, those dreams had to work in tandem, or nothing would work at all. But couldn't they be different? Weren't their dreams and their prospects the same?

"You know, Dad, it's not like with you and my mom. We had the same major, we have the same interests. Our job offers will take us down the same road, in the same places." *Unless he went to Seattle or California, and she went to Houston or D.C.* He shook away the thought. "Anyway, Dad, our paths are on the same route, not polar opposites."

Again, there was silence. Had he crossed a line? Had he made light of his father's own life decisions?

"You're right, son, but I still think you need to make these choices independently. If you both decide as individuals that you end up in the same place, that's great. Just don't bend your will to hers, and don't let her bend to yours."

Dustin closed his eyes. He could see the wedding photo in the album that still sat on their bookshelf in the family room. His parents looked so happy, so full of hope in the future. They'd already decided that Ted would take the job in Chicago, his dream job that he was offered right out of college, even though Alice longed to return to her hometown of San Francisco. Her dream was too out of reach for a young couple just starting out, so she applied to teach high school biology instead of applying to UCSF for medical school. Her wealthy parents were furious and cut off ties with their daughter and the husband they despised for taking her away from them.

Ted and Alice couldn't afford the tuition with Ted's starting salary, and they didn't want to take on loans. By the time Alice was twenty-five and had access to the trust fund left to her by her grandmother, she had a child, a mortgage, and a marriage in decline because she couldn't forgive Ted for getting what he'd always wanted while she worked with kids she didn't like in a career that held no promise for her.

Dustin didn't know when he started thinking of the couple as Ted and Alice instead of Dad and Mom. Maybe it had always been that way. To him, his father was a single man. As for his mother, Dustin had no memory of Alice, nobody named 'mom' in his life. On her twenty-fifth birthday, Alice packed a bag, claimed her trust fund, and drove off without ever looking back. He supposed she was a doctor somewhere, maybe even a virologist as she'd hoped, chasing down epicenters all over the world and establishing the moment of first contact. He didn't know, and he didn't care, but he knew better than to make their mistakes.

"You still there, son?"

"Yeah, I'm here. Thanks, Dad. I'll remember your advice. I promise."

"Good. Now, what about my visit? Are we still on?"

What could he say? He wanted to see his father, to have him meet Molly, to see that maybe she and Dustin had a chance of doing better than Ted and Alice. On the other hand, he couldn't let Molly or Dr. Stevenson down.

"Things are pretty busy at work. If you come, I might not have a ton of time to spend with you, but I've met lots of people you can hang with."

"Oh?" his father said, and Dustin could hear the disappointment in that one little word.

"I mean, I really want you to come. I'll try to make sure I've got time to do stuff with you, but I'll also introduce you to some of the people I've met in case I'm not able to get away. I really do want to see you."

"If you're sure I won't be in the way…"

"Dad, you could never be in the way. I can't wait for you to get here."

Besides, if we're still at this a week from now, who knows what that will mean for Dr. Stevenson.

✳✳✳

Nobody was supposed to know about the data. This could ruin everything. How did they find out? Would he still get his money? He'd been given one-third when he handed over the satellite parts and one-third upon delivery of the flash drive, but he wouldn't get the rest until they knew he'd gotten everything they wanted from the server. In the meantime, he'd better keep his head down, his nose to the grindstone, and his eyes and ears open.

Local Man Arrested by Federal Marshalls

Island resident and scientist at Wallops Island Flight Facility, Dr. Jared Stevenson, was taken in handcuffs by Federal Marshalls to Washington, D.C., last Monday on unknown charges. Facility manager and lead scientist, Dr. Simon Johnson, also an island resident, gave a brief statement to the press. "We are unaware of any wrongdoing by Dr. Stevenson and are relying on justice to prevail in this ongoing investigation." Stevenson's wife, home visitation nurse, Christy Stevenson, declined to comment.

The Chincoteague Herald, July 1

Chapter Twelve

"Hey, guys, what are you doing?"

Molly looked up to see Freddy in the doorway. "Oh, hey, Freddy. We're trying to keep Jared's research going while he's, uh, away."

"Yeah, I heard about that. I was on nights last week, so I wasn't here when it happened. I'm really sorry. Any news? Anything I can do?"

Molly shook her head. "No, but thanks. I appreciate the offer."

"Need me to talk to anyone, nose around, see what I can find out? The janitorial staff always knows more than people think we do."

Molly and Dustin exchanged a look. "Thanks, but we need to let the experts deal with that. Dustin and I just want to keep up Jared's work so he's not behind when he returns."

"You think he'll be back? I mean, have they let anyone know what he supposedly did? I heard they took all his computers and stuff."

"Nothing. His attorney can't really tell us anything, so we just have to hope and pray for the best. Fortunately, a lot of his research was backed up on the server, so we can keep that going." Molly hoped he would move on so they could continue working.

"That's good. Let me know if you need anything, though. The offer stands firm."

Molly smiled, grateful there were no hard feelings about her not going out with him again. "Thanks, Freddy. You're a good friend."

He emptied the trash and replaced the bag. He seemed to be stalling, but maybe that was Molly's imagination and impatience. Finally, he told them to have a good day and left the room.

"He might be onto something," Molly said. "Do we know when this breach took place? Could one of the custodians have seen something?"

"I don't know. They didn't give Dr. Johnson any details, as far as I know."

"He'd tell us, right?"

Dustin shrugged. "I guess so. I mean, he knows what we're doing. Then again, we're looking into people, not the actual crime."

"I don't want to drag Freddy or anyone else into this, but maybe we could find a way to talk to someone, see if they saw or heard anything suspicious."

"I think we should leave that to Jared's attorney and the investigators. We're only supposed to be digging for motives. We're not detectives."

Molly cocked her head to the side and frowned. "So, I've been told. More than once." She knew her mind was capable of more than just shuffling through employment records, but what could she do? She let out a frustrated sigh. "Okay, let's keep going. We've got a lot of backgrounds to look into."

***

"So, you seem to know everyone and everything that goes on around here," Ethan began, stirring his first cup of morning coffee. "What's up with the house that was raided by the Feds?"

Jenny blew on her own coffee a few times then took a cautious sip. "Jared and Christy are part of my sister's friend group. Christy's a local home health nurse. You remember her. Her daughter was your first patient, Molly's niece."

His eyes went wide. "The nurse with the little girl who needed stitches?"

Jenny nodded. "Yeah, that's the one. Jared works at Wallops, but I don't know that he works for Wallops. He's some kind of researcher, textbook writer, genius, moon expert." She shrugged and headed to their office. "Anyway, the Feds say he stole some kind of top-secret government files. Taylor and Nick say it's bogus. Some kind of set-up."

"Wow. This place really does have some incredible happenings, doesn't it?"

"You can say that again."

What Ethan really wanted to know was her family's impression of him, but he wasn't sure how to bring it up. He'd been wondering about it for a couple days.

"I don't know if I've told you how much I enjoyed dinner with your family on Sunday."

"You have, and I'm glad. Aunt Ronnie thought you were very—how did she put it?—'gentlemanly'." She took a seat at her desk.

Ethan frowned. "Is that good?"

Jenny laughed. "It's good. Nick said you were too good-looking to be a nice guy."

That caught him off guard, both the good-looking and the not a nice guy.

"What? What does that even mean?"

"It means my brother-in-law liked you and is giving me a hard time."

"Oh. Okay." He supposed that was good. "Do you guys do that every Sunday?"

Jenny was glancing over the day's charts but looked up with a puzzled expression. "Huh? Sorry. I got distracted. What did you say?"

"Do you get together for dinner every Sunday?"

She shook her head. "Aunt Ronnie's family does. Without fail. Of course, sometimes Aaron is working, or Kayla has a catering job, but they all try to keep that day and their dinners pretty sacred. We only go once a month or so, usually when Nick's off and I'm not on duty."

"It's nice. That she does that, I mean. And nice that everyone goes. After my grandparents passed, we rarely did any kind of family thing like that until my sisters got married and had babies. Then Mom started having family dinners." He shrugged. "I kind of miss that. Having dinners and regular get-togethers."

"You could still do that, you know," Jenny pointed out. "We're not that far from Richmond."

"Yeah, but it's far enough with having to work on Monday. I was thinking of heading home next weekend though. Maybe. I want to be here on the Fourth, but our community is celebrating on Saturday, so I thought I'd go home for the weekend since I'm not on the schedule."

"That sounds nice," Jenny said. "You should."

Ethan hesitated, not sure if he should ask, but he thought, what the heck?

"Would you like to go with me? Home for the weekend?"

Jenny froze, her eyes wide, a patient's paperwork dangling from her fingertips.

"I, um, I…"

"Never mind," Ethan said. "I shouldn't have asked. That's probably more like dating than being colleagues who are friends."

Jenny put down the file and sat back in the office chair.

"Maybe we should define exactly what we are," she said with no small amount of trepidation in her voice.

Ethan swallowed. This was the moment he'd been waiting for, but did he want to know the answer?

"Well, we don't have to define it. I mean, we can just continue as we have been and see how it progresses. What do you think?" He wanted to put the ball in her court, afraid Gram was right, but hoping that Jenny was ready to at least consider a relationship. With him, that is.

She nodded. "Okay. I'm willing to hold off on a label and see where this goes." She spoke slowly, as if uncertain that this was the right answer.

"I'm good with that. Nothing official, but maybe exploring that possibility?"

A knock at the door caused them both to jump. Stacey stuck her head inside the room. "Sorry, did you forget you have a patient, Dr. Edwards?"

His face became fiery hot. "No, uh, I just got sidetracked. Sorry."

He rushed from the room, still unsure where he stood with the woman he was certain he was falling in love with.

***

Molly and Dustin raced up the steps and burst into the house. They'd left as soon as Molly received the text to go home.

"Christy?" Molly called.

"We're in here."

They hurried to the kitchen. Jared and Christy sat at the kitchen table with a woman Molly didn't recognize. Without hesitation, Molly ran to Jared and wrapped her arms around him, burying her face in his chest. He smelled weird and looked awful, but he was home.

"We came as soon as I got Christy's text. Thank Heaven you're home. What's happening?"

"You must be Molly," the woman said. She was middle-aged with dark hair and eyes, wearing a suit Molly knew cost more than both Christy and Jared made in a month. Molly took her hand. "I'm Katherine, Jared's attorney."

Molly looked at Christy and tried to use telepathy to communicate with her to ask if Jared was off the hook. It must've worked because Christy gave an almost imperceptible shake of her head, her eyes filled with concern.

"So, what's going on?" Molly asked, taking a seat. She realized Dustin was still standing, probably unsure of his place. "Oh, this is my boyfriend, Dustin. He's Jared's intern."

Katherine looked him over. "Perhaps we should discuss all this later."

"No," Molly and Jared said at the same time.

"I want to discuss it now," Jared said. "We can trust everyone here."

"Are you sure about that?" Katherine asked, her eyes again going to Dustin.

"Unless you know something you haven't told me," Jared said. "This is my family, and Dustin has shown me that I can trust him." He gave Dustin an appraising look. "So far."

Molly saw Dustin's Adam's apple bob as he swallowed.

"You can trust me, Sir," Dustin said. "I'm one hundred percent on your side."

"Do you know something about Dustin that I should know?" Jared asked again.

Katherine cleared her throat. "He did have access to your office, your files, your computers, did he not?"

"Wait, do we know how this happened and when?" Molly asked.

"The Feds have narrowed it down. That's why Jared was released, though he's not totally off the hook. The breach happened on a Tuesday night, just after nine P.M. The date was June 13. The files were downloaded from Jared's computer onto some kind of external drive which in turn, left a hidden door that allowed outside servers access to information on NASA's servers."

Dustin and Molly met each other's eyes and nodded. "It wasn't Dustin."

"How do you know this?" Katherine asked.

"He was with me. And a whole bunch of others."

"Molly's on a trivia team that plays every Tuesday night at a local restaurant," Christy supplied.

"And you're on this team?" Katherine asked Dustin.

"No, Ma'am. I'm on an opposing team."

"And you know for sure you were at trivia on June 13?"

"For sure," Molly said. "It's the night he asked me out."

"And what time did you leave?"

"Right after I asked her. Trivia ended about 8:45, and I followed Molly to the bathroom so I could catch her alone. We talked for a bit, I asked her out, and the other interns and I headed back to Wallops after I got back to my seat and paid my tab."

"There's no way he could've gotten back to Wallops in time to ditch his friends, sneak into the building, and get into my office," Jared confirmed. "Besides, he doesn't have a key to my office or the password to my computer."

"That's not quite true," Dustin said, taking a seat next to Molly.

"What does that mean?" Jared asked.

"I don't have a key, but everyone knows your password. You're not good about hiding it when you type it in, and you've got it taped to the back of your monitor."

Katherine raised her brow. "Is this true?"

Jared's face reddened. "Probably. Yeah. Most likely."

"And it's taped to the monitor?"

Jared nodded and heaved a sigh. "Yeah. They don't call me the absent-minded professor for nothing."

"Well, that changes things," Katherine said. "A lot. I need a list of every person who has access to your office."

"We have that," Molly said.

Katherine raised her brow. "What do you mean, you have that?"

Molly and Dustin glanced at each other before turning back to Katherine. Molly answered, "We've been doing some digging."

"Please, tell me you're joking. Do you know how much that could compromise this case?"

"You said Jared was released. Is there still a case against him?"

"The Feds are still working on making their case. Jared was taken into custody and questioned, but he was released on bond pending charges, despite his relation to a crime family and his knowledge about disappearing."

"Because I have no ties with my relations and no knowledge of how to disappear." He ran his hand up under his glasses and rubbed his eyes a couple times before letting his glasses fall back on the bridge of his nose and pushing them into place. "I was five, for Heaven's sake."

"Which helped you in the eyes of the judge," Katherine said. "But it didn't clear you. And though they didn't place you on house arrest, you aren't allowed to leave the island."

Molly looked down at his ankle and saw the monitor he was wearing.

"Exactly what does all of this mean? I only know what I've seen on *Law and Order*." Dustin asked.

"Jared was arrested on grounds of a criminal charge, but that doesn't mean they have enough to convict him.

They need to prove their case, and so far, everything they have is circumstantial. They're looking for anything that shows he had a motive—money problems, blackmail, family allegiance, anything that proves Jared stole the information and has or will profit from it, and Jared has a storied past, which is why I need a solid case without any compromises."

"In other words," Molly said, "the FBI believes this ties to his mafia family."

"Precisely," Katherine concurred. "So, back to this list and your digging. Explain to me exactly what that means."

Molly proceeded to tell Katherine what they'd been up to and what they found. Dustin chimed in throughout her explanations, and as Katherine took notes, her expression went from angry to interested. She didn't speak right away after they finished, but she perused her notes and nodded, then sat back and looked at them.

"Okay, here's how we're going to proceed from this point on."

***

"I'm really sorry I won't get to see where you work," Dustin's father said after Dustin met him at his hotel.

"Me, too. I'm really enjoying it. I can see why so many of the people tend to stay here instead of moving on to one of the other sites."

"Do you like the work you're doing?"

"I do," Dustin told him. "I wish my boss didn't have to take a leave of absence and the center wasn't closed to the public for the time being, but otherwise, it's great."

"Any word on that?"

As they wandered outside, Dustin updated him with the bare minimum, leaving out everything having to do with the mission he and Molly had embarked upon.

"Not much. Hoping they can clear it up soon. On the bright side, at least I'm off while you're here."

"What did you say we're doing for the afternoon?" his dad asked as they walked down the busy, red brick sidewalk that lined Main Street.

"I'm giving you a different tour since we can't tour the center. I wanted to show you around Chincoteague, which is where I spend most of my free time."

"This is the place with the ponies, right?"

"Kind of. I made that same mistake, but Molly set me straight."

"Molly is the girl you've been hanging out with. The one from school."

"Yeah. The ponies are owned by the Chincoteague Island fire department, but they live on Assateague Island. They're only on Chincoteague at the end of July when they're rounded up and sold at auction to benefit the fire department."

"So, we won't run into them while we're out? I thought I'd seen pictures of them on the beach getting up close with visitors."

"When we're on Assateague, we'll see them. But don't get too up close. They're wild animals, not barnyard pets."

His dad looked at him and grinned. "Listen to you. You sound like an old man talking to a kid."

Dustin laughed. "Honestly, Dad, I feel like I've matured more this summer than I did in twenty-two years."

Dustin waved his father off when he reached over and tussled Dustin's sandy-brown hair. "Well, you still look like a kid. You need your hair cut."

Laughing louder, Dustin said, "Some things never change. Think your old legs can handle a climb to the top of the lighthouse?" Dustin asked, only half joking.

"Are you serious? I'm in the best shape of my life."

Dustin couldn't argue. "You do look good. What have you been doing?"

"I joined a gym. The doctor said I needed to lose some weight, start doing some cardio, lift a little. I never thought I'd say this, but I like it."

"The doctor?" Alarm bells went off in Dustin's head.

"Don't worry. Everything is fine. I'm just not getting any younger."

Relief spread through him. "Good. Are you going to a gym near your office?"

"We have one in the building, and the company pays half the cost. I don't know why I never took advantage of it before."

Dustin clapped his father on the back. "I'm proud of you, Dad."

When they reached the lighthouse, Dustin was impressed with his father's stamina and realized, as he struggled not to huff and puff himself, that maybe he should join a gym.

"This view is amazing," Ted said, and Dustin agreed. He pointed out Wallops in the distance and explained what they were looking down at—marshland, beaches, the town, and the ocean beyond. They could see all of Chincoteague and all of Assateague, including its famous residents.

"You're getting your first glimpse of the wild ponies, Dad." He pointed to the scene. "Want to see them a little closer?"

"But not too close," his father said with a smile.

"Yeah, not too close. Come on."

They made their way back down and headed to the beach. They walked on the sand, shoes in hand, and stopped when they saw a crowd of people taking pictures.

Dustin pointed and watched as a brown and white pony made its way toward the shoreline. She was followed by a sand-colored foal. Their tails swished back and forth as they walked, swatting away flies but completely unbothered by the paparazzi.

"Maybe while you're here we can book something with Saltwater Pony Tours. I've heard it's a great way to see the ponies."

"You know, I always wanted a horse," his dad said, throwing Dustin for a loop.

"You what? I never knew that."

He shrugged. "I wanted to be a cowboy when I was a kid. Once I grew up, met your mom, all that, I'd grown out of it."

Dustin laughed. "There aren't too many cowboys in or around Chicago."

"No, there sure aren't. And Chicago isn't all it's cracked up to be."

Dustin watched the expression on his father's face and wondered if he was thinking of moving. Did he have a new job or a girlfriend?

"Something you want to tell me, Dad? Are you planning on leaving the city? You just moved into your apartment when I went to college?"

"I'm thinking about taking early retirement," his father said, turning to face him. "I've got a good nest egg plus my inheritance. You're taken care of, thanks to your grandparents. I think I'd like to live a little."

Dustin's stomach clenched, thinking back to his father's earlier comment. "Dad, are you okay?" He grabbed his father's arm. "Are you sick? You're not...?" He couldn't say the word.

"No, no." His father shook his head as he assured him. "Nothing like that. I told you, I'm fine. I've gotten you through college. Your future's set. I've got the money. Why not enjoy it?"

"Wow," Dustin breathed. "I did not see that coming. You love your job. I never thought you'd retire, especially early."

"The job has changed. It's not the same as it was when I started. All this bitcoin stuff and round-the-clock trading, plus all the new technology. It's a different world, and not one I totally understand. Wow, would you look at that pony. What a beaut. You know, I may have to get me one of them after all."

Dustin watched another pony make his entrance, unafraid of the crowd that had gathered. He wondered if the three were a family. Did horses mate like that? Did they manage to have what he never had?

He was happy for his father, but he couldn't help but wonder what would happen to their family of two if his dad decided to move out west? What about Texas? Dustin might end up there. He had an offer. Maybe it was time to get serious about what he was going to do next.

***

Molly spent the day locked in her room going over every note she and Dustin had taken. She was missing something, but she didn't know what. As she sat staring into blank space, something came into view. She stood and walked to her dresser, picking up the framed photograph that stood there.

Molly and Dr. Johnson beamed at the camera after having been interviewed about the rocket they had just launched. It was the summer Molly turned eleven, their first on the island. They met Jared the first day of camp, and that day changed all their lives. Though the rocket was Jared's baby, his probe into the moon's resources, he refused to be interviewed. Nobody knew why at the time, but he'd always been told not to be photographed or have his picture in any national publication. He never questioned why but obeyed his mother as he'd been taught. Molly was as proud as a peacock to be able to talk to the reporter about the rocket she had helped Jared build.

What was it about that photo that made Molly's pulse quicken? What did it have to do with—

Her eyes widened, and she ran down the hall shouting Jared's name.

"What's up, Molly?" Jared said, coming out of the nursery with Nicky in his arms.

"Earlier in the summer, you said you were missing parts to your rocket. Did you ever find them?"

Jared shook his head. "No, I have no idea what happened to them."

"And did other things go missing? Other parts or models or designs?"

Jared nodded. "Yeah. There were a couple times we realized things were gone. We thought they'd been misplaced or that someone else saw them and used them without realizing what they were for. Why?"

"What if it's all connected? What if whoever got into your laptop wasn't just after information? What if he or she was selling the parts that went along with what you're working on? Did you tell the Feds about that missing stuff?"

Jared shook his head. "They didn't seem to know about it, and I was so busy focusing on clearing my name and answering their questions about the breach, I never thought about it. By that time, they'd been missing for over a month, I'd ordered new parts, and it seemed like ancient history."

"I think we should call Katherine. This might explain what they were looking for on your hard drive and why they wanted it. Your research on the moon's resources and the M29 you're working on might be the keys to everything."

***

"My son is doing an internship at Wallops," Dustin heard his father say proudly.

They spent the morning on Assateague, had lunch at Holly's café, and then spent the afternoon going in and out of the shops.

"How nice. I've always heard it's a great place to work."

"Hey, Dad, you ready?" Dustin hurried over after paying for his dad's shirt and smiled at the woman. "Sorry. I don't mean to interrupt, but we have dinner reservations. I've got the shirt you liked, Dad. Thanks for letting me buy it for you."

"What a nice thing to do. I was just hearing about your internship." The woman held out her hand. "I'm Donna Murray."

"Murray," Dustin said, assessing her features. She had dark, stylish hair, and big brown eyes. She was average height, and he was sure he'd never met her, but there was something so familiar about her. "You look really familiar. Have we met? I'm Dustin Howard."

She shook her head. "I don't think so, but I'm often told that my daughter and I look a lot alike. One of my daughters, not the redhead." She laughed. "Are you a friend of Jenny's? She's a doctor at the island clinic."

That's it! They do look alike.

"I know Jenny. She's friends with Molly."

Jenny's mother frowned. "She is. Shame what's going on with them. Jared's a gem. I just can't believe what they're saying about him."

"He's got a good lawyer, and we're, they're, doing everything they can to clear him."

"I'm glad to hear that. We've got a great family attorney, not a criminal attorney, but great nonetheless. And Taylor worked with an attorney who helped immensely when she was trying to become a Saltwater Cowgirl. If Jared needs anyone else on his team, let me know."

"A Saltwater Cowgirl?" Dustin's father asked.

"I can explain, Dad. We should let Mrs. Murray get on with her shopping."

"Oh, I'm not really shopping. I have all the Chincoteague clothing I need. I was just looking for something for my great-niece. Her birthday is coming up, and she's obsessed with the ponies. I guess it runs in the family," she said. "Even my grandson, Wesley, loves the ponies as much as his mother does.

"You can't possibly have a grandson," Dustin's father said, causing Dustin to do a double take. Was his father flirting?

"Oh, stop," Mrs. Murray said in amusement. "My Taylor is almost thirty."

She was blushing, and Dustin forced his mouth from falling open. His father had been single pretty much Dustin's entire life, and as far as Dustin knew, he'd never even looked at a woman.

Did Dad go on dates? When I went to college, did my father suddenly develop a social life?

"Oh, come on, you must've had her when you were no more than eighteen."

What is going on here? I can't believe this!

"Um, Dad, we should probably get going."

"Oh, sure, son. Well," he reached his hand out to Mrs. Murray. "It was my pleasure meeting you, Donna. I hope we run into each other again."

"It truly was a pleasure, Ted. You enjoy your visit with Dustin. Maybe we'll run into each other again before you leave."

Both men watched her walk out, rooted in their spots.

"Well, she was nice," Dustin's father said. Dustin turned to him in amazement.

"Nice? The first woman I've ever seen you show any interest in, and all you say is 'she was nice'?"

"What do you want me to say, Dustin? That was one beautiful woman I might like to get to know better?"

For a moment, Dustin wasn't able to speak, then he blew out a brash laugh. Before he knew it, he was laughing so hard he couldn't stop. Finally, he looked at his father and said, "Yeah, Dad. That's exactly what you should be saying. And it's about time."

They left the store and headed toward the Ropewalk, one of the restaurants Dustin had yet to try.

"Speaking of getting to know a woman, when do I get to meet this gal of yours?"

"I'm not sure I'd call her a *gal*."

"Okay, your girlfriend then. I'm not blind or deaf. Every time we talk, it's Molly this and Molly that. You never mentioned this girl in the whole four years you went to school together, and now you can't stop talking about her. Is she the reason you took this internship? Does she work at Wallops, too?"

"Dad, Dad, slow down. No, she's not the reason I came here. To be honest, if I had known she lived here and had ties to the center, I probably wouldn't have applied." He held his hand up and kept walking. "That's another story. Anyway, her brother-in-law is my boss, the one who's on leave. Molly and I have been hanging out this summer, and yeah, she's become my girlfriend, but we don't know where we'll end up come fall. Right now, I'm trying to help her family figure out what's happening with Jared, I mean Dr. Stevenson."

"Helping how?" His father stopped abruptly in the middle of the sidewalk, earning a nasty look from both a woman and her dog who were in a hurry to get somewhere.

"Just helping him gather info for his attorney."

"I don't know that that's a good idea, Dustin. If this man did something illegal, I don't want you caught up in it. Did this Molly put you up to this?"

"I'm not 'this Molly' and no, I did not. And furthermore, Jared didn't do anything illegal."

They turned to see a red-faced Molly behind them.

Dustin watched his father look her up and down before he reached out his hand. "My apologies, Molly. I didn't mean to insult you."

Molly didn't hesitate in taking his hand. "Thank you, Mr. Howard. There's been a lot of assuming going around lately, and I'd appreciate it if you didn't join the crowd in making assumptions about Jared or about me."

"Um, Dad, this is Molly, and this isn't exactly how I pictured this going," Dustin managed to say before swallowing the lump in his throat.

"I am sorry, Molly. Dustin's my only son, my only family, and I worry about him. Please, forgive me."

"And my sister, Jared, and their kids are my only family, so forgive me if I'm a little defensive right now." Molly's tone was forgiving, but her eyes were still on fire.

"How about we go inside and get some dinner," Dustin said, gesturing to Molly to go ahead. As she led the way, he and his father looked at each other, one with an expression of worry and the other with an expression of amusement. Even with the rough start, Dustin knew his father found Molly as intriguing as he did.

***

Per usual, Molly was greeted like the Queen of Sheba, and they were led to the best table in the house. The treatment was getting old, and Molly didn't appreciate it at the moment. All she could think of was that the apple didn't fall far from the tree, and Dustin's father was as big a jerk as Dustin had been back in school.

When they arrived at their table, Molly spied Aaron, Kate, and their daughters having dinner at a table nearby. She caught Aaron's eye and gave him a slight nod, acknowledging his presence. She knew his family wasn't there by coincidence. She'd told Zach where she and Dustin were having dinner with his father that evening, and Zach had obviously passed it on to his sister or her husband.

"Molly's kind of a local celebrity, Dad," Dustin said after they were seated. Molly didn't know which of them he was trying to placate.

"Is that so?" Dustin's father asked, picking up the menu and looking it over.

"It's no big deal," Molly said, picking up her menu and following his lead.

"Molly saved all the restaurants on the island by cracking the case of the restaurant saboteur."

Molly glowered at Dustin. "You make it sound like a bad detective story."

"You know, I bet Dad would love to hear the story. I know I enjoyed hearing you tell it."

Finally, Dustin's father put down his menu and looked at Molly. "I think what my son is trying to say is that he'd like us to get to know each other. Maybe we should start over."

Why does this feel like déjà vu? Like father like son?

Molly looked at Dustin and saw the pleading in his eyes. He wasn't really a jerk, and she knew it. She took a deep breath. "Okay, we can do that." She reached across the table. "Hello, Mr. Howard. I'm Molly McLane. Dustin and I went to school together, and we've become good friends this summer. He's told me what a wonderful father you are."

Dustin's father smiled. "Thank you, Molly. Please, call me Ted. None of Dustin's friends ever called me Mr. Howard. Tell me about yourself. Did you grow up here?"

Molly gave the shortened version of her life—she was born and lived just outside of D.C. as a child, her parents died in a car accident when she was ten, and she and her sister were forced to sell their big house and move to the island where they found a community and her sister found love. She didn't spend a lot of time on her school experiences except to say she went away to boarding school, graduated early, and went to Harvard. Dustin unnecessarily filled in some gaps.

"Molly's a genius, Dad. A bona fide genius. She was valedictorian of both her high school and our college class. She knows more about space science than Goddard did."

Molly found herself blushing. "I wouldn't go that far."

"Wait a minute. You gave the speech at graduation. I should've recognized you, or your name. You look different with your hair down like that. Your speech was fantastic. Very inspirational."

Molly blushed again as she ran a hand though her long tresses, still wavy from the braid she'd had in earlier. Dustin looked pleased.

"I told you. Jared told me Molly knew more about satellites and space travel at ten than most college graduates know by the time they finish school." Dustin beamed, and Molly had the sudden realization that he was proud of her, as a person and a girlfriend.

"Jared exaggerates." Molly uncharacteristically blushed with humility just as their waitress arrived.

"Sorry to keep you waiting. We just got slammed. Can I get you drinks?"

Dustin and his father ordered beer, and Molly said she'd stick with water, grateful that Ted didn't ask why she wasn't ordering an alcoholic drink.

"So, what do you like to do other than study space travel, Molly?"

"Well, I like to kayak and go to the beach, mostly at night when I can see the stars. I love bike riding, and I've been horseback riding a few times with my friend, Jenny, but mostly, I read. Sometimes about things other than space, mostly mystery and crime novels. I like to solve things, here and up there." She gestured above and smiled, and he smiled back.

"Jenny? Isn't that Donna's daughter?"

"You know Mrs. Murray?" Molly asked.

"We just met, and I thought she said she had a daughter named Jenny who was a friend of yours."

Molly felt a nudge under the table and looked to Dustin who was raising just one eyebrow. A small 'O' formed on her lips as she realized what he was insinuating.

"Oh, really? Where did you meet?"

"Before meeting up with you, Dustin took me around town to the shops. Dustin was buying me a shirt in one of them when we ran into her. Nice woman." He nonchalantly took a sip of the water that was on the table.

"You guys ordered beer?" a young man said, holding a tray with two bottles and two beer mugs. "Hey, Molly."

"Hi, Dave."

"We did, thanks," Dustin said.

"Shelly will be back to get your orders." He left the beers and hurried away.

"We went to middle school together," Molly told them, nodding toward the waiter. "So, what else did you and Mrs. Murray talk about?"

"Not much, really. She was very welcoming."

"Everyone here is," Molly said before taking a drink of water. "You're going to enjoy your stay."

They ordered their meal and talked about the island, what it was like to live there. Ted shared stories about Dustin's youth, sometimes making him blush, and other times causing him to laugh out loud and say to his father, "Not that one!"

By the end of the evening, all awkwardness was gone, and Molly decided she really liked Ted Howard. And she couldn't help but wonder what Jenny would think about Ted's interest in her mother.

Music at the Dock Opens This Weekend

Don't miss your opportunity to listen and dance to local favorite, Rosie and the Lunatics, this Saturday night at the Robert Reed Downtown Waterfront Park. The park is located in the historic downtown. Beginning this weekend, live bands will take the stage every Saturday at 7pm.

This free event is the hottest ticket in town every week and is sponsored by the Chincoteague Cultural Alliance. Bring the whole family for a night of dancing under the moonlight.

The Chincoteague Herald July 8

Chapter Thirteen

"That wasn't as bad as I thought it would be," Ethan said as he and Jenny walked to their cars.

"You never know, I guess. With so many people on the island, anything could happen, but I'm glad it was a slow day."

Ethan hesitated at her car. "So, you've never mentioned what you do for the Fourth? How do you celebrate?"

"I'm heading to Taylor's to pick up my nephew. The baby is due in a few weeks, and she's having a rough time. Wesley wants to watch the fireworks, but Nick is working, so Mom and I volunteered to take Wesley for the night. We can see the fireworks from the ranch, so Taylor can rest inside where it's cool, or she can join us. Either way, Wesley will stay with Mom, so Taylor can have a break."

"That sounds nice," he gave her a weak smile. "Have fun."

"You could join us," she said slowly, reaching up tuck a hair behind her ear though nothing was out of place. He'd seen her do that many times when she was reading over a puzzling medical case or even doing the morning crossword while sipping her coffee.

There were many little things he'd begun noticing about her. She wore very little makeup, but her lips were always moist and shiny. She had a quiet laugh except when something really tickled her, and she'd let out an adorable snort. She was always working on a word game or reading a book when things were slow, or she was taking a break.

"I wouldn't want to impose," he said, though he wanted to spend the holiday with her more than anything, "on your time with your mom and your nephew."

Jenny shook her head. "It wouldn't be an imposition. My mother loves you, and Wesley will enjoy having a guy around. Unless…" Her expression changed, "you already have plans."

He rushed to assure her otherwise. "No, nothing at all. I wasn't sure what today would bring, and I'm heading home tomorrow, so I didn't make any plans."

They were both aware that she had yet to take him up on his invitation to go home with him to meet his family. He hadn't pushed, but he really wanted her to go with him, despite the fact that he'd already asked someone else. He was sure Jenny would understand since she hadn't given him an answer.

"Well, I'd hate for you to be alone on the holiday."

"Give me your mom's address, and I'll head over after I go home and change. Is that okay?"

"That's perfect," she said with a smile.

On the way back to his rental, Ethan turned up the radio and sang loudly. It was too hot to roll the windows down, but he was tempted. He wanted the entire island to know how he felt about spending the holiday with Jenny Murray.

***

The dark sky overhead, unobstructed by clouds, was a canvas of multi-colored glitter that left trails of red, blue, white, yellow, green, and purple lights twinkling through the smoke that billowed around them. Molly was stretched across Lizzie's parents' dock, her head on Dustin's stomach, his body perpendicular to hers. Beside them, little Sally oohed and aahed at each burst of color. Jared begged off, not wanting to talk to anyone, so he and Christy stayed home with Nicky.

"I love this," Adrienne said. "I don't care what your politics are or what your ethnicity is, I love coming together as a people united and celebrating under a sparkling sky."

"I think you missed your calling," Lizzie said. "You should've been a poet."

Adrienne laughed. "A science poet. I kind of like that."

"The next Vladimir Zakharov," Dustin said, referring to the renown mathematical physicist and poet.

"Look at that one," Molly said, pointing to a burst that covered the sky and turned from one color to another. "That's my favorite one so far."

"Haven't you said that about five times?" Ben chided her.

"Leave her alone. A woman has a prerogative to change her mind," said, Lori, Ben's date for the evening. Molly had learned not to become too attached to anyone Ben brought around, but she liked Lori and thanked her for defending her.

"Where do you think we'll all be next year?" Adrienne asked.

"I'll be in the Big Easy," Lizzie told them.

"What?" Gwen and Molly both said at the same time.

"New Orleans?" Molly said, sad that Lizzie would no longer be on the island. It just didn't seem possible.

"EJ got his orders this morning. He's relocating next spring. We're relocating next spring." Molly heard the tinge of sadness in her voice and knew they were thinking the same thing. The island wouldn't be the same without Lizzie, and Lizzie would have to make a life off the island.

"Well, I know where Dustin and Molly will be," Cam said, breaking the melancholy moment. "They'll be on the west coast making more money than any of us could dream of."

Molly thought about that. "I don't know. I'm not sure I want to work for a corporation whose primary goal is to make money."

"Why not?" Nathan asked. "Money makes the world go round, and it would provide you with a lifetime of doing what you love. Besides, no matter where you work, their main goal will be to make money. That's the system we live under."

Molly took in a breath and stared at the sky. "I know," she said in a long sigh. "It's just that… I want something else, something more."

"More what?" Cam asked. "You won't make more money than you will with Musk or Bezos."

Molly noticed that Dustin remained silent, and she wondered where he was with his decision. It was a topic they'd been avoiding since they became *official.*

"I don't know. Something more exciting."

Adrienne sat up and looked at her. "What could be more exciting to you than watching rockets launch and learning about the moon and space and all that's out there? You might even get to go into space on one of those rockets."

"Isn't that the kind of opportunity you've wanted your entire life?" Lizzie asked.

"It is, and I still do want exciting opportunities involving space. It's just…" Her mind wandered back to the excitement she felt years ago when she pedaled her bike across the island to tell Zach that she knew who was sabotaging the restaurants. She thought about the riddle they were trying to solve now, how the pieces needed to fit just right, not unlike any scientific endeavor.

"I don't know. I've got another month to decide."

"You'll make the right decision," Dustin's father said. Molly hadn't realized he and Mrs. Parker had joined them on the dock. Maybe that's why Dustin was so quiet.

"Thanks. I've got a lot to think about," Molly said.

"We both do," Dustin said.

"Look at that one." Sally cried, pointing to the sky, and the conversation ceased. But Molly's thoughts kept bursting and spreading through her mind in a shower of lights and shadows.

***

Jenny felt a bit self-conscious about her perfume of choice that evening—eau de DEET—but she had doused Ethan with an equal amount of spray when he'd arrived, and it was all that was allowing them to sit outside this time of year. They sat on the swing under a blanket of stars. The night had grown dark and quiet after the sparkles and barrage of booms had subsided.

"That was spectacular," Ethan said. "Even better than the big shows I grew up with."

"Really? I heard you tell Mom that your family frequently went into D.C. to watch the fireworks on the Mall. How can this even compare?"

He reached over and took her hand. "Maybe it's the company."

She couldn't quite make out his features in the dark, but she saw his smile and the sparks in his eyes. Her heart was swelling in her chest. She'd been trying all summer to push these thoughts, these emotions away, but her feelings were becoming undeniable.

"Did you mean it when you said you'd like me to meet your parents?" Her heart quickened its pace. Had he meant it?

Ethan didn't answer right away, and Jenny swallowed, waiting for him to say he'd changed his mind, that he'd invited someone else, though she couldn't imagine who since he was at work or with her all the time. Almost all the time, she reminded herself. He could've met someone...

Before she finished the thought, she felt his hand reach up and caress her cheek.

"Would you like to go with me?" He asked quietly. "Because the answer to your question is, I meant it with all my heart."

Her heart was now beating so hard, she could feel the pulsing in her throat, especially when he dragged his fingers down her chin onto that same throat, then trailed them around the back of her neck. She let him gently pull her face toward his.

Jenny couldn't speak, couldn't tell him how much she wanted to go. He didn't wait for her to find her words. He leaned forward and placed his lips on hers, tentatively at first, but she allowed her lips to answer his in a way that needed no words.

Her mind went blank, and her chest swelled. Butterflies took wing in her stomach as she reached her arms around his neck and opened her heart to his.

The next morning, after returning Wesley to his mother, Jenny found herself sitting at the breakfast table with her own mother, explaining that she was leaving in a few hours to go home with Ethan to meet his family.

"Are you sure about this?" Donna asked over her cup of tea.

"I wasn't. I kept trying to keep things casual, but…" She closed her eyes and let out a sweet sigh before looking back at her mother. "Yes, yes, I'm sure."

"And you're ready to spend a three-and-a-half-hour drive with Arlene?"

Jenny threw her head back and laughed. Ethan waited until she accepted his invitation to tell her that his grandmother would be accompanying them on the trip to Richmond.

"It wasn't what I was expecting, but I don't know why. I mean, I didn't say yes when he first asked me, and of course, he would take his grandmother home with him. Ethan's a gentleman, and he'd never think of not including her on a trip to see his parents."

"Well, you'll win her over along with the rest of his family."

"I have to win her over? What's that supposed to mean? Ethan's grandmother doesn't like me?" Jenny was taken aback. Neither Ethan nor her mother had said anything about this. She put down her fork and stared at her mom.

"No, she likes you just fine. She and I just had a disagreement about you, that's all."

"What kind of disagreement?"

"It's nothing."

"Does she think I'm not good enough for her grandson or something?" Jenny wasn't sure she wanted to go after all. Why didn't his grandmother like her?

What the heck?

"She just thinks you're too career oriented. She's old fashioned. It's nothing to worry about."

"Then why did you bring it up? And what does that mean? Too 'career oriented'? Does she think that about Ethan, or is he allowed to focus on his career because he's a man?"

"Oh, dear, I shouldn't have said anything."

Jenny shook her head. "No, I'm glad you did. I'll just have to show her that I can have a career and be a good, a good…" She huffed. "What does she want me to be?"

"A wife."

Jenny coughed out a laugh. "Well, we're a long way from that."

"Good. You just met this man. You should take your time. But as for this trip, go, and be yourself. Show them why he fell in love with you, and they'll do the same."

"What did you just say?" Jenny's mind was reeling.

"Take your time and be yourself."

"No. You said Ethan fell in love with me."

"Jenny, are you telling me that you're the only one on this island who hasn't seen how he looks at you? I saw Paula the other day, and she was gushing about Ethan and how wonderful it is that you're together. Everyone can see that the man is head over heels."

"They can? He is? But he's never said anything."

"And have you encouraged him to? Have you ever treated him as more than a friend and colleague?"

"Well, not really. I've tried to keep it low key, and I didn't think anyone else knew. I mean, we've gone on dates, but we're still getting to know each other."

"Yet he asked you to drive all the way to Richmond for a forty-eight-hour trip to see his family?"

Jenny sat back in the chair. "I mean, I had a feeling he liked me, but until last night…" She shook her head. "Don't you think you're jumping the gun a little?"

Donna wiped her mouth with her napkin and stood. "You'd better get going. Ethan's going to be at your house before you have your bags packed."

Jenny didn't remember anything about the drive back to her house in town. All she could think about was their kisses, how much emotion they contained, what her mother had said, and that constant churning in her gut she had felt since the day she'd taken Ethan to Aunt Ronnie's house. She'd been discounting her feelings all this time, but now, the elephant had grown too large to be ignored.

***

Katherine told Molly and Dustin to act normal, not to defend nor reproach Jared in public, and not to let on to anyone what they were up to, so they tried their best to live as normal. They joined their friends on Friday for game night at Lizzie's. Dustin almost didn't go, but his father claimed that he was tired, and encouraged him to go with his friends. Molly had a hard time keeping her thoughts from going to the investigation.

All the interns were included, and Molly found it difficult to avoid their questions about her brother-in-law. Eventually, though, they all got the message and stopped asking. Nobody except Molly and Dustin knew that Zach was sitting in his truck down the street, making sure they were all safe.

"Yes! Hot dog!" Nathan said, pumping his arm in triumph. "Give me that green wedgie!"

Lizzie groaned. "Of course you got it. It's a space question."

"We should be playing for money. I'm hot tonight, and I need the cash."

"Don't we all," Todd said, and everyone laughed.

"Go again, Nathan," Dustin said. "I'm pulling for you to land a pink question."

Nathan snarled at Dustin before throwing the die, but said, "Can someone get me another beer. I need some brain fuel."

"Maybe it will dull his senses," Gwen said.

They finished the game, with the more well-rounded Adrienne taking the top prize. Between games, Molly followed Adrienne into the kitchen for a snack refill.

"I'm so glad you came," Molly said. "It's nice to all hang out as a group without being on opposing teams."

"Yet somehow, we're all still competing over trivia," Adrienne said with a laugh.

"Yeah, true." Molly filled up the bowl of chips. "How's your summer going? I know this is your second year here. Will you come back next year?"

"I'm not sure," Adrienne said. "I was weighing whether to do a summer internship after graduation, like Dustin is, or go straight into a job. I think I'm just going to go for it. What about you? Why didn't you take one of your offers right away?"

Molly shrugged. "I still can't decide what I want to do."

"I had no idea at your age what I wanted to do for the rest of my life, so I would imagine already having gone to college doesn't necessarily change that."

"It's so daunting," Molly admitted. "I mean, I know that I can change jobs anytime, so it's not like I'm stuck forever, but I'm afraid of making the wrong choice."

"I don't think there is a wrong choice," Adrienne said. "Life is all about making choices, and some are good for us and work out, and others, not so much, which is why life is also about adapting and learning. Humans aren't plants. We're not stagnant. We move and change and grow, and that requires trying out new and different things, sometimes different places. If you don't like where you are or what you're doing, you aren't planted there. You can uproot yourself and move on."

Molly hummed a thoughtful response. "Nobody has ever explained it like that to me."

Adrienne nodded. "I'm not surprised. Our society is all about moving ahead, making big bucks, gaining power. So many confuse a career with a vocation. Sure, they can be the same thing, but often a career is just what we do while a vocation defines who we are, who we are meant to be."

Molly inclined her head. "That sounds an awful lot like theology."

Adrienne's dark skin almost hid her blush, but Molly saw her face grow a tad darker. "Sorry. I assumed that since Jared is a Christian…" Her words trailed, and Molly felt a little flutter in her gut.

"You mean, you…?"

Adrienne bit her bottom lip and slowly nodded. She reached inside the neck of her t-shirt and pulled out a chain dangling a small gold cross.

Molly couldn't resist. She put down the bowl she was about to carry to the other room and threw her arms around Adrienne.

"You have no idea how happy that makes me," she gushed. "I thought I'd be the only one. It's one of the things that scares me most about taking a job in our field. You've just boosted my confidence more than you'll ever know."

Adrienne laughed. "I'm glad to hear that, sister. Now, let's get back to the games."

Molly felt so much joy as they continued to play games, she almost forgot everything that was going on with Jared. Before she headed home, she excused herself to use the bathroom. As she walked down the hall, she heard a voice coming from behind a closed door. It was the room where the guys were staying the night rather than driving back to Wallops. Adrienne was staying in

Lizzie's room, but Dustin, Nathan, and Cam were bunking in the guest room.

"I told you, it's all under control. There's nothing to worry about. You got what you wanted, and I've got an ace in the hole. I'll know everything that goes on with the investigation, and I can report back. I think that deserves a little more than promised."

Molly gasped. She knew that voice, very well, and she was afraid she knew exactly what he was talking about.

"Molly, it's nice to see you."

Molly turned to see Lizzie's mom coming down the stairs. "Hi, Mrs. Parker. I was just on my way to the bathroom, but I think someone beat me to it."

"You can use the one upstairs. You know where it is."

Molly hesitated for a moment but didn't want to get caught outside the door. Besides, he might not have been talking about the stuff at the center. She smiled, thanked Mrs. Parker, and hurried up the steps.

A pair of eyes peeked through the cracked doorway and watched her all the way.

***

Arlene snored lightly in the backseat of the car. A light rain dappled the windshield, but ahead, the clouds swelled with the promise of heavy showers.

"I'm glad the rain held off until we left," Jenny said. "It would've ruined your mother's plans for dinner last night."

"Dad would've been more upset than Mom. He spent all last summer putting in that stone patio."

"You mean, he did it himself? I hadn't realized that. I assumed he hired someone. I should have gushed over it more."

Ethan laughed. "He kept asking, over and over, 'how do you like my patio'? That didn't clue you in?"

She turned toward him and narrowed her eyes. "He's a doctor, and your parents have money. Why would I ever think he did all that work himself."

"True. You don't know my dad. If there's a project he can figure out how to do on his own, he does it. And it's not even a money thing. He likes to take on huge jobs like that, especially if my mother tells him he isn't capable of doing it. Sometimes, I think the projects are actually her idea and that she plants these seeds so that he, A, is kept busy and out of her hair, and B, she gets some fancy thing done to the house that she can show off to her friends."

It was Jenny's turn to laugh. "That's pretty ingenious. I liked your parents a lot. You take after them both in many ways."

"You did notice that my father is bald, right? Are you trying to tell me something?"

"Don't worry. You definitely have your mother's thick locks. Sammi does, too. She looks just like your mom."

"Yeah, and Victoria looks just like Dad and me, with my hair, of course."

"Except blonde."

"Yeah, Gram's side is all blonde. Dad was, too, at one time."

The shower picked up its pace and the sky became murky as they drew closer to the island. The clouds were illuminated by distant flashes followed by a loud crack, reminiscent of the lights and booms from the recent holiday. Ethan slowed as water surged onto the roads of the coastal byway.

Jenny watched as the wipers battelled the rain. "I enjoyed the morning tour of the clinic. Your father sure is proud of it."

Ethan nodded. "He is. It wasn't nearly as up to date when he took over. He's worked hard to make it state of the art."

Jenny thought that over. "Ever since you've been at the island clinic, you've complained about the paperwork versus tablets and the lack of modern equipment. What your dad did with his clinic, what you'd like to see done at ours, is that because…?"

"Because of Jamie? Yeah. If we don't have the right tools to save a life, then what are we doing it for?"

"You don't believe that. You know that providing the best care isn't always about the tools you have. It's more about the skills and knowledge you possess, the gifts from God that allow us to do what we do."

"But that only takes us so far."

"We only need to stabilize them until they can get to the hospital. That's what we did with that boy a few weeks ago. Without our skills, our talents, he would've died before the medivac arrived."

"Sure, but there's so much more we could do if we had the right stuff. I've been making a list of what we need to give our patients better care."

"Ethan, that's great, and I applaud your desire to improve the clinic, but the Board will never approve high tech, big dollar equipment. Not for a place as small as we are."

Ethan let out a breath. "I have to try."

"I know you do, and I think it's commendable. I just don't want you to get your hopes up."

Ethan was subdued for the rest of the ride, and Jenny didn't know if it was because of her comments or the worsening storm. The wind and light rain were now coming like the waves that crashed on the beach—hard and heavy, knocking against the car and pushing it from side to side. Lightning split the sky as a crash of thunder shook the island.

When they reached Arlene's house, Ethan helped his grandmother cut through the falling water and driving wind that battered them as they ran and shredded the umbrella he fruitlessly held over her head. He returned to the car with every thread of his clothing soaked and headed to Jenny's house, where she toyed with the idea of asking him inside until the storm subsided, her own emotions churning like the wind and waves.

"Ethan, I'm sorry about all the stuff I said about the clinic. I admire you for wanting to make things better."

He turned toward her, his eyes as cloudy as the skies. "It's okay. I know it won't be easy."

"I wish there was a way to upgrade the clinic, but I just don't think that's going to happen."

The clouds in his eyes gave way to light as he said, "Maybe there's a way to provide what's needed without the Board having to pay for anything."

She tilted her head and gestured for him to continue.

"What if we opened our own practice?"

"Here?"

"Sure, why not?"

"Well, for starters, we hardly have any experience. We're new at this, in case you forgot. We both just finished our residencies and started working as real doctors."

"I don't mean now. I mean in a few years, after we have the experience and some money put away. We could do this, you and me. We make a great team."

Her heart did a little leap before she came to her senses and realized what he was saying.

"It's no small task," she said, thinking of both the commitment he was asking her to make, to a practice and to him.

"It's not, but we have time. I'm not planning on going anywhere." He smiled. "I'm happy right where I am."

Jenny smiled back. "Okay, so let's see how this all plays out. I'm willing to give it a try."

Ethan leaned over and kissed her, and she savored the moment as rain beat down above them, wind rocked the car back and forth, and a light beamed in her heart as brightly as the sun in the summer sky.

***

As the rain pummeled the house, Molly tried to concentrate, but she was having a hard time dismissing what she heard the night before. On the other hand, she could have misinterpreted the whole thing. She only heard one side, and it wasn't specific about anything. She needed to talk to Dustin. No, she needed to confront him about what she heard. Was he involved? She didn't want to think so, but what else could that have been about?

"Here's my list," Jared said. "Where's yours?"

Molly handed him what she'd jotted down, knowing it wasn't complete. She shuddered at a crash of thunder, feeling on edge, but not because of the storm.

"I've narrowed it down to a few who have access and possible motive." She frowned as she looked over Jared's names. "Freddy? Really?"

"Freddy? Oh, you mean the kid who used to work at the café."

"Why is he on your list?"

"Why isn't he on yours?" Jared pushed up his glasses and looked at her across the paper-strewn table.

"I mean, he's Freddy. I've known him forever. He's just a kid."

"He's older than you are." Jared stood, picked up his glass, and went to the sink for a refill. He downed a whole glass and filled it again. Molly resisted the urge to roll her eyes at his comment about their ages.

"Yeah, but why him?"

"Did you know his mom kicked him out of the house? And that he's been couch surfing all summer?"

"What?" Molly was genuinely shocked. "How do you know that?"

Jared shrugged. "I hear things."

"No, seriously, how do you know that?"

Jared sat back down and put the glass on a napkin. "You should know by now that I'm pretty good at blending into the background. People don't pay a lot of attention to me. I can be right behind someone, and they talk as though I'm not even there."

Molly nodded. "Yeah, I know how that is, more so now than when I was an outspoken kid."

"You'll always be an outspoken kid to me," Jared said with a grin.

"Funny." She leaned toward him. "But Freddy? I mean, I know he has a reputation as a playboy, but a spy and a thief?"

"Or someone being paid to spy and steal, or just being paid to gather info and equipment. Didn't he get in trouble once for doing something with the school computers?"

"Hmm… You know, I think he did. I was already gone when that happened, but I think I remember hearing about it. Hacking in and changing grades or something?"

"Not too far a leap from that to breaking into someone's computer to steal information."

Molly sat back and stared at Jared, her mouth slightly open. Would Freddy do that? Was he that desperate? And would he frame Jared? Her family? She and Freddy were friends, though she did tell him she didn't want to date him. And by text, which she later found out was the lowest form of low. But he was still nice to her. Still, if he was that desperate…

"That's certainly something to think about," she said quietly. Then she remembered something. "And you know, he did tell Dustin and me that he wanted to help us gather information about," she gestured to their papers and laptops in front of them, "all of this."

"You told him what we're doing?"

"No," she insisted. "Absolutely not. He was just saying, well, it was a little weird actually. He was cleaning and kept asking questions." As much as she didn't want it to be Freddy, there was someone else she wanted it to be even less, so she filled Jared in on Freddy's eagerness to help.

"I'm giving all these names to Katherine to have her people dig deeper. Including Freddy's," Jared said.

Molly nodded, and Jared stood to leave. Another explosive rumble rattled the shingles followed by a flare of light.

"Wait," she said with reluctance. "I have a name to add."

Jared handed her the list, and she added the name. The thundering of her heart matched the crashing bass above, and her hand shook as she wrote. Jared looked at her with sympathy as she explained her reasoning.

"Are you sure? This could be very problematic for both of you."

"I'm sure." Molly nodded. "I just have this feeling."

Jared nodded and left the room with the papers in hand.

The more she thought about the night that Jared's computer was compromised, the more she realized there had been an opportunity that Dustin hadn't told Katherine about. She remembered something important Dustin had left out, and she couldn't help but wonder if he had omitted the information on purpose.

Molly stared out the glass doors looking into the backyard as wind shook the trees, and rain fell like Victoria Falls. Should she cancel her plans with Dustin? Could she spend the entire evening with him and his father without Dustin seeing that she was bothered by something? Molly had no answers, so she continued staring ahead long after Jared had left the table.

***

"Yeah, it's all messed up. I don't know what's going on, but the island has been crawling with Feds... No, this has nothing to do with us, but the guy they arrested, on the other hand..." He told the man all he knew about the situation.

When he finished, he closed his eyes and listened to the rant on the other end of the phone. Once the line was silent, he spoke.

"Another thing, they've circled the wagons. They're all looking out for each other, and there's no way I'm going to get to any of them until this mess dies down. I'm leaving town for a couple weeks, and then I'll come back once the heat is off. As long as they don't arrest the scientist again, I can take care of him along with the others. I'll take them all out in one night. You still want the wives and kids, too?"

He listened, and his gut twisted. He didn't mind taking out women and children. Heck, sometimes they were the intended targets, but this job was going to be messy. And it was taking a lot more time than planned. He had hoped to be in the tropics by now, and this little island that he'd liked at first had become suffocating, even with its miles of beaches.

"Sure, I can do it, but that's a lot of people to hit all at once. Lots of logistics to get just right with all this heat going on now, and I've already been here long enough. I think the price just went up."

Again, he listened to the diatribe. He'd get what he wanted because they both knew that other than one of the intended targets—who was now retired—he was the best in the business.

In the end, a deal was struck for twice what he was originally promised. He and the boss man knew there was plenty of money in the bank, wherever the bank was. This job had so many backers from around the world, he could hardly keep them straight, but that was okay. The less he knew, the better.

He had another job, though not as lucrative as this one. He'd take care of that, and then he'd be back.

It's Okay to Be Blue When it's Festival Time!

One of Chincoteague's most beloved events is back this weekend. Make your way to the community center on Saturday for the Annual Chincoteague Blueberry Festival, the largest fine arts and crafts event on the Eastern Shore of Virginia. Don't miss your chance to hear live music while sampling blueberry pancakes and blueberry ice cream. Enjoy a slice of Kayla Middleton's award-winning blueberry-lemon cake at the Second Helpings table. There are plenty of goodies to take home with you from blueberry pies and blueberry cakes to all the best handmade items collected in one place.

For more information, see the festival website, or call the Chincoteague Chamber of Commerce.

The Chincoteague Herald, July 16

Chapter Fourteen

The afternoon storm cleared, and the sun took the temperature right back up to where it belonged for early July, but the humidity was gone. At least, for the time being. It didn't take long before everything on the island was dry, the air smelled fresh and clean, and any thoughts of the brash wind or battering rain were banished. Some of the coastal towns hadn't fared as well, with swelling tides and flooded roads and buildings, but Chincoteague seemed to make it through unscathed.

Dustin, his father, and Molly made their way to an open spot on the lawn in the park and opened their chairs.

"This band is great," Molly told them. "They sing everything from country to pop to oldies from the 70s and 80s."

"You call those oldies?" Ted asked, and Molly laughed.

"Oldies but goodies?" Molly teased with her question.

She and Ted continued to talk and laugh throughout the night, but something was off. Molly hardly paid attention to Dustin, and when she did, her smile wasn't genuine. Several times, Dustin caught her staring at him intensely, like he was a riddle she couldn't figure out. He hadn't seen those expressions since the first couple weeks of the summer.

"Hey, Molly, want to dance?" he asked, and she smiled politely and took his offered hand but without showing any excitement or even desire. She felt stiff when he took her in his arms, and he knew something was wrong.

"What's going on?" he asked.

"What do you mean?" Her eyes didn't meet his.

"You've barely acknowledged me all night. You're acting like my dad is the one who asked you here, not me. You haven't touched me, and I know you pretended not to notice when I tried to hold your hand."

"We're dancing, aren't we?" Her tone wasn't reassuring.

"Did I do something? Say something? I feel like we're back to ground zero."

Molly looked down and sighed. She shook her head and raised her gaze to look him in the eye.

"I'm sorry. I really am. I'm trying to have fun, but all this stuff with Jared. It's starting to get to me. I'm scared. I'm afraid we'll uncover something earth-shattering, and everything will come crashing down."

Dustin pulled her tightly to himself. "I'm so sorry. Here I am, spending all this time with my dad, not helping you, and then taking you away from your family. I haven't been very considerate about your feelings. What can I do to make things better for you?"

"Thanks, Dustin." She squeezed him tighter, and he held onto her until the song finished. When he reluctantly let go, she pulled back and faced him with a heart-breaking look in her eyes.

"Dustin, if you don't mind, I think I'm going to walk home. I'm not really in the mood to be out tonight."

"I understand. Let's get our stuff together. Dad will understand. I'll drive you home." He remembered what happened last time she told him she was walking.

"Thanks, but it's not far, and I really need to clear my head."

"Are you sure?" He had a bad feeling about this.

"I'm sure." She smiled at him, and it almost looked sincere. "Thanks, Dustin."

He nodded, and gave her a quick kiss. He stood by as she told his father goodbye and swallowed a wave of bile that rose to his throat as he watched her walk away.

Had she learned something about Jared that she didn't feel she could share with him? Had they decided to shut him out of the investigation? What exactly did Molly know that had her so upset, and why did he feel like his world was the one that was about to come crashing down?

***

"Oh, it all sounds so nice. I'm glad you went," Donna said over dinner. She texted Jenny just after the storm ended and asked her to join her for dinner after Mass. Jenny didn't feel like cooking, so she agreed even though she was beat. "It's a shame you couldn't stay all weekend."

"I have to work tomorrow," Jenny said. "It didn't seem right to ask someone to switch with me over the holiday weekend. We broke up the work so none of us has to be there every day. Ethan would've been on yesterday if he hadn't already made plans to go home, which meant Joanne had to work both Friday and Saturday. I couldn't take Sunday from her, too."

"You're so thoughtful," her mother told her, and Jenny wondered what was going on. Her mother was buttering her up for something.

"You know, I was thinking that it would be nice to have a get-together of our own tomorrow after you're done working. I think we should ask your sister and her friend, Christy, and her family. We haven't had them over in a while. I can't even remember when." Donna took a long sip of wine while Jenny stared at her over their meal.

"Mom, we've never 'had them over.' I babysat Molly, and Christy and Taylor became friends after Nick and Taylor were married. Taylor had already moved out by then."

Her mother waved her hand in dismissal. "Well, with everything they have going on right now, we should invite them over. I thought about it the whole time you were gone. We need to have more get-togethers, like Ronnie and Trevor have, and since we don't have any family left on the island, we can invite friends who have family."

"Yeah, that's weird, but okay." Jenny took a bite of fish and wondered what this was all about.

"I'll call Taylor and tell her to invite Christy and the family. You make sure Molly knows that her boyfriend is welcome. And any family he has in the area are welcome, too."

"Family? I don't think he has any family around here. I'm pretty sure he stays at Wallops with the other interns."

"Well, ask anyway. Just to be polite."

Jenny looked at her mother, trying to decipher where all this was coming from, but her mother never looked back at her. Donna continued to eat, paying an extraordinary amount of attention to her food.

****

"Another family dinner?" Ethan asked, though he wasn't opposed to going. The more time he spent with Jenny, the more time he wanted to spend with her.

"Inspired by my trip to meet your family, supposedly." Jenny said, holding her hand over her mouth as she hastily chewed a bite of her sandwich.

They stood in the lunchroom having a quick bite between patients. Ethan had volunteered to work on his day off, and Jenny suspected it was so they could spend another day together. She wasn't complaining.

"How's that?" Ethan took a large bite of the sub he picked up on the way over.

"I'm not sure. I had dinner with Mom last night after you dropped me off, and she suggested it."

"You don't look happy about it."

"Confused is more like it. She hasn't had a dinner party or entertained since my dad died, and that was several years ago."

"Maybe she didn't feel ready until now. I know my dad took a long time to want to be around people after his father died."

Jenny considered that. "I guess you could be right, but what's odd is who she's inviting. For her first time entertaining in years, I would've thought she'd invite her garden club or her church friends, even Aunt Ronnie and Uncle Trevor, not Christy, Jared, and Molly."

"Maybe she's starting with a group that has low expectations," Ethan said. "I mean, garden clubs and church friends sound intimidating."

Jenny frowned. "I don't know. I think there's something else going on, and it's not morbid curiosity about Jared. Mom's not like that."

"Well, I guess we'll find out tomorrow night, won't we?" Ethan asked before heading to see a patient, leaving Jenny alone to wonder what her mother was up to.

***

"I don't want to do this," Jared said, looking at Christy behind him in the mirror while trying to contain his unruly hair. "Why did she even invite us?"

"I don't know," Christy answered, pulling a clean shirt over her head. "She told Taylor she wanted to do something nice for us because of everything going on."

"I feel like I'm going to be on display." He turned and looked at his wife. "You know how I hate having the attention focused on me."

"You won't be on display. With three small children at the table, there will be plenty of attention mongering."

"It just doesn't feel right. Maybe we should've taken my mother up on her offer to go visit her for a few days."

Christy huffed out a breath and shook her head. "You know you can't leave the island." She pointed to his monitor. " Be realistic."

"Not even to visit my mother? I'm sure Katherine could work that out somehow." He looked at her with a pained expression.

"Your mother, who lives several states away and is an expert at hiding out and keeping her location and identity—and yours—a secret from everyone."

"With the government's help! I hardly think they're going to rush in to protect me now. They're the ones I need protecting from. They'd be the ones escorting me to see her." He made a noise of disgust and tossed the brush onto the dresser.

"Jared," Christy said calmly, wrapping her arms around him. "It's going to be okay. The government is wrong, and they're going to admit it once this is all solved."

Jared rested his chin on her head and closed his eyes. "I'm not sure the government likes to admit when it's wrong," he said wearily. "I'm so sorry I've dragged all of you into this."

Christy pulled back and looked up at him. "How did you drag all of us into this? You didn't do anything."

"I let someone have access to my computer. I was stupid and too trusting. I knew there was top-secret stuff on the server. Anyone who works for NASA knows that. I can't believe I was such an idiot."

He let go of Christy and sat on the edge of the bed, his tall frame hunching over in defeat. Christy inserted herself between his legs and put her arms around his neck.

"Stop it, Jared. Don't beat yourself up over this. You are not the one who did something wrong. Look at me." She waited until he lifted his head and met her gaze.

"I'm going to tell you something that you won't want to hear and probably won't believe, but Jared Giovanni Francesco Stevenson, you are a human being. You make mistakes. You do stupid things. And you have to live with them. Nobody in this house is blaming you for anything. Nobody at Wallops is blaming you for anything. The people who know and love you know that you aren't perfect, and we know that you aren't a criminal. Yes, you were too trusting. Yes, you were an idiot for putting your password in the number one, most obvious place. That does not make you a bad guy. It makes you human. You need to stop beating yourself up and start thinking about how we can fight this. Katherine can't do her job without your help, and you can't help if your head's not where it should be."

She leaned down and planted a long, loving kiss on his mouth.

"Now, we're getting out of this house for the first time in a week, other than church, and going to Mrs. Murray's dinner party. You got it?"

Jared gave her a small smile. "Yes, Ma'am," he said before pulling her down for another kiss. "Thank you for all that. I needed to hear it."

"Yes, you did. Now, get up and finish getting ready before we're late."

He watched her leave the room and listened as she and Molly began rounding up the kids. Jared would never know or understand what he'd done to deserve this wonderful life with this incredible woman, but he was going to fight to save it.

***

"Oh, Ted," Donna gushed, leaning up to place a kiss on Dustin's father's cheek. "I'm so glad you came. Come in, come in."

"Thanks for the invitation."

Molly and Dustin exchanged surprised looks as they were ushered into the ranch house, which was the understatement of the century. The house had a grand entryway with a large, round table in the center holding nothing but a giant vase of flowers. Twin staircases wrapped around the space and ended in a balcony, along which could be seen several closed doors. Open doorways flanked the base of the stairs, and revealed a large sitting room on one side and a dining room on the other that could rival the one Dustin had seen in photos of the White House. Beneath the stairs was another room with a wide opening that lead to a sunroom overlooking a channel.

Though Dustin's extended family wasn't hurting for money, he had never seen anything like this place outside of the house tours he'd once done on a visit to Newport, Rhode Island, while in high school.

"This place is incredible," he whispered to Molly.

She made a thoughtful noise and looked around as if assessing the house for the first time. "Yeah, I guess you're right. I've been coming here for so long, and the Murrays are so down to earth, I guess I never really noticed."

Her voice seemed off, and Dustin wished they'd had a chance to talk since the previous night. Dustin had spent all day with his father, and Molly wasn't texting as much or as openly as usual. He knew she was keeping something from him.

"Wow," Dustin heard his father say. "This is even more beautiful than you described. It more than rivals the view from the restaurant."

"Restaurant?" Dustin said, turning to Molly.

"Don't look at me. I don't know what they're talking about."

"Come on out here," Mrs. Murray called to them. "I've prepared a few appetizers and cocktails for us."

"She means she slaved all day making crab dip, bacon-wrapped shrimp, and a charcuterie tray to die for," said Jenny, sneaking up behind Molly and Dustin. "She went all out, and I think I just figured out why."

They all looked toward the wall of glass where Donna and Ted stood, her arm linked in his as he asked, and she answered, questions about her property.

"We probably should have warned you," Dustin said. "They met for, like, five minutes last week, and my father hasn't stopped talking about her. I think that's why he extended his stay a few days."

"You were right," Ted was saying. "Your crab dip is better than what we had on Friday."

Dustin's jaw dropped. "Friday?"

"While we were at Lizzie's," Molly supplied.

"I knew something was up," Jenny said. "I just didn't know it was this kind of something."

"What are we whispering about?" Ethan leaned in and asked.

Molly motioned ahead, and Ethan nodded. "Is this a good thing, or a bad thing?" he asked.

Jenny and Molly looked at each other and both shrugged.

"The verdict's still out," Jenny said. "But apparently, when we were away, my mother and Dustin's father went on a date."

"I think they look cute together," Christy said quietly as the group continued to grow, each one assessing the scene before them.

"What the heck is going on?" a loud, male voice asked from behind, and the entire group turned to see Taylor, Nick, and Wesley standing in the entranceway. "Why are you all huddled together, and who's the man Mom is swooning over?"

***

Considering Taylor was the biggest daddy's girl who ever lived, Jenny and Molly agreed that she was being quite gracious toward Dustin's father. Dinner was a lovely affair, consisting of roasted lamb, an heirloom tomato salad, a summer pasta with fresh vegetables and lime vinaigrette, and fresh, homemade cornbread. Molly didn't think she could eat another bite, but she'd caught a glimpse of blueberry pie cooling on the counter before dinner, and she loved Mrs. Murray's pies.

"Mom, you've outdone yourself," Nick told his mother-in-law. "You should join forces with Kayla. The two of you would make a killing."

Mrs. Murray smiled. "Thank you, Nick. It was fun to plan this and spend all day cooking. I haven't done this in so long, and I'd forgotten how much I enjoy it."

"I can't thank you enough for having us over," Christy said, wiping the food from Sally's face. "This was such a nice treat."

"Well, I figured you needed a break," she said sympathetically. "Why don't we go out back and sit by the water for dessert? Those picnic tables Trevor made haven't been used in much too long, and I had Taylor's crew spray for mosquitoes this weekend, so we should take advantage of it while we can."

"That sounds nice, Mom," Jenny said. "Why don't you go out, and Molly and I will clear the table and get dessert ready."

"Oh, honey, that can wait."

Christy shook her head. "We've got this, Mrs. Murray. You all go out. You too, Taylor, go put your feet up."

"I'm not going to argue," Taylor said as she used her hands to push herself up from her seat. "I've got under two weeks to go, and all I want to do is put my feet up."

Molly stood, too, and started clearing the table. She was about to take Dustin's plate when she saw the look on his face. He had his phone in his lap and was staring at a text message. Before she could ask what was wrong, Jared shot up, holding his phone in his hand.

"They got him. They made an arrest," he exclaimed.

"What?" Christy said, turning around to look at him. "Who? When?"

Molly noticed that Dustin didn't look surprised by Jared's announcement. In fact, he never looked up from his phone.

Please don't let him be involved, please don't let him have known, she prayed.

"I don't know," Jared answered Christy. "Simon just sent me a text. He said he'd call me as soon as he had a chance."

"Is he at the center?" Christy asked.

"I don't know. He just said they arrested someone, and they're sure he's the one who broke into my office and downloaded the files, and he was the one who stole the missing parts."

Christy squealed and threw her arms around Jared. "I can't believe it. How did they—?"

"I really don't know," Jared said, shaking his head.

"Well, isn't this wonderful news," Mrs. Murray said. "I just happen to have a bottle of champagne in the fridge. I think we should open it."

"I'm all for that," Christy said as most of the group moved toward the outside though Jared looked shell shocked as he followed them.

Molly stayed rooted in place. Ted, Jenny, and Ethan must have noticed because they stayed put as well.

"Dustin, are you okay?" Molly asked hesitantly.

Dustin finally looked up with a look of bewilderment on his face.

"It was Nathan," he said, looking at Molly. "Nathan, my roommate. My friend. He…he knows how I feel about you. He knew this could destroy your family, Jared's future, *my* future."

Molly sat back down beside him, her heart thudding. "Nathan?"

"He was at the fireworks," Ted said. "He shook my hand and acted like it was so nice to meet me, like he was the nicest guy in the world."

"He is a nice guy," Dustin said. "At least, I thought he was."

Jenny and Ethan sat back down, too. "Can we do anything?" Jenny asked.

Dustin looked at them as though he didn't know who they were or where he was. "I… I don't know. I don't understand how, or, or why."

"Who texted you?" Molly asked.

"Adrienne. She said he was just taken away in handcuffs. She and Cam are shocked. I'm shocked."

Then Molly asked what had been on her mind for the past few days.

"Dustin, he's your roommate. You don't think you'll be implicated, do you?"

At that moment, there was a knock on the door, and they all turned. Through the tall glass panes on each side of the door, they could see an unmistakable black SUV in the driveway.

Molly's heart sank when she saw the look of terror on Dustin's face.

***

The same two men who took Jared to Washington in handcuffs offered to escort him to Wallops, where everyone was being briefed on the events of the day. Jared declined their offer, but he and Christy followed the men with Molly, Dustin, and Ted completing the caravan. Jenny and Ethan volunteered to watch Sally and Nicky and help Donna clean up.

Molly held her breath as they entered the large conference room where reporters lined the back wall. Jared followed Molly and was instantly surrounded by cameras and microphones but declined comment. A hush fell over the room as everyone awaited the director of NASA and the deputy director of the FBI, who they were told would address the crowd. All attention turned to the front when the door behind the podium opened, and the two highly regarded officials stepped up to speak.

"Good evening. I'm Deputy Director Caruso of the FBI. Since it's late in the day, I'll be brief but concise. In an unprecedented, speedy turnaround, the FBI, working in conjunction with NASA, and through the help of AI, was able to trace the breach of information at this facility to a particular person. As you all know, Dr. Jared Stevenson, whose computer was identified as the point of the breach, was taken into custody for three days of intense scrutiny before being released. He cooperated fully, and through his attorney and the work of a select group at Wallops over the past few weeks, we gained valuable information that led us to an arrest this afternoon."

Molly bristled at the phrase, 'small select group' but even more so at 'in conjunction' since the FBI had nothing to do with the break in the case. She and Jared, along with Katherine, were the only ones outside the agencies who knew the truth about the tip that led to the identification of Nathan as the perpetrator.

"While certain aspects of our investigation are ongoing, we have reinstated Dr. Stevenson and are allowing the facility to return to normal operations. I'll let Director Esper take it from here."

"Thank you, Deputy Director Caruso. I'm NASA Director Esper. As you just heard, the center will be opening back up, and summer camps will continue. The annual July Fourth launch that was postponed will take place next weekend. Are there any questions?"

An explosion of enquiries spewed from the reporters. Most wanted to know the same things.

"Deputy Director Caruso, can you tell us who was arrested and has it been determined conclusively that he was the perpetrator?"

"I cannot comment on that at this time."

"Director Esper, what was the information that was stolen, and to where was it sent?"

"I cannot comment on that at this time."

"Director Esper, have any other employees been implicated in the crime?"

"Not as of now. The person arrested has assured us that he is willing to testify under oath that nobody else was involved, but our investigation is ongoing. It does not appear, at this time, that any other persons at Wallops were involved, but again, the investigation is ongoing."

Molly let out an audible sigh of relief, and Dustin reached over to take her hand. He leaned over and said, "You must be so relieved."

"You have no idea," she admitted, knowing she'd have to level with him at some point, hoping he would forgive her for thinking the worst.

The press conference continued with a barrage of questions, almost all of them receiving the same answer, "I cannot comment on that at this time."

***

Nothing felt right over the course of the next week. Dustin was questioned over and over despite Nathan's statement that none of the interns knew anything about his actions. Ted wanted to stick around, but Dustin convinced him to go back to work. Ted grudgingly left with the promise he'd be back for Molly's birthday party the following month, assuming they were still invited.

Dustin hadn't seen Molly since the press conference. Technically, he was allowed to leave Wallops, but he was discouraged from doing so until the questioning was complete to the satisfaction of all agencies involved. He didn't see Jared most of the week except in small glimpses when they arrived in the mornings and left in the afternoons. Molly's brother-in-law kept to himself, presumably reassembling his office, and not wanting to garner any attention from his colleagues.

Since Dustin was unable to assist Jared any longer— he didn't know if that was Jared's choice or someone else's—he began answering to Dr. Jeffries, another scientist who worked exclusively in the lab. Dustin could deal with the changes at work, and he enjoyed working in the lab. He'd even made a decision about where he wanted to work come September.

It didn't take long to get used to having no roommate for the first time in over four years. The room was a lot quieter, and the nights seemed to drag on forever, but he had a greater ability to read and to think. He missed going to the beach. He missed trivia. Most of all, he missed Molly.

He couldn't understand why he hadn't heard from her and why nobody would tell him if she was okay. Did she honestly believe that he had something to do with all this? Did she trust him so little, see him as such a bad guy? Why wouldn't she answer his texts? He thought they really meant something to each other.

"Dustin," Dr. Jeffries said, breaking into Dustin's thoughts. "You have someone here to see you. You can use the meeting room."

The scientist led Dustin to the room at the end of the hall to which the interns had been given limited access since the breach. When he walked in, Molly turned around and faced him. They stood, looking at one another, both seemingly at a loss for words. Dustin opened his mouth to speak, but Molly ran across the room and threw herself into his arms. He held her while she cried and said over and over, "I'm sorry. I'm so sorry."

Once she stopped crying and heaving big, sobbing breaths, Dustin took her hand and led her to one of the chairs.

"What happened?"

Molly proceeded to tell him about the phone call she overheard the night they played games at Lizzie's house and her realization that Nathan was not at trivia the night someone broke into Jared's office. She confessed that she suspected Dustin was covering for his roommate and that Katherine believed Dustin might be involved.

"I wanted to ask you. There were so many times I wanted to say something, but I couldn't." She shook her head. "Katherine gave me strict instructions not to say anything. I didn't want to believe that you knew about Nathan, but there wasn't any way to be sure. I'm sorry. I know that sounds like I didn't trust you, but…"

Dustin let her words fill the air between them until silence pushed them away and filled the void. He swallowed and closed his eyes for a moment before looking back at her.

"I didn't know."

"I know you didn't," she gushed, taking his hands in hers. "I really did know that, deep inside, but everything was so confusing, and Katherine never trusted you. I didn't know what to do."

"And Jared? Did he think I had something to do with it? Does he think that now?"

Molly shook her head. "He kept an open mind, as he always does, but he never wanted to believe it."

"Why won't he let me work for him? Why didn't you answer my calls and texts?"

"I wasn't allowed, not until they finished questioning all of you. As far as Jared, he just wants some peace and quiet to put his research back together. He told me today that he needs your help, that you're the only other person up to speed on what he's been doing, and he's hoping they'll let you work with him again. Right now, though, none of you are allowed to have access to the offices."

"I get that." He looked down at their entwined hands. "Are we…?" He lifted his gaze to hers. "Are we okay?"

Molly shook her head. "I don't know. Are we? I mean, I doubted you. I shut you out. I don't know if you can forgive me." His heart broke as he watched her hold back more tears.

Dustin smiled and tucked a piece of hair behind her ear as he spoke. "Remember that jerk you went to school with? The one who was so mean to you? He wasn't worth trusting, and he wasn't worth forgiving, but you let him make it up to you. He put you through hell for four years, and you opened your heart to him, at least, I think you did."

"I did, I do." She nodded emphatically.

"If you could forgive him for everything he put you through, I can forgive you for thinking he had returned. But Molly?"

"Yes," she breathed.

"That guy is never coming back. Never. You got that?"

One last tear slid down her face as she bobbed her head up and down. Dustin wanted to kiss every one of her tears away, but instead, he reached his thumb up and gently wiped the drops from her cheek.

"There's something else about that guy that you should know. He was cynical and closed minded and didn't want to believe everything you believe. But earlier this week, I was in the center's library and ran across a book called *Cosmic Christology and Christian Cosmology* on the writings of a priest named Pierre Teilhard de Chardin and his contributions to science and theology. I was fascinated by it and couldn't put it down."

"You were fascinated by Teilhard?" Molly asked in disbelief.

Dustin nodded enthusiastically. "I was especially intrigued by his definition of the soul, and it made me discover more than the existence of God, at least the possibility of his existence."

Molly nodded, beckoning him to continue.

"You might not be ready to hear this, Molly McLane, but I discovered love. I discovered that I love you, that my soul longs for you. I hated being apart this past week, and I don't want to be away from you for the rest of the summer. Do you hear me?"

She smiled, and Dustin marveled at her eyes ability to secrete even more tears.

"Yes, but Dustin, I think you should know that I may have made a decision about my future, and I'm not sure you're going to like it very much."

"I have, too, and I want to talk to you about it, but right now, I just want to kiss you. The rest can wait."

She laughed and granted his request.

Pony Penning Week is Here!

The 104th Annual Pony Swim will take place this Wednesday at slack tide. The time is predicted to be somewhere between 10:00 AM and 12:30 PM.

The Chincoteague Volunteer Fire Company makes the following requests:

- Please keep at least fifty feet away from the wild ponies at all times.
- Please do not attempt to feed the ponies. A change in their diet can lead to sickness, even death, and the ponies do bite.
- Please do not approach the ponies, or you will risk being bitten or kicked.

Enjoy your time on the island, and remember, this is our home. Help us take care of it.

The Chincoteague Chamber of Commerce

Chapter Fifteen

"Today is the first day since Jared was taken into custody that I'm glad I'm not working for Holly anymore," Molly said as she stood on the wooden fence at the pony corral. Dustin stood on the ground beside her, his hand laid protectively on her back as she craned to get a better look.

"I'm just sad that Taylor can't be here," Jenny said. "She really did a very poor job of timing Maureen's entrance into the world."

"Oh, but what a joy it is to have another baby girl in the family," Donna said. "And she looks just like her aunt."

"She does," Jenny admitted, "which is so cool."

"Maureen's a pretty name," Ethan said. "What made her pick it?"

All eyes turned toward Ethan.

"What? Is it a family name?"

Jenny laughed. "You could say that."

"You should've gone with us to the movies yesterday," Ted told him. "You'd know that Maureen is the little girl in the Misty book."

Ethan's brow furrowed in confusion for just a moment before he opened his mouth and said, "Ah, I get it. That makes total sense now."

Jenny rolled her eyes, and Molly laughed, feeling happy and light-hearted with all the stuff at Walllops behind them. She looked at Dustin as he gazed at the ponies and felt bad for him. He and Nathan had really bonded, and word was, Nathan was going to be tried for espionage, hindering a federal investigation, and theft. He was going to be in a federal prison for a very long time just because he'd made a deal with a foreign agent to pass along secrets and parts for Jared's rocket to the moon.

"Are you all ready for dinner?" Ted asked. "I'm starving."

"Like father, like son," Molly said. "Dustin is always hungry."

"Hey, am not."

"Yes, you are," Molly said, jumping down from the fence and taking his hand.

"I'm ready, but I hope the restaurant isn't absolutely packed," Donna said.

"It will be," Jenny told her, "but we'll be fine. Molly has connections."

They made their way to the Ropewalk where they stopped outside to take photos in front of the mural on the side of the building. A grey pony eating marsh grass was at the forefront of the mural with three other ponies behind her, and the Assateague Lighthouse stood in the distance, shining golden beams into a gull-filled sky.

Inside the restaurant, people were lined up for photos with the interior mural, depicting three ponies standing near the shoreline amid the sand and beach grasses. The place was overflowing with people, but their waitress led the group to one of the best tables, a six top on the shadowed deck where overhead palms swayed in the sea breeze.

Once they were seated and ordered drinks and appetizers, the conversation flowed. Ted told them of his week back at work and the filing of his retirement papers.

"I've been thinking about it for a while, but after what happened with Jared, I realized just how much I wanted to be able to enjoy life and spend time with Dustin."

Ethan and Jenny shared stories about the clinic, and Donna told them about her garden club's plans for the upcoming year, which included making arrangements for the annual Veteran's Day Breakfast and decorations for the island's Christmas festivities.

Molly listened to everyone's plans and wondered about her own. She knew what she wanted to do, but she also knew that others would not understand her choice. She just had to convince them that, despite her age, she knew what she was doing. They had to realize it was her choice to make.

***

"Would you believe, I've never actually watched the live auction?" Molly asked as she sliced into a watermelon. "That was so cool." Dustin loved the way her words rushed and her eyes lit up when she was excited.

"I wish I could've seen it," Ethan said as he filled a container with ice. "One of these years, we have to close the clinic just long enough to get to the carnival grounds and see what it's like."

"I don't understand the buyback stuff," Dustin said. "How does that work?"

"It's not that complicated," Jenny told him. She helped Molly cut the slices into chunks while Dustin and Ethan filled glasses with lemonade.

They'd all spent a lot of time together that week while Ted was back in town. He and Donna seemed inseparable, and Dustin was okay with that. He was glad his father found someone who made him happy, whether this was a fleeting thing or not.

"Every year, a small number of the foals are designated as buybacks," Jenny explained. "The winner gets a certificate of purchase from the fire company and is allowed to name the pony. Then, the fire company buys the pony back to replenish the herd. That way, the ponies live on, and the tradition continues."

"Huh." Dustin nodded. "That makes so much sense."

"It does," Jenny agreed, "and it allows the fire company to keep track of the ponies while they're young and vulnerable. Once they're weaned, the mothers are returned to Assateague, but the foals are cared for at the carnival grounds until spring to ensure they are kept safe from the harsh weather and limited food supply during the winter."

"Taylor has a buyback, doesn't she?" Molly asked.

"She does. She's had him since she was in elementary school. She goes to visit him all the time, but she can't get close. Even after spending the winter here, once the ponies are released back to Assateague, they're wild horses again. She has a pony she bought and kept, too. He's in the barn with her horses."

"How did the auction go?" A voice asked from the doorway to the kitchen.

"Speak of the devil," Jenny said.

"It was so cool," Molly told Taylor, hastily wiping her hands and running over to coo over little Maureen. "But not as cool as you are," Molly said in a sing-song voice.

"I know I am, but my daughter's not bad either," Nick said, coming up behind Taylor. Dustin was getting used to Nick's humor and saw what everyone liked about the guy.

"Where's Aunt Jenny?" Wesley asked. He spotted his favorite person and ran to her for a hug.

"Are Christy and Jared here yet?" Taylor asked, looking around.

"Not yet," Molly told them. "They'll be here soon. Jared had to work. He gave Dustin some time off this week so he could do the pony stuff with his dad."

"How about you, Molly? You staying out of trouble?" Nick asked.

"Yes," she said, and Dustin could hear the eye roll in her tone. "I'm helping out at Wallops, but only part time. I'm working on applications and stuff, trying to get things straight for my future."

Molly smiled at Nick, but Dustin noted how her answer sounded rehearsed. He knew her well enough to know she had given very serious thought to her future, but he also knew she was nervous about her decision. She'd spent the past three weeks working on applications, attending online and in-person interviews, and assuring everyone, especially herself, that she was the right person for the job.

"And have you made a decision?" Nick asked, but Molly was saved by the bell, literally, when the timer went off on the oven, and she hurried to remove the brownies she'd made.

A few moments later, Christy and Jared arrived with the kids, and Ted was right behind them bearing large platters of party food. While Taylor and Nick were the official hosts of the get-together, everyone else was doing the work, and Donna's house was the location for the big announcement her daughter and son-in-law wanted to make.

Once they all had food, Taylor handed Maureen to Nick and stood.

"Okay, you guys know that we chose Wesley's Godparents pretty easily. Jenny was always my first choice, and we knew Zach was a no-brainer."

Dustin listened with a new appreciation. He didn't have Godparents, and his parents had never practiced any religion. Understanding what it truly meant to be a Godparent—to represent the Church and guide a child to grow in his or her faith within the Church—allowed him to comprehend the weight of the decision and the importance of the role. This was something Taylor and Nick hadn't taken lightly, and everyone was waiting to hear who that important couple would be for Maureen.

Taylor continued. "We've put a lot of thought into this, and in case you hadn't already guessed by the invitees here this evening, we'd really love it if Christy and Jared would do us the honor of being Godparents to Maureen.

Amid the sounds of acceptance and approval, Dustin saw Christy wipe a tear from her eye.

"The honor would be all ours. Can I hold my Goddaughter?"

They all laughed as Christy reached for Maureen.

Talk turned to the date of the ceremony and plans for a huge reception, and Dustin went back for more food. Molly appeared at his side.

"I'm sorry I'll miss it," she said. "I wish I could be here."

"You don't think they'll let you come home for the baptism?"

She shrugged. "I don't know, but I doubt it. The regimen is supposed to be pretty intense."

"Are you nervous?" he asked.

Her smile was tentative. "A little. More nervous about..." She gestured toward her sister.

"She's supporting you. She always does." He knew it had been a tough sell, but Molly was pretty persuasive, and though they had their doubts, Christy and Jared were in her corner.

The evening grew late and turned to night, but everyone except Nick—who left to work the night shift—had taken off the next day, so a round of board games had ensued once the kids were asleep in their room at Grandma's house.

Dustin agreed with Molly. There was a lot he was going to miss when they were gone.

***

He returned to the island to finish the job he wished he'd never taken. The payout would be good, though, which is what he reminded himself as he hacked through the security system and made his way inside.

Children's toys littered the floor, and he had to watch every step. He hopped over a doll and maneuvered around a pile of blocks. He was nimble on the stairs, careful to place just enough weight to avoid any creaks. He would take care of the adults first then the kids. His boss wanted to send a message to any relatives who might even think about double crossing the family. Once he was done here, he'd give the word for things to be taken care of in Michigan. First the son, then the mother.

Moments later, he hurried from the house, his blood on fire with fury. Every room was empty, not a soul in sight. He cursed but kept his cool. How had he not noticed the missing car? One didn't reach his level of expertise or demand by making those kinds of mistakes or giving in to emotion. He had made another sweep through the house, making sure he hadn't missed a room, but nobody was home. It was late, on a weeknight, so where would an entire family be other than home and in bed?

He had hoped to hit all the houses in one night, but that would not be possible unless he saved all of them for another night, and he couldn't do that because he was needed elsewhere. Perhaps he'd have time to circle back, but time was ticking, and he had two more houses to visit. His price just went up. Again.

***

Zach sat up in bed. The hairs on the back of his neck stood. This was not the first time he'd been awakened during the night by an almost imperceptible noise, a scent, or even a shift in the air. Kayla stirred beside him as he eased himself from bed.

With the prowess of a panther, he looked up and down the hallway before making his way toward the stairs. He had memorized every board in the floor, every minute squeak on the steps. He knew how to approach without a sound and move through the house undetected. These were habits that died hard, even all these years later.

Zach stopped halfway down the steps and stooped to look at the alarm which was not flashing. It had been disengaged. Zach's heart remained steady, his eyes continued scanning, his ears alert to even the softest movement.

A floorboard creaked nearby, and Zach felt the air leave him. He wasn't wrong. Someone was in the house. Easing himself back up the staircase without turning around, he was already forming a plan.

***

"Stop," Molly said when they reached the entryway.

"Molly, move," Christy whispered a protest. "Before we drop a child."

Christy and Jared had both managed to get Sally and Nicky into and out of their car seats without waking them up. Molly knew they were in a tenuous situation, but she also knew something was wrong.

"Christy, did you set the alarm?"

"What? Of course. You know Jared insists on it. Why?"

Molly felt her insides grow cold, sending a shiver down her spine. "Someone turned it off." She looked around the room. "I think someone was in the house."

"What? Why would you think that?"

Something in the air made her shake her head again. "Something's wrong. I can feel it. Back up. Get back in the car. I'm calling Nick."

"What's wrong?" Jared asked closing the space in the small area.

"Get out," Molly said through clenched teeth, pushing her sister toward the door. "I mean it. Get out."

"Christy, come on," Jared said. "Maybe they sent someone…"

He didn't finish the thought before Christy hastily retreated from the house and followed him down the wooden steps. Molly pulled the door closed as she backed out and reached for her phone.

"Come on, Nick. Pick up. Pick up." The phone rang until it went to voicemail. Molly punched the button again, apprehension increasing with each ring.

***

Kayla knew not to argue. She huddled in the bathroom and prayed silently, wishing Zach had stayed with her and deeply grateful that Todd was camping with Ben and their other friends.

She had no idea what was happening. There wasn't time to ask questions, and she didn't know what to do other than follow Zach's unspoken commands. When she heard the faint, almost inaudible sound of shots, she froze, praying the sound of her pounding heart wouldn't give her away but more than that, she prayed she wouldn't lose another husband to someone holding a gun.

***

He pulled out his phone to take photos for the man who hired him. He was required to send proof of death in order to get the wire, though he knew the figures in the bed had no chance of survival. He needed to hurry so he could get to the next house and return to the first one before the bodies were discovered.

As he reached for the bed covers, he felt the blow to the back of his head, and for the first time since being held captive in a Taliban prison, his whole world went black.

***

By the time Jared pulled the car into Diane's driveway, Molly had almost given up on reaching Nick. She didn't call 911 because she knew, logically, that she could be wrong, and she didn't want to waste police resources. But she also knew that one's instincts were almost always correct, and she had Zach to thank for that. Finally, Nick answered.

"Listen, Molly, I can't talk. I'm on my way to Zach's—"

"Zach's? Why? Did something happen?"

"He called us. Something about an intruder."

Molly gasped, and her breath quickened.

"At his house? We had one at our house. I'm sure of it."

"Your house? You're sure?"

"No, but the alarm system was off, and something just didn't feel right."

"Molly, I know you think you're some kind of modern Nancy Drew, but just because the alarm was off doesn't mean there was a break-in. Look, I've got to go. Go to bed."

And with that, he was gone, and Molly knew she needed to get to the other side of the island to find out what was going on at Zach and Kayla's.

It took a lot of convincing, but after several attempts, Jared gave in to Molly's pleas and drove her to Zach and Kayla's house. There were too many flashing red and blue lights to count, and Molly felt sick to her stomach. Were Zach and Kayla okay? She knew Todd was away, but was EJ home? Was Lizzie there?

"Chief Parker," Molly called to Lizzie's father who was talking to another officer in front of the house. Sawhorses were connected with yellow police tape, and Molly was desperate to break the perimeter.

Chief Parker looked up but didn't answer before turning back to the officer.

"Chief Parker, please. It's important."

Lizzie's father looked at her again, and even in the random flashing of the police lights, Molly could see the look of annoyance on his face. He did, however, make his way through the crowd of police and EMTs to tell her to go home.

"We can't go home," Molly told him. Someone broke into our house."

"She thinks," Jared clarified. "We're not sure."

The chief's head straightened, and his eyes widened.

"You think someone broke into your house? How? Why? I mean, what makes you think that?"

"The alarm was off, and I just had this sense." Molly shook her head. "I know, that doesn't mean anything but—"

"Hold on." He turned and looked around. "Tom, come take Molly's statement."

Another officer, one Molly didn't know, hurried over with a pen and small notebook in hand.

"Another possible break-in. Alarm off. I'll send someone over to check it out." He looked at Jared. "Okay with you?"

He nodded. "Do you really think someone broke in? I mean, maybe we didn't turn on the alarm."

"Jared, has there ever been a single day, since you discovered who your family is, that you haven't set the alarm? One single time?"

Jared shook his head.

"That's what I thought. I'll be back." He turned and headed back to the house.

"Officer, can you tell me what's going on?" Molly asked once she was done giving Officer Tom Whalen what few details they had. "Is everyone okay?"

"As far as we know, Ma'am. I'm sure the chief will be back to talk to you soon."

"Kayla, Kayla! Where's Kayla?" A frantic Aaron ran toward them as they waited for Lizzie's father to return. He was still in uniform, and Molly assumed he was on duty that night.

"We don't know anything," Molly told him.

He threw up the police tape and ran toward the house, still calling his twin's name. Molly looked at Jared and wondered if he was saying the same silent prayer she was. Before she could whisper, *Amen*, Lizzie's father motioned for her and Jared to follow him inside.

*****

Molly saw Aaron looking Kayla over, surveying her from head to toe, as she stood in a bathrobe that was, undoubtedly, way too hot for July.

"I came as soon as I got the call. They said he shot you. You and Zach."

"No," Kayla assured him. "He tried to. Zach made me hide in the bathroom, and I heard him shoot the pillows." Her voice cracked, and Molly and Jared exchanged horrified looks. "What about you? Kate and the kids? Is everyone okay?"

"We're fine. Why wouldn't we be?"

"Aaron, Jared, Molly," the chief called from the steps. "Can you please join us up here?"

Outside Zach and Kayla's bedroom, Chief Parker paused. "We need Jared and Aaron to take a look at the guy we've apprehended. See if he looks familiar."

"I don't understand," Jared said. "Why Aaron and me?"

"I'll explain everything shortly. The Feds are on their way to take him into custody."

Jared's jaw dropped. "The Feds? Is this related—"

"We don't think so, but we're not sure," Chief Parker said. "Because of the delicate nature of everything that's happened, and the parties involved, I called and asked if they could send someone over. They agreed that it seemed suspicious on the heels of what happened with you, so they're sending a chopper. They should be here soon." He looked at Molly. "You're up here only out of courtesy. Don't touch anything or ask any questions. Just wait, and we'll all see if we can get to the bottom of this."

Molly nodded. "Yes, Sir."

They went into the room where Molly saw an unconscious man folded over in a desk chair, his wrists cuffed to the arms of the chair.

"Do you know this man?" the chief asked, looking at both Jared and Aaron.

Jared looked at the man and shook his head. He looked at Aaron, who also shook his head.

"Should we?"

"Probably not," Zach said, stepping into the room.

"But you do," Aaron said, sizing up his brother-in-law. "Who is he?"

"I wasn't sure at first," Zach said. "I had to wake up a friend at DOD, and he confirmed my suspicion."

"Care to enlighten us?" Chief Parker asked just before two more men appeared in the hallway.

"We'll take it from here," the men said, pushing their way into the room.

"I don't think so," the chief said, putting his arm out to block them. "You're here at my invitation, but only because I thought this might have to do with your investigation. Zach, you want to fill us in?"

Zach nodded. "William Jackson, former Army, spent time as a POW in Afghanistan. Honorably discharged but disappeared shortly after. He's been off the grid for about fifteen years."

"Did you know him?" Aaron asked.

Zach took in a long breath and let it out. "Not well. We mainly worked in different parts of the country, under different COs, but when you do what we did, you know each other, cross paths now and then."

Molly felt her breath catch. Jackson was a sniper, someone hired to kill people, but why Zach and Kayla?

"Why is he here?" Aaron asked. "Why your house?"

"Show him," Zach said to the chief.

"Aaron, Jared," he hesitated before adding, "Molly, this is going to be hard, shocking even." He walked to the dresser and picked up a phone in his gloved hand. It was a model Molly had never seen before.

"It's a burner," the chief said. "No code, no saved information. Calls, texts, DMs, everything set to delete after each transmission. It has nothing on it, but these."

He held up the phone and began flipping through photos. Molly gasped as she looked at the first picture. It was Christy, holding Nicky on her lap, looking slightly away, but with enough of her face in the camera's range to positively identify her. Molly felt sick as she forced herself to stay focused as Lizzie's father went from one photo to the next.

There was one of Jared, another of little Sally, and a professional portrait of Kate and Aaron's kids. In one photo, Aaron looked out at the water from his Coast Guard vessel, and in another, Kate was in the island grocery store. Kayla's photo was taken on the beach, as was Todd's. She assumed from the photo's background that EJ's was taken on his base. Then there was her picture, taken on her graduation day as she gave her valedictory speech. She felt her throat constrict as she tried to swallow a cry. A small sound escaped her lips, and Jared turned to look at her, his eyes filled with concern.

"What does this all mean?" he managed to ask.

"Jackson was hired to perform a hit, multiple hits," Zach said.

"He was in our house," Molly said, her voice small, her breathing shallow. "I could feel it when we walked in."

"I think so, Molly," Zach agreed. "Lucky for you, none of you were home when he showed up."

"How did you know?" Aaron asked. "I mean, how did you and Kayla not…" He didn't finish his question, and Molly saw the pain on his face.

"Sixth sense?" Zach said with a shrug. "The same way I knew that time someone broke into Kayla's storage room several years back. I can't explain it other than years in the field."

"Thank you," Aaron breathed. "Thank you. You saved my sister, again. And you saved me and my family. I can't…"

Molly had never seen Aaron like this, but she knew what he was feeling. Not one of them, nor any of their immediate family, should be alive at this moment.

"But why?" Jared asked. "What connection do we all have?"

"Your pasts," Molly supplied. "Your family, Zach's targets in the Middle East, Aaron's takedowns in the Gulf. Somewhere, somehow, there's a thread that ties you all together."

Gaining his composure, Aaron nodded. "She's right. There was a time when all those people, those groups operated independently, but not anymore."

Zach agreed. "Drugs that come into the US from Latin American drug cartels are often funded by American crime families. Those same families, nowadays, have ties with the Russian mob, which has ties with ISIS, the Taliban, Hamas, you name it."

"This was some kind of revenge?" Chief Parker asked with unbelief.

"I'd bet on it," Zach said.

The two men in suits had been quiet up to this point. "We're going to have to call this in," one of them said. "If you're right, this crosses several department lines."

Chief Parker nodded. "Be my guest, but I want assurance that my department will be kept in the loop. If there's any danger to my citizens—my friends," he corrected, "or anyone else on this island, I want to know about it."

One of the men shook his head. "Noted, but above my pay grade." He left the room with his phone in his hand.

Molly walked out and slowly made her way down the stairs. Her head was spinning. Her summer had not gone at all the way she'd planned, the way she expected, and she had a lot to process, a lot to think about. One thing was for sure. She had made the right career choice. She knew it as surely as she knew the sun would rise in the morning.

Wallops to Launch Two Rockets this Summer

Wallops Flight Center, which had been closed to the public for several weeks earlier this summer, invites everyone to a rocket launch on Wednesday. The launch of an M29 rocket is the culmination of a project to discover essential minerals on the moon. Jared Stevenson, the science who has been working on the M29 for approximately five years, was arrested earlier this summer when his computer was identified as the point of an information breach in NASA's security system, allowing critical information to be accessed by a foreign entity. Stevenson was cleared of all charges.

Nathan Lovell, an intern at the facility, was arrested and indicted for espionage, among other charges. A trial is pending, and details about Lovell's involvement remain forthcoming. There is no relation between Nathan and former Apollo 13 astronaut, Jim Lovell.

A second rocket launch, which will take place in August, has been in the works for the past two years and will deliver crucial supplies to the International Space Station (ISS). The project was put on hold when the breach took place, but all systems are now ready for the launch.

Wallops opens to the public at 10 AM for tours and informational talks about the rockets and their missions. The launches will take place at 4 PM on the respective days, weather dependent.

The Chincoteague Herald, August 1

Chapter Sixteen

"Do we know anything else?" Molly asked Jared when he got home from work. "It's been a week. We should know something."

Jared shook his head and gave Nicky a hug before plopping him back on his play mat. "Jackson isn't talking. His phone contained no info, and even the best techs at the bureau couldn't find anything."

"But they think your family was behind it? Along with the cartel and one of the terrorist organizations?"

"Looks that way. It's the only thing that ties us all together. My family doesn't typically target entire families, though, so they're probably not the ringleaders."

"But the cartel does," Molly said as she set the table for dinner.

Jared nodded. "Yeah, and ISIS usually likes grand gestures and hits they can claim, not like this."

"So, if they were involved, they weren't making the decisions. They would've just gone after Zach, and in some big public display."

"You got it." He gave her a lopsided grin "You're kind of good at this."

"I'm an expert at setting the table," she said, taking a plate from the stack she carried and placing it in its place.

"That, too, kid." He tussled her hair like she was still ten and went to fill himself a glass of water.

"And Nathan's part in this?" she asked.

"They weren't sure it was connected at first, but it looks like everything may have been connected in some way."

Molly nodded. "I thought so. It makes sense. They could sell the info to an interested third party and launder the money to pay Jackson without anything coming out of their own accounts or tracing back to them."

Jared paused, the glass hovering in the air. "You really are good at this."

Molly just shrugged. "Christy will be home soon. She picked up a new patient today." She saw Jared tense. "Someone local, someone known by the staff at the clinic. Don't worry. Besides, Zach went with her, just in case."

Molly didn't voice her thoughts.

If it wasn't for Zach, we'd all be dead.

Nicky started to cry, and Molly picked him up and strapped him into his highchair.

Still standing by the sink, Jared startled and reached into his pocket for his phone. "Dr. Stevenson…Yes…" He walked to the table, sat down, and immediately started playing with the silverware while he listened. "Yes, Sir, that's right… So, there was a connection?" He looked at Molly as she gave Nicky some pieces of cheese to munch on. "Anything on the other guy?" He shook his head, and she felt deflated. "Okay, thank you… Yes, goodbye."

"Well?" she asked without giving him a chance to put down his phone.

"Still looking into Jackson. But Nathan finally broke after they offered him a deal. He was working for someone from South Korea. Someone he connected with through a kid in school. His name was funneled through some channels by this other kid, and Nathan got a call with an offer he couldn't refuse. He never met the guy, never knew who he was or where he was from. He only cared about the dollar signs that were dangled in front of him."

"So, not someone who had anything to do with Jackson?"

"On the surface, it doesn't look that way, but you were right. There's some kind of connection to Jackson, but they aren't saying what it is."

Molly sighed. "Okay, well, part of the mystery solved." She called Sally to come for dinner and began putting food on the table as Christy walked in the door.

Their dinner conversation consisted of tales from Sally's day with Marge and Diane and updates on the rocket launch from Jared. Molly listened intently to the details while the wheels of her multifaceted brain turned. There had to be a way to connect the dots between the hit on their three families. She just wished she had the clearance and approval to help figure it out.

***

"Three, two, one," the crowd shouted, and Dustin beamed, his heart palpitating as though he was on board the rocket. He'd seen launches before, but not like this— not up close, and certainly not as one of the people responsible for its construction and flight plan.

As he watched the smoke billow out from around the rocket and the waves of fire expel from the boosters, he held his breath. The ground shook beneath him, and the fishy smell of propellant fuel and exhaust flames filled the air, making his eyes water. The rocket lifted, picking up speed, and Dustin's heart soared into the clear, blue sky with it. His father had flown in once again, wanting to be there on his son's special day—a day that only five weeks prior, Dustin wasn't sure would take place—and Dustin was thrilled to share this day with his best friend.

He looked over at his father and grinned, then shifted his gaze to Molly who stood next to Ted on the other side of the fence. He knew she was used to standing right where Dustin stood, and her eyes conveyed that she knew just how he felt.

"Good work, boys," Dr. Johnson said to the crew standing on deck, including Dustin and Jared. "Who knows, maybe you'll be headed up there someday," he said to Dustin. "Maybe the ISS, maybe beyond."

While Dustin appreciated the encouragement, right now, he was just in awe over his small part in the launch.

As soon as the area was declared safe, and the gate was opened, Molly rushed in and threw herself in his arms. "Way, to go, Dustin. Congratulations!"

Ted shook his son's hand. "I'm so proud of you, son."

"Thank you, both. This has to be one of the best days of my life so far." He had never been an emotional person, but he felt the tears well in his eyes, and he couldn't stop smiling. He looked up into the expansive blue sky, placing his hand above his eyes, and tried his best to locate the rocket, but it was already out of sight. He knew the crew in the control room were tracking it, but he didn't want to go inside. He just wanted to stare into the atmosphere above and remind himself that his summer had been a series of dreams come true. How blessed he was, and how happy he was to be able to look upward and know, for the first time in his life, where those blessings came from.

***

"Dr. Edwards," Jenny called from the exam room. "I need you. Stat. Joanne, you, too. All hands on deck."

"What's up?" Ethan said when he walked in. Holly was on the exam table, a sheet draped over her bottom half, with Steph wiping the sweat from Holly's brow.

"There's no time to get her to the hospital. Joanne and I are going to deliver. You'll take the baby and check him or her out."

"Got it," he said, and Jenny knew he was no longer the cocky baby doc who she met back in May. Dr. Edwards was capable, caring, and calm in every situation, and that's just what they needed right now.

Holly let out a groan.

"Okay, Holly, this is it," Jenny said. "Scream if you want, but push with all your might. Right. Now."

Holly's screams filled the room, but Jenny's heart leapt with joy as the baby's head slid into her hands.

"I've got the head, Holly! Just one more good push."

"I can't," she panted. "I can't. I'm too—"

"You've got this," Ethan said as Steph squeezed Holly's hand. "Bear down and give us one more big push."

Another earth-shattering scream erupted from Holly, and baby DeAngelo eased herself into Jenny's hands. Jenny felt tears gush from her eyes as she held the baby. She barely had time to register the sex before the door flew open and Lorenzo hurried into the room.

"You're just in time, Dad. Want to cut the cord?"

Lorenzo looked at the baby, his breath coming in little gasps.

"Is she? He? Is the baby—"

"She's perfect," Jenny said as Joanne cleared the baby's mouth, and a small, high-pitched cry rang out. "Mama still has work to do, but as soon as you cut the cord, you can go with Dr. Edwards when he gives her a full exam."

Joanne handed Lorenzo a pair of gloves, which he hastily pulled on before taking the scissors offered and cutting the cord as instructed.

Joanne took the baby from Jenny, wrapped her in a blanket, and handed her to Lorenzo. "Take her to Mommy," Joanne instructed, and he did as told, unable to take his eyes off his daughter.

"It took so long," he said. "We waited so long. I never thought…" He went silent as he handed the baby to Holly, and they both cried along with their little girl.

Jenny looked up at Ethan, and she knew she was seeing her own awestruck expression mirrored in his face. She knew there would be days like this, but she never imagined they would feel this exhilarating.

"You did that," Ethan said to her, his voice low and filled with emotion.

"I did that," Jenny breathed before turning back to Holly to finish the job.

***

"Happy birthday, dear Molly. Happy birthday to you."

Molly beamed as she looked at all the smiling faces. She leaned forward, took a deep breath, and blew out eighteen candles. A cry rang out from one of the picnic tables, and both Holly and Taylor looked down at their little girls.

Taylor had family on the island, but neither Holly nor Lorenzo did, so Kayla was helping at the café until Holly was ready to go back to work. Anna was pitching in at Speziato so Lorenzo could spend time with his wife and daughter. That's what they did here. They were family, and they looked out for and helped each other.

Molly bit her lip and wished she would be around to help and babysit. Thinking of babysitting, her eyes found Jenny, who looked happier than ever sitting with Ethan's arm around her shoulders. Molly would bet money that Taylor's baby would have a cousin not too far behind her, at least within the next couple years. Molly, Jenny, Ethan, and Dustin had become close, and Dustin's father was spending a lot of his weekends on the island and most of his time with Donna Murray. Everyone's families seemed to be growing.

And nobody was more like family to her, Christy, and Jared than Diane, Simon, and Marge. Diane had already jumped in and started passing out cake while Simon helped Christy scoop out ice cream. Marge was helping Kate refill the punch bowl and serve more drinks. Molly thought about how different this birthday party was from her eleventh, her first one on the island, when Diane, Marge, Simon, Jared, and the two interns from Wallops were the only attendees. My, how things had changed.

Molly caught Zach's eye, and he winked at her. She still thought he was the best-looking guy on the island.

The FBI, working with the CIA, Homeland Security, and the DEA were finally able to trace Jackson to Jared's mob family in New Jersey, a powerful cartel working out of Venezuela, and a Taliban cell in Afghanistan with ties to Russia and South Korea. Molly didn't know how they'd managed it, but more arrests were made, and the foreign parties were being monitored. Word was spread through lines of chatter that retaliation toward former American military or government operatives would not be tolerated, and Molly wondered what steps had been necessary to make that known and understood. She would find out soon, and that made her pulse race with excitement.

They all knew that threats were still possible, that danger would never be eradicated, but Molly trusted Zach, Aaron, and Nick to keep all her family safe when she was gone, and she was planning to do all she could on her end to do the same. Zach and Aaron both raised a bottle to her in a mock toast, and Molly felt immensely blessed to have them and their entire family in her life.

In fact, she felt blessed to have everyone on this island in her life. That's why the announcement she was going to make shortly would be both hard and easy. It was certainly going to shock almost everyone here, everyone except Dustin, her biggest confidant, and her sister and brother-in-law. Dustin wasn't even surprised when she told him her plans, but the other two took some convincing, which Molly was extremely good at.

She didn't know where things would ultimately go with Dustin, but he and his father had started attending Mass with them, and Molly was pleased with that, whether she and Dustin stayed together or not. For now, they had to follow their own paths and see if their winding roads continued to intersect or go in opposite directions.

Everyone ate, drank, basked in the afternoon sun, and swatted the mosquitoes that managed to survive the yard treatment. It was a festive birthday celebration and just the send-off Molly wanted.

Once the cake was distributed, she stood up on a chair and got everyone's attention. With a smile on her face and a song in heart, she said, "Thank you all for coming. You have no idea what it means to me that you're all here. I haven't made this public, but I'm leaving the island in one week, and I don't know when I'll be back." She looked around from one face to another, and announced, "I have something to tell you all."

***

"I can't believe this is goodbye," Molly said, and Dustin wiped away the tear that trailed down her cheek. They stood by her new-to-her car on a hot day near the end of August. She told him that she wanted him to be her last goodbye.

"Goodbye? You can't get rid of me that easily, especially with Dad moving here permanently. And we won't be living that far apart, at least for a while. We'll see each other plenty. I promise."

Molly nodded, her bottom lip trembling. "I know, but nothing will ever be the same." She looked up at him. "Am I making a mistake?"

"No, you're doing just what you're supposed to be doing. I don't think anybody was even surprised by your decision."

"I don't know about that. Christy was pretty upset at first, but she's being supportive."

"I told you she would be. I want you to know how proud I am of you," Dustin said. "You're going to make such a difference in this world."

"And you're going to make a difference in other worlds," she told him. "I'm proud of you, too. You've always wanted this, and you deserve it."

"You don't think I'm stupid for turning down a three-figure salary to follow my dream of working for NASA?"

"Do you think I'm stupid?"

Dustin laughed. "I think we're both very, very smart, and our respective agencies will be lucky to have us."

Dustin watched as Molly looked around at the happy families and end-of-summer visitors. They'd chosen the site of their first outing to say their farewells. She gazed across the parking lot and nodded toward the suspended beam rising above the fence.

"I kind of feel like I'm up there again, walking that beam, not sure of myself." She looked at Dustin. "What if I fall?"

"You won't," he assured her. "And if you do, I'll be there with my arms wide open. No matter what happens between us in the future, I'll always be there to catch you if you fall."

She smiled, and Dustin felt his heart breaking. "Take care, Molly. I'll miss you."

"I'll miss you, too. I hope you understand that it's not you."

"Molly, I told you, it's okay. I get it. You need to do this, to figure out if it's the right thing, to know if I'm the right thing." He grinned. "We agreed, right?"

"Right. Just some space and time to figure out life."

They hugged and shared one last, long kiss, the kind that knocks a person off his feet, and Dustin felt his heart snap in two as he let her go.

He watched her drive away and thought about their pact. They each had to find their way, to discover their paths. They needed to go their different directions, to find what they were both seeking, but they would always stay connected. He knew that what they were seeking separately was also what would always bring them together, those universal mysteries, one created by God and one invented by man - space and time.

Epilogue to the Chincoteague Island and Sunsets
Trilogies

"She's here," Christy called. "She's home!"

It had been almost a year since Molly had been back on the island. When she first left, she hoped she would be back often since she wasn't even leaving the state, but her time at the academy had gone by quickly, and she was immediately given assignments, spending the next several months flying around the world from one embassy to the next.

As an FBI agent, she worked with several organizations—Interpol, foreign police and security, and national and international law enforcement associations—but most of her work was with NASA and the ISS. She primarily investigated breaches within space agencies as more and more countries were entering the new space race, and many terrorist and crime organizations used space colonization groups as a front for illegal activity. Molly could spot one of those a lightyear away.

That's what had kept her in constant contact with Dustin. He was in Washington—D.C., that is—at NASA headquarters, and they often worked together on cases regarding American space interests. They kept their relationship platonic and professional, which was not hard to do since they rarely saw each other in person.

Molly ran up the stilted staircase and met Christy at the door.

"Welcome home," Christy said, her face buried in Molly's thick, shoulder-length hair. "I can't believe you're finally here." Christy pulled back to look at her sister. "I love the hair."

"Thanks," Molly said. "I love the bump."

Christy laughed as she reflexively put her hand on her stomach.

Molly was engulfed in the hugs of her niece and nephew. Jared brought up the rear and hugged her fiercely.

"We've missed you more than you could ever know," he said. "This place has never been the same without you."

"Is everyone else home yet?"

"Lizzie and EJ will be home later today, as will Todd and Susan and Ben and Nancy."

"And?" Molly asked, drawing out the word.

"Oh. Do you mean, Dustin?" Christy asked with a sly smile. "Yes. He and Denise arrived earlier. They came by to say hello."

"Great," Molly beamed. "I know I just got home, but—"

"Go, go. We've got all week together."

Molly took her bags to her old room, borrowed from Sally for the week, used the hall bathroom, and rushed back outside. As she drove across the island to Ted's house, she noticed all the changes. RJ's was closed, and AJ's on the Creek had taken its place. Sundial Books was under new ownership, and she'd heard that the former owners, Jonathan and Jane were traveling the world in their retirement.

Zach and Kayla and Mr. and Mrs. Parker were grandparents now, though EJ and Lizzie were stationed in California these days. Todd and Ben were both engaged to girls they met in college. It was hard to believe that all her friends were married and had kids or were getting married. And that included Jenny and Ethan as well as Ted and Donna, who were having a double wedding at St. Andrew's on Saturday. Molly was overjoyed for them all.

She slowed her car as she approached the house. She was nervous about seeing Dustin and the woman who had become central in his life over the past year.

Before she was even out of the car, Molly saw the front door open, and Dustin stepped out onto the front step. Denise stood beside him, and she looked as nervous as Molly felt.

Molly walked around the car and stood in place for a moment. The boy she knew was a man now, grown and mature, yet looking just like Molly remembered him when she first saw him across the classroom years before. She resisted the urge to break into a run, but not for long. As soon as she realized he was the one running toward her, Molly sprinted across the yard. Dustin pulled her to him and swung her around.

When he pulled away, his eyes were sparkling. "Come meet Denise," he said, pulling her toward the house.

Denise leapt off the step and hugged Molly. "I can't believe I'm finally meeting Molly, the famous FBI agent, saving the world from bad guys and alien invasions. I'm surprised you aren't wearing a black suit and dark sunglasses."

Molly laughed and shook her head in amazement. "You look so much alike. Even more in person than in your pictures."

"We get that a lot," Denise said. "I only wish I hadn't waited so long to search for him." She looked at Dustin and grinned. "Our mom had been dead for years before I even knew he existed, and then it took years more for me to get up the courage to look him up."

"I'm so glad you found him," Molly said. She looked at Dustin. "It's not just you and Ted anymore."

"Nope, and Ted adores Denise, so that makes it even better." Dustin grabbed Molly's hand. "Speaking of Ted, he can't wait to see you."

As they walked into the house, Molly mused. "You know, on my drive over here, I was thinking about how much has changed, yet how much has stayed the same."

"You know how this place is. It never changes too much."

"Everything changes," Molly said. "That's the way of the universe."

"Some things don't," Dustin said, looking at her with that familiar glint in his eyes.

Molly smiled up at him, knowing she had finally found what she had been seeking for so long.

***

The double wedding of Theodore Alan Howard to Donna Marie Murray and Ethan Frederick Edwards to Jennifer Teresa Murray took place on June 17 at St. Andrew's Church on Chincoteague Island. Standing up for Ted Howard was his son, Dustin. Donna Murray's Maid of Honor was her daughter, Taylor. Ethan Edwards' best man was his brother-in-law, Gavin MacPherson, and Jenny's Maid of Honor was friend, Molly McLane. Flower Girls were Sally Stevenson and Rose MacPherson. Ring Bearers were Wesley Black and Alana Pierson.

***

And they all lived happily ever after.

The End.

Maybe…

Acknowledgements

After Molly's debut in *Seeking Tranquility*, many of my readers commented on how much they loved her character and wanted more of the spunky child prodigy. Aging her five years between *Seeking Sugar and Spice* and *Seeking Space and Time*, allowed me to grow and mature Molly while still exhibiting her characteristics as a teenage girl. Not far from experiencing those days with my own children, I'm very familiar with the emotions and insecurities one has when transitioning from childhood into adulthood. Molly's transformation from child to adult was complicated by the fact that she was not even an adult when she was thrust into the adult world. It was sometimes difficult helping her make that conversion without losing the aspects of her character that my readers and I had grown to love. Thank you, Cayley Ross, my extraordinary editor, for helping me navigate that.

Thank you, Mom, for always being critical and kind and helping me keep the story real. Thank you for being my best friend and biggest supporter. Most of all, thank you for instilling in me a love for reading and encouraging my love for writing. I would not be doing this today if not for you. Thanks also goes to my father, my self-appointed publicist, who never meets anyone to whom he doesn't hand over one of my cards and say, "My daughter's a writer. You should read her books."

Thank you, Pat Woods, for your amazing cover designs. You make every book I write stand out with your magic touch and creative mind. I wouldn't want to work with anyone else.

Thank you, Anne, Cheryl, and Jeanne for reading, critiquing, and proofreading my books. Your help is invaluable but not nearly as priceless as your friendship. Thank you for being there for me and supporting me. "A faithful friend is a sturdy shelter: he who finds one finds treasure" (Sirach 6:14). You are among those who provide my shelter and are treasured greatly.

I would be remiss if I didn't thank all my readers on the island of Chincoteague, Virginia. I first started writing *Island of Miracles* about ten years ago but put it down because I couldn't fully envision the story. After a weekend in Chincoteague, about five years later, I knew I was ready to bring Kate and Aaron and their families to life in the pages of not one, but three books. Each character in these trilogies is so real to me (especially my beloved Nick), and I am truly grateful that so many of you embraced them as your friends and neighbors.

Thank you Rebecca, Katie Ann, Morgan, and my dear, Ken, for being my biggest cheerleaders. Thank you, Morgan, for attending so many conferences and festivals with me and making sure not a single person walks by without purchasing a book! Thank you, Rebecca, for sharing my books with friends, colleagues, and even professors, and for instilling in my granddaughter the same love for books we have. Thank you, Katie, for handling the finances at event after event over the years and for telling everyone you meet about my books. Thank you, Ken, for all your support, for making (or picking up) dinner when I'm engrossed in writing, for doing all the driving on those road trips when I was deep in editing, and for always encouraging me to pursue my dreams, even as they keep growing, expanding, and sometimes taking me far from home.

Finally, but most importantly, I give thanks to the Father, the Son, and the Holy Spirit for the gifts you have given me that have allowed me to spend the last fifteen years doing what I love.

About the Author

Amy began writing as a child and never stopped. She wrote articles for magazines and newspapers before writing children's books and adult fiction. A graduate of the University of Maryland with a Master of Library and Information Science, Amy worked as a librarian for fifteen years and, in 2010, began writing full time.

Amy writes inspirational women's fiction for people of all ages. She has published two children's books and numerous novels, including the award-winning Whispering Vines and the Chincoteague Island Trilogies. A former librarian, Amy enjoys a busy life on the Eastern Shore of Maryland.

The recipient of numerous national literary awards, including the Illumination Award, LYRA award, Independent Publisher Book Award, International Digital Award, the Golden Quill Award, and the Eric Hoffer Book Award as well as honors from the Catholic Press Association, Amy's writing has been hailed "a verbal masterpiece of art" (author Alexa Jacobs) and "Everything you want in a book" (Amazon reviewer). Amy's books are available internationally, wherever books are sold, in print and eBook formats.

Follow Amy at:
http://amyschislerauthor.com
http://facebook.com/amyschislerauthor
https://twitter.com/AmySchislerAuth
https://www.goodreads.com/amyschisler

Book Club Discussion Questions

1. Put yourself in Molly's shoes as she navigates college at the age of fifteen and graduation before she was seventeen. How would you have handled the trials and tribulations she had with her classmates and circumstances?

2. Dustin was twenty-two and Molly was just under eighteen when they began dating. Do you think their relationship would last in real life? Why or why not?

3. What do you think Dustin learned from his parents' mistakes. Do you think his life decisions reflected those lessons?

4. How did Ethan grow and change over the course of the summer? Other than Jenny, what influenced his growth and how?

5. Ted and Donna found each other in middle age. How would this have made their relationship different from their children's? As a longtime single father and widowed woman, how do you think they viewed what was happening between them?

6. What life decision did both Ethan and Dustin have in common? What influenced their choices? What path would you have chosen?

7. How was Molly's career decision different from theirs? What influenced her? How and why?

8. Were you surprised by Molly's career choice? Do you think she made the right decision?

9. Think about your favorite character from this book (or one of the previous Chincoteague books). Where do you think he or she would be in five years?

10. Has reading this book, or any of the Chincoteague books, made you want to visit this special place? Have you made the trip?

www.ingramcontent.com/pod-product-compliance
Lightning Source LLC
Chambersburg PA
CBHW032114310726